A Common Glory

A Common Glory

Robert Middlemiss

With best wishes,
Bob Middlemiss

IRIS PRESS
Oak Ridge, TN
www.irisbooks.com

Copyright © 2000 by Robert Middlemiss

Photographs used with permission

AUTHOR PHOTOGRAPH:
Copyright © 2000 by
Robert Middlemiss

BLACK AND WHITE PHOTOGRAPHS:
Copyright © 2000 by
Southeast Army Air Forces Training Center

COLOR COVER PHOTOGRAPH:
Copyright © 2000 by
James A. Rollow

book design by Robert B. Cumming, Jr.

Library of Congress Cataloging-in-Publication Data

Middlemiss, Robert, 1938-

A common glory / by Robert Middlemiss.
     p. cm.
   ISBN 0-916078-52-3 (alk. Paper)
   1. World War, 1939-1945—Georgia—Fiction. 2
British—Georgia—Fiction. 3. Women journalists—Fiction. 4.
Georgia—Fiction. I. Title.
   PS3563.I358 C66 2000
   813'.6—dc2l

                                      00-009799

For my Father-in-Law,
Harry F. Dixon USMC, DFC

and in memory of my Mother-in-Law
and fellow writer,
Mary Lou Dixon

Mary Lou Dixon

ACKNOWLEDGMENTS

Grateful acknowledgment is made to all those who gave so graciously and generously of their time and knowledge. Any errors contained in the narrative are mine alone.

—*R.M.*

ROYAL AIR FORCE PILOTS:

The Royal Air Force Arnold Scheme Register:

F. Norman Bate: *MBE*
George T. Shaw
Edgar Spridgeon

Flight Instructors at Cochran Field:

Captain Victor Hewes: *Delta* Ret'd
G.A. (Mac) Findlay

UNITED STATES ARMY AIR FORCES PILOTS:

Commandant of Aviation Cadets:

Lt. Colonel Frank Iseman: Cochran Field Ret'd
    in memorium
Captain Miles T. (Marty) Bennett: *Eastern* Ret'd
    in memorium
Captain Len Morgan: *Braniff* Ret'd
    and Contrib. Ed. of *Flying Magazine*
Maurice Johnson
Thomas W. Fischer
Captain Steve Yeagle: *Eastern* Ret'd

USAAF Historians:

Dr. William Head
Dr. Richard Iobst
Ms. Mary Ann Kan

Librarian at Middle Georia Tech Inst.:

Lillian Peterson

City of Hartlepool, England:

Mr. Bill Hunter: historian
Neil Hunter, Simon Walton: *The Mail* staff members
Mr. J.M. Ward: Photo-chronologies
Mr. D. Blackett
Mrs. Mary Shaw Stott: cousin
Mrs. John Presland: LTCL, sister
Mr. Ernie Dring
Mr. Mick Cannon
Ms. Hilda Maguire

•

Special Thanks

Imperial War Museum, London
Royal Air Force Museum, Hendon, London
The Royal Air Force Arnold Scheme Register

Connie Green
Jo Stafford

Chapter 1

IT WAS NEAR noon when I arrived in Americus. I parked at the Central of Georgia Depot and touched up my Max Factor in the rearview mirror, giving attention to my rather full jawline inherited from my mother. That curve of jaw was on the faces in all the old photos from Tennessee, some of which were now mounted in silver frames. My eyes, gray or blue depending on light and mood, were my best feature, and all in all Nature had been kind. In a few moments a young woman's conceit would have me position myself for a flattering shaft of sunlight. As I got out of the car I felt the sweat and pulled at my dress. Liberal dabs of talcum powder accomplished only so much.

I stared at the locals spilling around the raised train platform and out across the parking lot. The men's familiar greasy battered hats were worn low against the sun and thumbs were hooked into overalls. The women were turned out as custom required in freshly ironed dresses and wearing their flowered hats. But the British cadets dominated everything, as foreign to Georgia soil and custom as you could get. How can I describe them? They did not wear uniforms. They wore gray suits and black ties, and what I would learn later were "bloody silly elastic belts." Some wore pith helmets, others had them balanced on duffel bags.

There must have been forty or fifty cadets standing in small groups, talking to the locals who had come out to meet them, occasionally smiling or nodding. Some of their faces were quite red, either from embarrassment at the reception or from the relentless Georgia heat. Some had mustaches. A couple of them smoked pipes, their hands waving away smoke as they talked. Quite a few smoked cigarettes, and there were cigarette butts on the ground. I took it all in, standing by my car under a hard blue sky in the pulsing heat. My practical flat shoes eased the walk across cobblestones.

I heard a voice lift, the English accent dissonant and unexpected among the Southern questioning. The cadets had this exotic tang to them in this small working town. The train had long gone and the cadets spoke and nodded, taking questions from farmers and insurance agents, women in dresses and kids leaning on bikes. The colored hung back on the crowd fringes the way they did when politicians came through on the stump, a little uncertain and careful. The talk was relaxed between locals and cadets; they had crossed that first threshold. Good things were being said, insightful things, shared things, and I was late. My presence would be a slight shift in the delicate balance, in the rhythms and ease of the gathering. A couple of reporters I knew moved through the crowd, press cards stuck in hat bands, flash cameras angling against bodies. I edged forward with my notebook in hand and smiled. Several cadets responded and waited expectantly. They were about my age, nineteen or twenty, with bright complexions and hair worn long, so different from the crew cut boys I'd dated. And reserved. I didn't know if that was from a pep talk orientation for dealing with the locals or a natural British reserve.

"Hi," I said. "I'm Doreen Summers, with the *Macon Dispatch*." My voice lifted in a Southern inflection, something I was trying to get rid of. "Can I ask you a few questions?"

"Certainly, miss."

"Doreen. That's an interesting name."

"Is it Southern?"

"I wish we had some shade. It's awfully hot."

I stared at them, their accents impacting on me, so very different, the unexpected delivery of their comments exciting. How would Lombard have handled this? I looked at the boy who found my name interesting. His pale face was pink from the sun. "You sound Scottish, are you from Scotland?"

They all laughed, loosening up with me, youth surmounting reserve. Others gravitated into our small group.

"Yes, he's Scottish. Proper pest."

"Ruin of the Empire."

"Ask him what he wears under his kilt."

"Here, steady on, chaps..."

"Ask him about the bagpipes. They got 'em from the Ancient Greeks and they've been learnin' 'em ever since!"

Any final reserve dissipated on laughter and there was some elbow thumping and swipes with helmets. I worked my pencil and notes but I caught the movement to one side. A local, his overall loose on one strap over a red shirt, his cap proclaiming Jarrell's Feed and Seed, stepped forward. I kept my face impassive, knowing what was coming, my attention fixed on my note pad.

"Young fellah," he said, his voice rich in our ways as he addressed the cadet who had made the crack about the kilt.

"Sir?"

"We don't talk like that with ladies present. I know you're new here, but that's good to remember." He nodded his head to his own words, "Just some friendly advice."

The cadet blushed furiously. "I'm terribly sorry, sir. Certainly no harm was meant. I'm terribly sorry."

"We all are," another cadet said, "We do apologize, Doreen."

The local looked from one to the other. "Sure, I understand. Just our ways, like you got your ways."

"Yes, sir."

I stepped in after a respectful beat, addressing the hapless cadet. "You all sound like very close friends — did you come over together?"

The mood lightened.

"Yes, indeed. But we haven't seen very much except from the train. We stopped in New York and had a wizard view. And the food's jolly good."

"Marvelous food. Nothing like it at home, what with the rationing, the war..."

Out of the corner of my eye I watched another farmer turn to a friend. "Wizard. What the hell's wizard?"

"Everyone's been very kind, very friendly, all the way down here. Wouldn't you say, Roy?"

"I'll say."

I watched Roy cast a careful brief look at Jarrell's Feed and Seed. It was a familiar look on a very unfamiliar face, the kind of look offered by a negro who is unsure of his ground. Get some human interest, my editor, Billy had said. Play it against the war in Europe, and here we were in the Briar Patch. I gripped my notebook and readied my next question, but the other farmer spoke first, moving from 'wizard' to firmer ground.

"What do you think of our women?"

The cadet struggled with this first apparent paradox: they had been admonished about certain jokes in a lady's presence and now faced this, my presence be damned.

"Absolutely charming, sir."

"Top drawer," somebody said.

"A little more open than girls back home."

"How come?" A meaty hand shoved back his hat.

"Sorry?"

"How come your girls ain't open?"

"Well, we're a bit more reserved, sir. The ladies are too."

"English ways."

"Right, that's it."

I took back the initiative. "So you came down from where, Canada?"

"Yes. A lovely ride down, the food really is marvelous, and the size of the country is mindboggling. And of course we can't get over the kindness of everyone."

They were relaxed again and the answers were charming, but I felt a certain rote to them. And there had been a brief hesitancy when I had asked about Canada. I started to dig. "I see you're not wearing uniforms, why is that?"

"Better skip that one, Roy."

It was a new British voice and I turned to face him. He was tall, sinewy, and his face, neck and hands were deeply sunburned. He was much older than the others I had been talking with, about twenty-seven, I guessed. His brown eyes watched me, and I knew instinctively they had been on me for some time. I fought my blush and uncertainty and returned his look. He seemed apart from it all, all the talk between cadets and locals, the cultural miscues, and he seemed impervious to the Georgia heat beating down on him.

"S'okay, sergeant," Roy said.

His eyes were so brown they were almost black and I found myself holding my notebook like some barrier between us. I shoved it down. "You won't tell me why you're wearing suits, then?"

"Same as I told the other news people, Miss. Better check at Souther Field."

He spoke quietly, his diction clear. And I knew that kind of applied effort. I was working on my own Southern accent, trying to smooth it out, developing my vocabulary, carefully enunciating 'negro,' readying myself for New York. What was he readying himself for? Wherever I was going with that thought got lost against the sudden hard drone of an airplane engine. The Stearman biplane climbed above us against the cloudless blue. Shadow dappled its yellow wings as fabric shaped to the currents of air. I watched the upturned faces around me, thanking God for the presence of mind to do so. The sergeant stared skyward. White skin showed against his collar, a sharp contrast with the sunbeaten neck. Upturned faces followed the training plane's progress as it made a climbing turn; they took in the bright blue fuselage and yellow wings, the stars and the red and white stripes at its tail. It was to me like a brightly adorned jungle bird. Two coveralled figures, helmeted and goggled, hunched down in open cockpits. As I made a note about English eyes turned skyward I was all too conscious of those brown eyes again directed at me. Where the hell was he, what lay in the back reaches of that look?

"It's got a big engine," someone said, shading his eyes.

"Bigger than a Tiger Moth's," Roy said.

"Whole thing's bigger than a Moth."

The brown eyes stayed on me.

I listened to the accents sounding out in counterpoint, willing my pencil across the pad, so terribly conscious of the older Englishman. But when I looked up, steeling myself to meet his gaze, he was gone. I saw him edging through the cadets and locals, smiling a little, nodding politely, moving towards the other reporters. Taking a deep breath I said, "What's a Tiger Moth, a British plane?"

"Yes, a trainer. Decent old kite."

"Kite?"

"We sometimes call aeroplanes kites."

"Oh. So you want to be pilots," I said, aware that my voice was brittle. "What if you wash out, do you think you'll wash out?"

It was the Scotsman who lightened the mood for me. "Well, I'll have n'trouble lass, but these idiots I'm forced to associate with, well, that's another..."

There were more thumps on arms, jeers and laughter. I was getting used to them and enjoying them. I looked around for the sergeant. "What's your sergeant's name?" I said at last, hoping I had waited long enough, put in enough buffer questions.

The group went silent. A cadet with a full mustache spoke for the first time. "That's George Wescott. You've got a real story there, miss."

"Oh? Why is that?"

"George was at Dunkirk. One of the last out."

"An army bod," Roy said. "A call went out for volunteers for pilot training. He got to keep his stripes." He ran a hand through his brillianteened hair. "Sorry. Should mind my own business."

I made a note. "Don't worry, I won't use it. He has a

nice accent. Where's he from?"

"Cripes, he'll love that!"

"Don't tell him that. He'll think you're taking the mickey."

"He's from the north, Newcastle way."

"No he's not, he's from Hartlepool, near Sunderland."

"Well, we know that, don't we? But would Doreen know Hartlepool? Not bloomin' likely. But she might know Newcastle."

"I know Newcastle," I said. "That's coal and ships. I've read about it in school."

Roy smiled. "He's from the north, and that makes him a Geordie, a northcountryman."

"A Geordie," I said, savoring the word; it spoke of clans and tribes and insular ways.

"Right. And that chap over there is Welsh. All Welshmen are nicknamed Taffy. Like Taffy Jones. But that's not quite the same thing."

"Come on, you're confusing her."

"No," I said hastily, "it's okay, I..."

But that's as far as I got because the buses began pulling in, and there was a sudden milling around in the beating heat, a grabbing at pith helmets and duffel bags while the locals, the farmers and insurance men, and women in summer dresses and flowered hats, told them to come over for some 'real Southern cookin' when they had a chance.

Months went by before I saw George Westcott again. By that time America was in the war and increasing numbers of British cadets came through airfields like Souther and Cochran. This time they wore their RAF blue and the uniform provided by the USAAC. And the first of them died, falling to earth in their brightly plumed machines so very far from home.

Chapter 2

GEORGE WESTCOTT CAME back into my life one day in early February, 1942. I wasn't ready. It was a bad day shrouded in morning ground fog. I was at Cochran Field, a basic training flight school near Macon and the Dispatch office. This is where the successful graduates of the sturdy Stearman biplane come to grips with the BT-13, the Vultee Vindicator. Pilots called it the Vibrator. I looked out at these airplanes as I sat on a damp bench outside the dispersal shack. They had a menace to them with their enclosed canopies and big engines, a dark prelude to the waiting warbirds, and at that moment I hated them. The closest plane offered its blue and yellow markings but the others faded back into wet gray shapes, then shadows, then nothing. Painted over street lights offered a weak halo here and there, and an army truck groped its way forward in the shaping dawn.

This was one of those ghastly days when you are hammered and molded by something that reaches deep inside you and stirs up the fear. Most things you can hide away under the gloss of living, and keep them on that outer edge of your world, but not this. The plane crash breeched my world and shriveled me up. Thoughts of New York with its Park Avenue and Greenwich Village were now far away and questioned. And newsprint itself was no longer lifeblood but instead some gauze filter I used to distance what was real, and now the gauze was torn open.

I watched the fog. Planes crashed, I knew that. But I had only heard of them by word of mouth, and the accidents were distanced by time. There was lazy talk about flight training down in Florida, where the heady smell of the orange groves rose a thousand feet into the air, to touch the pilots in their Stearman biplanes. But a biplane strut had severed, and the wing had folded, and the airplane had spun towards the orange groves like a sycamore seed, spinning, spinning, through the perfumed air. At Gunter Field in Alabama a BT-13 had fallen to earth, the sustaining cushion of air slipping from under its wings. No height, no height to recover...

John Piggott was a slender young Englishman from London. He was fair and blue eyed, with a certain alertness to his gaze that smacked of rude streets and quick wits; and he taught me to foxtrot and I taught him to jitterbug.

John Piggott could not drive. I took him for a ride once, and we stood beside the Nash. "Smashing car, Doreen. Just like in the films with the white circles on the tires. And it's so big! Everything's big over here, even the birds. Your robin is huge compared to our English robin. But I love your Cardinals; what smashing color they have." We had a flat that day, what John called a puncture. The farm girl had to step in and help the well intentioned but inept cadet. I'll remember that drive always: glancing across at John, watching him take in our Georgia land and fields. "I saw some of England and Scotland when we were coming over here, but it was nothing like this. Here there's a looser look, wilder, a ranging of the land. In England we have small hedges around fields making them look rather neat, like a quilt. And it's all a far cry from London grime." John eyed me, declaring secrets. "I'm not from the fancy parts, you know, Doreen. No bowler hat for me. Dad was a train driver on the Underground. I got along well in school but my home life was modest, what we English like to call working class. The minute you open your gob in England they pigeonhole you."

"I know the feeling. I'm trying to improve my own way of talking. People up north make fun of us. So you're a Cockney? That's what Londoners are called?"

"Only some of us. Technically a Cockney is someone born to the sound of Bow Bells."

"And a Geordie...what's a Geordie?"

John laughed. "Cripes, a Geordie? Who told you about them? A Geordie's a Northerner, like from County Durham, up that way. A bit clannish. They come down to London looking for work but can't wait to get back north. Cockneys and Geordies take the mickey out of each other, but deep down we're all Englishmen."

"Not like us, then," I said.

"How'd you mean?"

"Well, the Civil War, North versus South. What we in the South call the War Between the States, We're still fighting it."

"Oh, the English are bloodthirsty, Doreen. England's history is full of bloodshed. The Thirty Years War, and fighting Robert the Bruce and the Scots."

"But not Cockneys against Geordies."

"No, but if we had a go at it, the Cockneys would win," John said flatly. "Blimey! Look at that eagle."
I followed his eye to an extended tree branch. "That's a hawk. They hunt for rodents mostly."

"He's beautiful. Got a menace to him."

"John, do you know George Westcott?"

Tires thrummed. The name hung on the sound, along with my own anxiety and hope.

"Westcott, Westcott. Can't say I do."

"He was at Dunkirk."

"Ah, an army type. Tough egg. What class is he?"

"The first one, when we were neutral and they had to wear suits and ties."

"Oh. 42A. No, he's too far ahead for me to know him. He must be through, now. Gone back to England and an OTU."

"OTU?"

"Operational Training Unit. Preparing to go on the squadrons, get into the fighting."

"Oh." I shrugged it off as best I could, thinking about the nights in my rented room in Macon, the map of the British Isles with Hartlepool circled, the library book and brief notes. And the quieted dark and secret thoughts. Those early dances when I kept glancing across a partner's shoulders, looking, searching. Never there... "Oh, Westcott? Sorry, luv, you won't see him here, I'm afraid. Bit of a loner."

I swallowed hard. "It must be exciting to live in London, John. I know it only from books at school, of course."

"Well, it's like most places. If you live there you don't go to see the sights. I did some for school, of course. Mum would make me some egg sandwiches and get me some lemon squash and off I'd go to the Science Museum in Kensington. Any kid would love it. But as I got older I went to the Victoria and Albert. Very interesting there. Period costumes, dress and so on. And we had a school trip once up to St. Alban's to see Verulanium, the old

Roman city. The remains of the baths are still there. Funny to think of it now: St. Alban's is only about twelve miles from Fighter Command."

I glanced at him, catching the change in his voice. "What is it?"

"Oh, nothing, really."

"Come on, John, spill it."

"Well, I want to be a good pilot, Doreen. Not some Battle of Britain type, obviously, but a good pilot. I did well in Primary, but I already had a few hours in Tiger Moths back home, so I had a head start. But..."

"But what?"

A possum lurched across the road in front of us, shuffling about its business.

"That's a possum, right?"

"But what, John?"

"Well, here at Cochran it's tougher for me. The BT-13's okay, it's the navigation. It's no longer seat of the pants flying. I'm worried about night flying too."

"You'll do fine."

We eased around a curve. Some negroes sat beside the road.

"They're a long way from anywhere," John said.

"What...the colored? Not really."

"Wouldn't like to walk it," he said, "no bus for Twickenham here."

I thought about that. I said carefully, "What do you think of our segregation, the negroes?"

He waved a dismissing hand. "It's not my place to..."

"No, come on. What do you think?"

"Well, I come from a class structure where I'm the underdog, Doreen. I guess I'm for live and let live." He smiled, dismissing it. "None of my business, really." As he looked out the car window his face was somber, reflective.

The last time I saw John and we had time alone was at a Cochran dance. I had a side job as PRO, public relations office, which got me into the thick of things taking photos and writing for the wires, but this moment was ours. It was a warm night and we sat beside the swimming pool. I slipped off a shoe and dangled my foot in the cool water. Folds of my evening dress were captured by moonlight, and the dance music and laughter flooded from the hall, and he talked about the King and Queen and how once, before the war, he had watched them ride by in their horsedrawn carriage. "No matter what station we have in life," he said, "we are all soldiers of the King. And you won't see our royal family running off to safety somewhere, like Canada." I commented on the pageantry, the beauty and pomp of it. John smiled. "Can you see 'em driving in their carriage down Main Street in Americus? There's a scene for you..." the band moved into Jimmy Dorsey's *Tangerine*. John stared at the glittering pool water. "Two things about us, Doreen. We honor our King and Country, and we don't shop our mates."

"What does that mean, you don't shop your mates?"

He shrugged. "You don't turn in your pals. This honor code you have over here, turning in your mates. It doesn't sit right with us. It's not our way. We had a lad who couldn't swim very well, so one of us took his swimming test. Bit of a fiddle, but we got him through. If we'd done it your way we'd have lost a mate and a damned fine pilot too." I can see him now, brooding, a Cockney underdog, who ate egg sandwiches in museums and got himself an education, enough to qualify for pilot training. "You don't shop your mates..."

When I heard about the plane crash I got there fast, asking my reporter questions. *Yes, weather was good...*

no, the engine just quit on takeoff... the ship hung in the air then slowly rolled over and down...worst thing, I could see the instructor in the rear seat fighting it, and the student up front, frozen, looking out... No, the instructor was from Miami, Ohio, a good ball player. I don't know the student, some English guy...

The autopsies of Jimmy Peterson, ball player, and John Piggott, soldier of the King, would be done in Hawkinsville. Peterson would go home to Ohio. Piggott would be buried at Oakwood Cemetery in Montgomery, Alabama, far from the sound of Bow Bells.

"That you, Doreen?"

"Bill?"

Lieutenant Bill Trepick loomed in the shaded yellow light, a bulk in the fog, his A-2 jacket beaded with moisture. I had dated Bill several times and enjoyed his homespun tales about Wisconsin red barns and cows. We had stopped dating in a mutual unease when he got too insistent, his hands too adventurous.

"What're you doin' out here, and where's your authorization?"

I handed him the chit.

"You've got pull to wangle this. Anyway, come into Dispersal."

"I wanted some time alone," I said.

"Like me to shove off?"

"No." I fingered my public relations office badge and ran a thumb over my smiling, too confident face. It was slippery to the touch.

"Damned ground fog's gonna knock flights off schedule. Won't get the weather ship up until 1100." He glanced at me, sizing me up. "Look, you'd better stick close. You shouldn't be in here, even with that pass you got."

"Bill?"

"What."

"Did you know them?"

"Know them?" His brow cleared. "Oh. Yeah, I knew the instructor, Jimmy, a good guy. I don't remember the English cadet." His hand moved apologetically. "We just keep shoving them through. Primary, Basic, Advanced—get 'em back to England."

"I've done some interviewing on that."

"Gonna do a story on this?"

I shook my head. "My editor said no."

"Oh."

"I talked to him about it. He didn't like references to 'flying coffin.' Not good for the war effort."

Bill looked at me with his eyes flashing a first impatience. "Come on, drop that talk. The BT's a sweet ship."

"I hear its engine is too big, too much torque or something."

"No."

"That's why its wing loading is too sensitive. Isn't that what it's called, wing loading?"

"Lady, where'd you pick up the technical stuff?"

"Talking with cadets."

"Well, knock it off. At least on that subject. The BT's accident rate is within limits and it's a good ship." The eyes steadied on me. "And it's the only good basic trainer we got, at least for now. And watch what you say in your stories, you'll have the FBI after you. There's a war on, you know." His hand dug into his leather flight jacket. "Cigarette?"

"No, thanks."

"That's right, I forgot. They make you cough."

"And stain my fingers."

"Yeah."

Somebody in Dispersal turned on a radio. Glenn Miller brass drove a sweet beat at the fog.

"You like the English guys," Bill said, exhaling smoke at the ground.

"Sure. I like all the cadets."

"Yes, but you really like these English guys. What is it, because they're foreign?"

I thought about it. "A couple of them gave me books to read. Poetry. And a Madame Butterfly record. I've never listened to opera before."

Bill smiled mischievously. "That how I get to you, Doreen...woo you with a little opera?"

I went red, off balance, moving from thoughts about death and airplanes and war to a spastic protection of sexual urges. And Mama's warning, delivered *sotto voce* in the parlor. 'You must remain pure, Doreen, chaste... Northern men are no different in that regard, I'm sure...' Bill drew deep on his cigarette. "They're bringing in a replacement instructor for Peterson. Fresh out of Maxwell's instructor course."

"Oh?"

Ash sparked and fell. "English guy. Sent him up to Canada, got fitted out in RAF blues, RAF wings. They're holding him back instead of sending him home. We're short of instructors."

Something moved inside me, some strange echo like a fingertap on a base drum. I saw the Stearman biplane, climbing against the blue, and the sergeant's upturned, impassive face, the white skin stark against the deep suntan line at his collar. "Know who it is?"

"Why, you gonna interview him?"

"Maybe."

"He's on the roster, new arrivals. Pilot Officer Westcott. George."

"Pilot Officer?"

"British rank."

"I know. I thought he was a sergeant."

Bill's eyes skewered me. "No. How come you know him?"

"I covered the arrival of the first cadets over in Americus. He was one of them."

Bill grinned. "Helluva memory. Made an impression, huh? Maybe he reads poetry."

"Anyway," Bill said, standing up and grinding out his cigarette under his shoe, "he's coming here. Maybe by train, maybe fly in when this all lets up. What's happening about the dance tonight?"

"It's still on. They would've wanted it that way."

"Save one for me."

I was alone again but now suddenly glad of it. The fog clung thick as ever, but now his life beat thumped in me. George Westcott was suddenly real again; the man I thought was gone, beyond reach, was reentering my world. And I felt a wash of guilt as John Piggott faded back like the airplanes, into shadows, then nothing. I struggled with that. But then I thought about what he would say, and in some deep release I gave myself up to waiting for Westcott.

Chapter 3

A LEMON SUN kept its promise, sending the training planes up, bright blue and yellow birds stiff winged against a cloud flecked sky. The sound of their engines drove away all ghosts and fears summoned on the early morning fog. The sun revealed a field resonating to the movement of airplanes: BT-13 trainers zigzagged along taxiways, trailing their tailwheels (thumping a pilot's spine, cadets told me, and the rudder banged like an old tin can). Pilots peered around the big engine cowlings and whirling propellers, staying on track. Some took off in flights of three, wings lifting and rocking; others took off alone, heading for practice areas to master the stalls and spins, the pylon eights — all the dances of survival I had witnessed in enthusiastic hand movements and sketches on cocktail napkins, this ultimate slow melding of man and machine. Some of the first combat losses were getting back to us, boys who had themselves sketched on cocktail napkins. We would absorb the losses, then move on to a swing beat. They flew off into the rapidly heating air, gathering height in a carefully choreographed ballet, climbing, climbing, away from the dark scorching where one of their number had fallen to earth. Under the Plexiglas canopies that winked in the sun were British boys I knew. Archie Watkins, a Yorkshireman who would play piano tonight and speak knowledgeably of jazzmen in New Orleans and Memphis; Freddie Latham was up there, a Cornwall boy who loved Keats and bad puns; and Stuart 'Haggis' McKay from Glasgow, who tonight would sit as he always did with his gin and tonic, rolling a shilling coin expertly across his knuckles and talking about his racing pigeons.

But a strengthening sun also put in clear light my own doubts and insecurities about meeting George Westcott. How would I meet this enigmatic Englishman, how could I engage the interests of a man seasoned by life's experiences, who was so self possessed, sure of who he was; while I was playing at it, pushing at life with a reporter's pencil, diligently documenting things I knew nothing about? And who was he, really? What I knew of him was a first impression on a hot June day in Americus, and I had taken that and fragments of his background gleaned from his countrymen and created someone who inhabited my reveries indulged in against a soft pillow during long and empty nights. Truth be told, I was waiting to meet someone I did not know. Too cerebral, Doreen. Let the feelings out. Let loose the thumping heart and hot images. I sat there, blinking in the sun, crushing a candy wrapper in my coat pocket, and looked around at what was driving the energies of a military base: far off bulldozers gouged at the red Georgia crust; men marched to ground school; jeeps whipped through their gears, all sound lost against the airplane engines. Some planes were quiet, parked near hangars and curiously mute, abandoned, their propellers stilled.

Let the hot images out.

I rubbed at my face, sighed and took stock. How was I? Seams straight, some Max Factor touch up needed, no candy crumbs. Only a nervous twisting of an earring and my high school ring gave evidence of the emotional buffeting I was going through. There had been a one time meeting at the Americus train depot, then nothing. Nothing. At Souther Field's socials and public relations assignments I had burned for contact with him, keeping up conversations over swizzle sticks, dancing and looking across shoulders. No Westcott of the brown almost black eyes, sinewy build and careful composure. George. What would it be like to call him that? *So, do you have a girl back home, George? I'm sure you must.* Fantasies were relentless and I confided in my one good friend, Wendy Clinkscales; my last friend really since being ostracized as a snob by everyone else. What were his dreams, his pet peeves, did he like eggs for breakfast, did he smoke? Restless thoughts, superficial and so terribly important. Images. His bemused eyes and our shared concern for good diction. What kind of relationship was that?

But George Westcott was always there, in back of every conversation, at every dance where I made wet circles with my cocktail glass while I listened to a cadet talk about home; or while I tapped my foot to Tommy Dorsey's *Song of India* and a boy talked excitedly about his flying that morning. He was always there, in my images, holding it all together, a dimension of excitement and mystery.

"If you come over to England after the war, Doreen, you must stay with us. My insufferable sister can sleep on the settee."

"That would be great, Freddie. I hope to go to New York after the war, maybe sooner."

"Smashing. And do what?"

"Become a reporter on a big newspaper. But I'll have to work my way up like Dorothy Kilgallen did."

"Don't know her. We came through New York on the train down from Canada. Two of us got off and had an ice cream soda."

"New York's exciting, challenging. And glamorous — Ginger Rogers and Fred Astaire."

"Mum likes those films. Takes her mind off things, she says. How did you like Madame Butterfly?"

"Great. Gave me goose bumps."

"You'll have to hear me and Haggis do the Pirates of Penzance. Spot on, we are, if I do say so myself. Sometimes he keeps rolling that shilling across his knuckles but he never messes up."

"I'm inviting some of the guys to the farm. Mama and Daddy like the company. Can you come — can Haggis come?"

"Absolutely. As long as we don't do anything barmy and get demerits. By the way, do you know John Piggott? Hey, Piggott! Get over here. Doreen, this chap wants to learn how to jitterbug. He's got three left feet but can you salvage him?"

On those weekends at the farm you could count the pairs of shoes removed by cadets who didn't want to wake anybody. Those well shined shoes were always in a neat row at the foot of the stairs. And odd things, British things, marked the guys' presence as they slept. On tables and dressers were cigarette packets with unfamiliar brand names like Churchill's and Players, Capstans and Woodbines. And there were always British coins and playing cards and score pads with handwriting that was so distinctive and to me elegant. Sometimes in that quiet I would romanticize about Westcott. His coins. His handwriting. For me, tiptoeing around, my home held the echoes of British voices, shouts in northcountry and southcountry accents, or Scottish and Welsh and Irish twangs. And I would listen carefully to the northcountry accents. He was always there, always there.

"Come on, Taffy, get off it!"

"He played the nine of hearts, the twit."

"Les, I hope you ride that Royal Enfield better than you play cards."

"Enfield's no good, anyway. You need a 1,000 CC Panther."

"How about an Indian?"

"Nice bike in its own way. Definitely American looking."

"I think there's a difference in national character, like in the design of warships and aeroplanes. Like in the lines on a Spitfire versus a P-40."

"Think they'll let you near a Spit, Taffy? Dream on."

"Hey, he's done it again. He's gone with the eight of clubs..."

"Oh, belt up."

But there was only an occasional word about George Westcott and that came from Wendy Clinkscales delivered in her affected British accent. "Oh, he doesn't come to the swimming pool, dances or anything. Sticks to himself mostly." All of which I knew already. Well, today would be different and I would handle it. I'd waited all morning for him and now I'd maintain a detachment. P/O George Westcott would be no different to any other airman, American or British. I would quiz him from my list of questions, such as what did he think of becoming an instructor, being held back and not going overseas for active duty. Then there was the dance tonight. Should I mention it? Why not? Afterall, I had a job to do; take PRO pictures.

A BT-13 moved through its landing pattern towards the runway, dropping a wing into final approach. I stared at it. BTs were everywhere — why this one? I got anxious. My heart thumped against my business suit, and I felt again that finger tap on a base drum. The BT descended, flaring delicately, settling its yellow wings, the wide set wheels reaching for the runway, over the scorching, God bless you John and Jimmy...touch...touch...down. I jammed my hand into my coat pocket and crushed the candy wrapper. The basic trainer moved along the taxiway, its canopy slid open. Two men. One to fly it back to Maxwell Field? It swung around on a pulsing rev of engine then parked off by itself, away from other maneuvering planes. Both men climbed down. I watched the taller man in RAF blues and white coverall. He carried a flat case, stuff he would need, obviously. In Americus he had stared skyward at the Stearman biplane, an Englishman in a gray suit and black tie. And now he was walking towards me.

"Hey, Summers! Better freshen up."

I jumped at Bill Trepick's words and felt instinctively for my skirt seams, shoving a hand at my hair, worrying about my jawline.

"I'll introduce you," Bill said. "But let him get signed in, okay?"

I nodded and studied my notebook. When I knew Westcott was close to the dispersal shack I dragged my head up, my heartbeat driving the blood to my cheeks. The calm brown eyes were on me. I had the delirious feeling they had been on me for some time. Like before. "Good morning," I said, barren months washing away. There were small lines etched into the corners of his eyes. A trainer blared its path from the runway, scattering my words.

"Morning." He nodded pleasantly, a questioning look — was it recognition?...then he went inside. His

RAF blues and wing brevet were brand new in the sun. That was it. He was gone. Gone inside with Trepick. God, what would Bill say, what if he talked about our dating? Bill could be cutting sometimes. And he was both possessive and competitive. Not a good combination. I watched through the window as P/O George Westcott from Hartlepool near Sunderland, survivor of Dunkirk, made log entries. Bill said something and suddenly Westcott was staring at me. It was Americus all over again, my talcum gumming into sweat, me off balance, my notebook coming up instinctively to hold him off. They came out together and hulked over me.

"She's been here since 0530, George. Knew the English cadet in the crash. How she pulled strings to get here I don't know, but her pass is in order."

"Miss Summers." Westcott said.

I nodded. No handshake. No touch. I should offer my hand. Southern gentility said so, Emily Post said so. The moment passed and was lost.

"She wants to interview you, George. Says she knows you from Americus."

Dammit Bill, let me talk! But I couldn't talk. I who had preened at interviewing company executives about the war effort, who had watched the faces of ruined farmers as they stared at the dry cracked earth, who had watched gaunt mothers holding malnourished babies — I had no words.

Westcott smiled. He had very white teeth but a crooked front tooth. All these months and pillow reveries and I had not known that. "That must have been at the train depot. When we first arrived."

Three BTs took off in formation, rattling the windows, and I watched him turn, shading a critical eye from the sun as he watched their progress. The lines at the corners of his eyes deepened, then he abruptly turned back to me again. "You wore suits and ties," I said, finally getting it together.

"And I discouraged you, didn't I. I remember."

"Do you? You told me to check at Souther Field."

His eyes stayed on mine. "And did you?"

"Yes. You were wearing suits because America was neutral." It came out like a child's answer to a classroom arithmetic problem. I knew Bill was watching me. He had never seen me like this, awkward and girlish. It was getting to him, something he couldn't handle. Well, I couldn't worry about that.

Bill shifted his feet. "Not much time, George."

A concern touched the sunburned angles of his face. "I'm very sorry, Miss Summers, but I've got to get ready for some instructing." He took a step, hefting his leather case. "Everything's running behind."

"Can I see you tonight, then? For an interview I mean." My mouth was dry, the words coming out wrong, everything slipping away. "There's a dance."

"Doreen's with the PRO, she'll be working this evening." Bill said quietly.

Bless you, Bill Trepick, and all your unborn children. I watched as Westcott smiled again and said, "Yes, we can do that. Since you knew the English cadet who died…"

That's as far as he got. Tension unleashed from inside me, from deep hidden places, shearing through private mists and self doubt, driving the anger. "I don't trade on dead friends, Westcott. See me, but not because of John." It was like he imploded, sucking me into the vortex. Not anger, more an instantly guarded surprise. "No, of course not. I said that badly. A bit tired, I suspect. See you tonight, then."

I nodded, wanting to say something, to save it, but I was numbed, jammed up inside.

Bill broke the ghastly tension. "Stuff coming by bus, you say?"

"Yes."

"Don't count on it today. Tomorrow if you're lucky. Meantime let's get over to BOQ. You're in with Martinelli."

They were walking away.

"What's his Christian name?"

"First name? Alphonse. But you'd be wise to call him Butch. Good second looey though, natural pilot." Bill looked back at me, his grin wicked, the message clear: You blew it, honey.

I just stood there. Of all the emotions, that was the last I had expected. Straight ahead, Doreen. Mama would be proud.

Chapter 4

"I DON'T CARE if he looks like Dracula," Wendy Clinkscales was saying, "just so long as he can dance!"

Archie Watkins laughed. "Good news for you, Freddie."

I kept quiet, slowly turning my glass, clinking ice cubes. The dance was off to its usual comfortable start with cadets and girls sitting at tables around the dance floor under the draped Stars and Stripes, Union Jack, and RAF ensign. Colorful streamers were looped across the walls. There was a good turnout and the band was good. The musicians as usual were older, well above draft age. They wore tuxedos and their saxophones and trumpets gleamed in the smoky artificial light. I had spent some time at the newspaper phoning around for the ever willing girls I knew from my reporter job. This time I had to force myself to sound upbeat, but the girls made it easier. They were girls with plans of their own. Even Wendy, a real farm girl, had applied to the FBI hoping to train as a fingerprint clerk in Washington. And tonight we all looked good. Wendy had borrowed my second best dancing shoes to go with her new red and white sequined dress. I was wearing my emerald green dress with the flowered top, and I had my hair up and braided in a popular Esther Williams style. I looked around. Ashtrays were filling up, there were the first empty glasses with melted ice, a first napkin drawing of an aerobatic maneuver.

"How are you, Doreen?" Freddie Latham asked.

I stared at my drink.

"I just wish he would hurry up."

"At least you know he's coming."

I laughed at that. Freddie had cut close to the bone. All those nights when I had looked and never seen him. At least this night he was coming.

"What do you plan to say?" Wendy asked.

I shrugged. "Apologize. I was rude and touchy and I need to apologize."

Haggis shook his head. "I think you're being hard on yourself. You were upset about John Piggott, he told you he was tired. It'll smooth over, he's a good type." He patted his pockets. "I'm out. Got a fag, Arch?"

Archie reached across the table with the cigarettes then offered a match.

"Cheers," Haggis said, through a puff of smoke, picking up his shilling.

"I still have trouble with that word," Wendy said.

"What...cheers?"

"Fag."

"It's just a word for cigarette, like dumper."

"Dumper?"

"A dog-end."

"A butt?" Wendy's eyes were wide.

"Right."

I forced myself to talk, join in. "Like 'homely' Remember when Freddie recited some Keats at the Davidson's dinner party, then told them what a homely house they had?"

"Poor Freddie," Wendy grinned, her brown eyes sparkling as she sipped her rum and coke.

Freddie's eyes widened. "Well, I didn't know, did I? In England 'homely's' a nice word."

"So, do you say 'homey' now?" I asked.

"I don't use the word at all, thank you very much. I try and think of something else nice to say." Freddie's face was reddening. "God, that was embarrassing."

"And the pun you used on Mr. Davidson," Wendy went on. "Alimentary, my dear Watson."

"It lost something because of British and Southern accents. Anyway, isn't it time to pick on somebody else? I've had my two penneth."

"The Keats was good," Archie said quickly. "Everyone loved your Keats."

I tried to stay in the banter but my mind kept wandering back to my own concerns. Yes, I would apologize, but how would we get together. Would he come to our table, beckon me outside, smile, not smile? I glanced across at the instructors' table. Bill Trepick was lost in airmanship, his coveted wings gleaming in the subdued light, his hands turning, diving at the table cloth, while his date stared wide eyed, hanging on every word. There would be adventurous hands tonight.

I looked away and found Haggis watching me, his gaze thoughtful, the shilling rolling on its knuckled journey. "Look, he said he was coming to talk with you, so he couldn't have taken it too badly, or he'd have told you to buzz off."

"That's true."

Freddie chimed in. "With respect, Doreen, Westcott's been through a lot, and I don't think you could've put much of a dent in him."

"That's true too." Archie said. "The bombing at

Dunkirk, being in Class 42A — their lot got the worst of it."

I looked at him. "You mean 42A had no introduction to American ways, Southern ways, straight off the boat? I did a piece on that at Turner."

"Then you know, don't you?" Archie said. "It's been up hill for him all the way through. Lots of his classmates got washed out for stupid reasons…"

"Oh, come on," Wendy said, "not again."

"…and some of them had already soloed in England before coming here. Crackers, just crackers. Washing out good men for nothing."

"And remember, Doreen," Freddie said quietly, "Westcott was in the air instructing in less than an hour. He hardly had time to pee."

I smiled in spite of myself. "Sorry, I guess I'm spoiling the evening."

Freddie leaned over and pressed my hand. "You'll do fine. He shouldn't be too long."

"Nigel washed out today." Archie said.

The shilling fell off Haggis's knuckles. "Oh Christ. What for?"

"Froze during a sideslip. His instructor had to kick the stick to knock him loose."

A trumpet offered a quiet rippling phrase signaling a break. Cadets and girls moved slowly back to their tables.

"I liked Nigel," Wendy said.

"A good man." Haggis drew on his cigarette and stared at the coin but he didn't pick it up. "He'll head up to Canada, I expect. Train as an observer or something."

"He could get his wings," Freddie said. "The RCAF has different training methods, more like the RAF's. Didn't Dusty Miller get through that way?"

"Yeah. He's on ops now, or so I hear."

Archie grimaced. "I hear our instructors have new orders. Don't waste time on a cadet if he muffs it, plenty more coming through."

I opened my clutch purse and rummaged for a tissue, poking aside my gasoline coupons. Westcott had imploded, just retreated on me, not giving up anything. I would go to him, apologize, and ask him to dance. Could I do that? Yes. I could do that. The musicians came back, sitting, twisting, turning pages on their music stands, checking reeds and mouthpieces, talking to each other and looking around. Then they settled, hunching into *I Hear a Rhapsody*, a nice choice to bring back the mood. I decided to wait a while before taking PRO pics; let things get more settled. Usually the evening began with lively tunes like *Kalamazoo*, then moved into slower, dreamier numbers like Frankie's *All or Nothing at All*, then moving on into nostalgic British songs like *Lambeth Walk*, or *White Cliffs of Dover*, or *Roll Out the Barrel*. I dragged my thoughts back to the table. They were commiserating again on American ways, Army Air Corps ways, anyway. I know it got to some girls. They preferred to date American cadets, turned off by it all. Wendy's sister would not date a British cadet, which caused occasional matching up problems. But I loved it, reveled in it. It was all life beyond my own experience.

"And God help you if you don't hit it off with your instructor." Freddie was saying. "Higginbotham got it that way, remember?"

Archie nodded. "Primary at Souther. That bush pilot didn't like his posh accent."

"Higginbotham brought a lot on himself." Haggis said quietly. "He baited him with that superior air. I tried to talk to him once about my pigeons. He looked at me like I was dirt. They're all toffee nosed snots."

"Don't write off your fellow cadets who've had privileged upbringings, Haggis," Archie said. "Remember Aubrey Pym? Eton and Cambridge, the lot. You couldn't find a nicer bloke."

"Yeah, I suppose. I was forgetting Aubrey."

Archie slit open another pack of Player's with his thumb. "Thing was, before Pearl Harbor we were at war and the Americans weren't. Damned hard for us to get serious about hazing and eating by the square while families back home were being bombed. They couldn't understand that. 'Course, now they're in the war and the penny's dropped."

"Still eating by the square, though. And memorizing barmy quotations."

"Give 'em some Keats."

"Right, and I'm on my way back to Canada."

"Higginbotham's parents bought it in London, didn't they?" Haggis said.

Archie picked up the shilling and looked at it, King George the Sixth's profile glittering, a talisman from home. "His father did. He was an air raid warden who marked exam papers for a local school. Got it just before Christmas. Y'know, I think the American money system is better than ours. Shillings are okay, they're like quarters, but think about our halfcrown — not even a whole crown..."

"What happened to his mother?" I asked.

"Don't know. With family, I expect." Archie handed the coin back to Haggis.

Wendy stopped the serious drift to the talk by lunging in with her characteristic zest, forgetting to put on her English accent. "Hey, guys we're here to dance, okay? Who wants to hold me in wild abandon?"

Archie had his chair back in an instant. "Wendy, my luv, here I am. Once around the garden as they say."

"It's a foxtrot, you kicked me last time."

"You just hang on, girl."

Freddie pressed my hand again. "Care to dance, Doreen?"

"What if he comes in?"

"Well, you can ignore him and let him come to you, or leave me standing — which under the circumstances would be okay with me."

"You're sweet, Freddie." I said, as I shoved the camera under the table. Jokes about Freddie's looks aside, the man danced like a dream. We went into our familiar embrace and moved to *Moonlight and Shadows*. I tried to let myself go, let Freddie guide me under the subdued lights.

"I like your hair in plaits," he said.

"Plaits...you mean my braids?"

"Braids, yes. Very nice."

"Thank you."

We turned slowly, watching faces. It didn't take long.

"You're on, Doreen. He's here."

"Where!"

"Over to your right. What would you like to do?"

We were still dancing.

"I want to go over to him. Take the initiative and apologize."

"Why don't you then. See you back at the table some time."

Freddie turned me with the minimum of fuss, then I was edging through dancing couples and moving towards Westcott. I should have stepped to the tables and simply walked around, but there I was, edging towards him. He saw me then. I tried to smile, still edging through, then I was beside him.

"Miss Summers. I'm a bit late..."

"Doreen, please call me Doreen." I let the words out, not wanting to stop them. "George, I'm so terribly sorry, I don't know where that anger came from. It just burst loose and I lashed out at you, and I was rude beyond belief..."

"Here, steady on." He smiled at me. "It wasn't..."

"Yes it was."

We were on the fringe of the dance floor, couples slowly turning. I took a bump and fell forward a step. His hand came out to steady me, taking my arm. It was our first touch, and I shall remember it always. It came across reverie and dream, hope and yearning, and he was suddenly real.

Then he let go. "You and Piggott were close."

"Yes. A couple of underdogs, misfits." I watched his eyes, dark in the smoky hall.

"Grieving does strange things. It always has anger in it." He glanced around at the slow sinuous turning of dancers. "Look, this isn't the place to talk like this, let's..."

"Dance with me, George."

"What?" He looked startled. "I haven't danced in years."

Wordlessly I took his hand, half expecting him to pull back, but then we were in with other couples and beyond retreat. His arm came around me and he grasped my hand, his now holding mine, then we were dancing, and for me, the reporter always tuned in to observation and fact, I just let everything go and it was indescribably lovely. The new RAF wings held a luster in the light and I wanted to lay my head against his chest, but I was able to hold back, to wait, intoxicated with things as they were. Then, to my surprise, I caught a whiff of Lifebuoy soap coming from his shirt. "It's crowded," I said. "You just have to shuffle." Touch. Touch. "You dance fine."

He was looking around at the dancers, the cadets at the tables. He was not comfortable, but I sensed that he was glad to be there. And it was true, he hadn't danced in years. As he turned me I became aware of quizzical looks, a girl's profile lifted as she whispered into her partner's ear. Westcott was oblivious to it. Bill Trepick watched us, then turned back to his date.

"It's odd being back," he said at last. "Look at those cadets. They're not relaxed, y'know. Their brains are going a mile a minute. I remember how it was."

"And now you've completed Advanced and Instructor's training."

"Hard to believe, but yes."

He was still looking around, a touch of small boy to him. Where was my enigmatic Englishman, a man seasoned by life's experiences, self possessed? "What did you do at Advanced?"

"Multi-engine. AT-9s."

"Isn't that the one where they say if you can fly it, you can fly anything?"

"That's right." He smiled again, more comfortable now.

"How were you selected as an instructor?"

"Heaven only knows. I'm older, of course."

"And more mature. You were at Dunkirk, you've seen action." I felt his body tighten. "I'm sorry. Occupational hazard of being a reporter. But you must know the cadets here are talking about you. Their destiny is in your hands."

"Destiny?" His foot hit my ankle. "I'm sorry, I kicked you."

"It's okay."

"Destiny's laying it on a bit thick."

"Worries about washing out, then."

"Well, I'm an unknown quantity. They were comfortable with Peterson." He looked down at me then, looking into my eyes. "Is this an interview, Doreen?"

I listened to my name echo back. He emphasized the first syllable. DOReen. Another joke on my reveries. "No, of course not. Sorry. I'm just filling in spaces. To tell you the truth I'm a little nervous."

"So am I."

I wanted him to say something else but he glanced away, watching the couples dance. "There's Bill," he said. I looked across at Trepick who was dancing snuggled close to the wide-eyed girl, his turns precise and sensual. I knew those turns. A perceptive cadet once said he flew the same way.

"He dances well." George said.

"He's a smoothie."

"Ah."

George guided me around the floor, avoiding bumps and elbow jabs. "You really do dance just fine."

"I guess it's coming back, like riding a bike."

"That's not too flattering, George. I'd rather think I inspire you."

It was a long moment, a long musical beat. "I think you do."

I wanted more, greedy for it, and I held the silence hoping he would fill it, but he glanced away again, slowly gliding us to the music. He held my body half distant, but not with the easy comfort of John or Freddie; it was as if he were recording old senses and pleasures, not sure of himself, but not wanting to let go, disengage, give them up. And he smelled of Lifebuoy soap.

"The band is pretty good," I said at last.

"Yes. Trumpets could be stronger. The chap on tenor sax steals the show."

"You talk like you play, do you play?"

He smiled and shook his head. "No. I had little time for that in the army. But I have a good jazz record collection from school days. Louis Armstrong, Art Tatum, Chick Webb, some early cuts of Sidney Bechet. And Duke Ellington, of course."

"You should meet Archie Watkins. He's great on piano, and once you get him talking about New Orleans and Chicago you can't shut him up." I waited, then had to fill in again. "I've noticed so many British guys love jazz."

"Don't you?"

"Frankly, no. It's just noise to me. Except for Benny Goodman, of course, and Glenn Miller, and the Dorseys. I understand Swing and their playing. But..."

"But?"

"Well, I don't get the real jazz stuff. Like Louis Armstrong. What's so good about his playing, why is he better than Harry James?"

George smiled, but this time it was more open, a matching of eyes and mouth. "There are people all over the British Isles with American record collections who could answer that for you. Fact is, by 1926 Louis Armstrong had changed the face of music, and Harry James would be the first to acknowledge that. If Armstrong had done nothing after 1926 he would still be remembered." He turned my hand in his, pressing it. "Some people go back to Jelly Roll Morton, of course, and his phrasing lifted from Seventeenth Century French classics. It was a big hit in New Orleans, then the river boats took it north to Kansas City. But I stick with Louis.

And Duke Ellington."

He was a boy engrossed, quiet, holding my hand in a tighter grip but unaware of it, opening up to me. I sensed he was offering old talk, cared about talk, but talk not used in some time, like a boy discovering a long lost stamp album and going through it, page by page, remembering. "Now I feel silly calling it jazz stuff." I said.

"Put it this way. Duke Ellington was playing in London back in 1933, his first trip to England. A woman there said she didn't understand it, she had just come along with her boyfriend. Duke said something like, 'She listened for five minutes to something I had practiced and studied for over ten years to get me to this point on this evening. It's not a fair swap.' Something like that. The fans applauded. I got his autograph, his and Cootie Williams'...now there's a trumpet player!"

"You were in London for it?"

"Just before signing on with the army. I went down by train. The fans just about tore Duke's clothes off, and they were hanging on the running boards of his car."

We turned under the subdued lights and I watched the musicians. 1933. I was listening to Uncle Remus stories, and he was in glittering London listening to jazz concerts. He was relaxed now, speaking easily, but what he said next tore my world apart.

"Both Ellington and Armstrong wanted to come back to England. That pleased us."

"They loved England?"

"Well, they liked their acceptance as negroes. Not by everyone, of course, some hotels didn't permit them to stay, but by and large they were accepted. Integrated couples too, but that was more in Paris than London. The Left Bank art crowd, rather like Greenwich Village." He leaned back a little from me. "Are you all right? You look a little pale."

And pale or not, I had looked around, anxious that no one had over heard his words. I found my own words in a fear-dried mouth. It was as if I had been kicked in the stomach. I felt sick. "Yes, sorry. I suddenly remembered I have to take photos tonight for the PRO."

"I see. Well, I think I've taken enough of your time..."

He was retreating again, going back into his shell.

I struggled over my own feelings, then blindly knocked them down, pushing through. "No, please. I'd like to talk a while." But I needed time, time to recover from this man who had stood my world on end. The band moved into the opening phrases of *Serenade in Blue*. I took a shallow breath. "I love this song."

He didn't say anything, we just danced with me too rigid. If he felt it he didn't say anything. We danced, turning and gliding. I looked across at Wendy and Freddie at our table. Freddie gave me the thumbs up; Wendy just watched with her hand propped under her chin. She was grinning at me. Wendy had firm Southern views on negroes. But now she was delighting in me, and later she would say, 'Did you see Bill Trepick? Had a face on him like two cents looking for change.'

Negroes mixing with whites. Integrated couples. And he didn't care. I stared at his new RAF wings and cast around for something neutral to say. "Did your stuff arrive?"

"No, I had to wash things in the sink and round up an iron. Do I pass inspection?"

I managed a smile. My every sense took him in, matching reality with brushstrokes from a darkened bedroom. Only now there was this savage stroke revealing my own essence, and John's words came back: *I come from a class structure where I'm the underdog, Doreen. I guess I'm for live and let live.* And Daddy in the parlor with friends, his Jack Daniels and cigars: *Gotta look after 'em when they get sick, bail 'em out when they land in jail, an' bury 'em when they die. But we gotta preserve ah Southern ways...*I'd have to talk to my editor, Billy Odum, and recover some balance. It always came back to this. It was like pushing against a membrane, pressing against its translucence, held inside. Why was life like this, why did it set you up in delight and wonder, then...knock you down? The band gave a last flourish, the trumpet rippled down, and couples began walking back to their tables.

Outside dark clouds layered the sky. Hangars were black humps on the landscape. Somewhere an airplane droned. I fought with my feelings, summoning conversation. "A lovely moon tonight."

"Yes, it is."

He pulled out his pipe and tobacco pouch and began tamping tobacco into the bowl. His strong fingers kneaded and pushed. "Piano fingers," I said.

He smiled around his pipe and waved out the Swan Vesta match. "Mum's a piano teacher, and my sister's very good. I think the war's holding up her exams. But I was a lost cause. Mum would give me lessons during the winter months, then I'd ignore it during the summer and play cricket and go to the shows."

"Shows, you mean movies?"

"No, the carnival. Came every year on the Town Moor. And there was the firework display. Roundabouts, chairaplanes, all the kids loved it; the lights, the noise, the excitement. Then you could go down on The Prom and look at the sea. I liked to watch the drifters going out."

"Drifters."

"Fishing boats. They'd go out overnight, leaving at

around five in the afternoon. You could watch their bows appear from beyond the promenade, their hulls bobbing as they took the swells."

To my surprise his accent broadened, a lyrical north country. A rum tang came from his pipe. "That would be Hartlepool." I said.

He looked at me, startled. "Now how did you know that?"

"Roy told me in Americus, when you all arrived in your gray suits and black ties. Remember Roy?"

"Ah. He's oversees now. Good man."

"You were different that day. Withdrawn. Now you talk about jazz and fishing boats."

"I was working."

"Tell me, why don't you go to dances? Why do you stay out of things?"

He looked away, fiddling with his pipe. I kept my own concerns pushed back and pushed gently at his. "You're described as a loner. Standoffish. It must have given you a dilemma to come to the dance to see me."

His eyes were as black as the night around us. "I needed to correct things. And I must say you know a lot about me. I'm not sure I'm comfortable with it."

"I'm sorry. A reporter on the job."

"Yes, you said that before." He was distant again, his diction clear and crisp, all Royal Air Force officer and instructor. *Not a good sideslip, cadet, do it again. Good left hand spin, now do a right one. Flaring out too high, how's your depth perception?* I knew the litany. I had seen it on napkins.

"Tell me, just how did you get on post so early this morning?"

"Oh, that. I wrote a piece on the military police, how they really ran everything and kept democracy safe. The major was very pleased. He was fed up with the pilots getting all the glory."

"Ah. You say you knew Piggott well?"

"Yes. We were good friends." I turned aside the rising ache and waited for George to speak, to soften again around the edges, but he said nothing else. For a moment the moonlight caught his eyes to reveal a haunting look that on top of everything else made me anxious. "So how far did you get with the piano." I asked, too brightly.

He laughed quietly and things eased. "Chopin's famous nocturne. That was it."

"I made it through *Für Elise*."

The band started in on *Lambeth Walk*, and singing voices tumbled out into the night. I really did need to take photos.

"Bill Trepick says you want to go to New York."

My words lunged at him. "What else did he say?"

"Only that you don't like our basic trainers."

"Oh." I felt my face go red. "Well, I just talk to cadets. When John died I wanted to know all I could."

"Of course."

Again the conversation had changed, shading back into darker tones, like the layered cloud above us. I shivered, but it was not the coolness of the evening etching into me. If he was so casually accepting of negroes, how could I take him home to the farm? That had been my reverie, his voice echoing in quiet hours when cadets were asleep; and showing him the land, the crops, and maybe going giggin' for frogs, show him where I played as a child, the corn crib...

"Here, let's get back inside. Don't want you catching cold."

"No, I want to stay here, at least for a few more minutes." I looked at the now calm eyes. "How about you, do you like flying the BT-13?"

"Frankly, yes. It's like anything else mechanical. You have to understand its temperament, its character. There isn't an aeroplane flying that won't give you the chop if you don't stay on top of it."

"You think Jimmy Peterson didn't stay on top of it?"

"Look," he said gently, "flying is a risky business. Brilliant pilots, far more competent than I, sometimes get killed. You do everything right, then..."

His hand moved expressively. "This is not for publication, but do you realize that not all of these cadets want to become pilots?"

"What?"

"It happens. It affects only a handful, but it happens. I know cadets who washed out and they were relieved. You could see it in their faces. I know one cadet who gulped down sodas because he'd heard that could give him ulcers."

I stared. "Was it a British cadet or an American cadet?"

His hand came up and wiped at his jaw and I saw the fatigue there. "Does it matter?"

I loved him for that. I uttered my fantasy line then, but it was soured by my fear that the cultural chasms between us were too wide. "So, do you have a girl back home, George? I'm sure you must."

He smiled. "Not as a young soldier travelling the world with the army." He took my arm and gently steered us towards the music. "I guess we should get back inside, I need to get you to your table and friends."

The light grew sharper, the music and voices louder, and it was all going to whirl me away, and this moment would be lost, perhaps for always. I turned to him, stopping him in his tracks, and changed my life forever.

"Look, here's my phone number at the Dispatch." I said the number. "Call me."

"Well, I don't think..."

I gave it to him again, riding over his words. "Call me." This time he reached for a pen. It was unthinkable for a Southern girl to ask. And I had no idea how things would go for us. But gut deep I wanted to try, I ached to try.

"Things are so hectic right now..." as he jotted down my number.

A light note was needed. Think like a reporter, Doreen, keep the initiative. Do it. "What kind of tobacco is that?" I interrupted.

"This? St. Bruno Flake. A touch of rum to it."

"It goes well with your Lifebuoy soap."

And he laughed, open and to the night, and to my sudden lifting heart, I swear the moon got brighter.

Chapter 5

THAT YEAR, 1942, we were losing the war and retreating on all fronts, so the academy award went to Greer Garson for 'Mrs. Miniver', a portrait of a British house-wife bearing up. But 'Casablanca' was the most popular movie, and it was Bogie's words to Ingrid Bergman that fired young hearts and carried the day. Millions of young servicemen and women knew that their love didn't amount to a hill of beans in this crazy world. So they clung close and shared their dreams and wrote dreamy, ruthlessly censored letters.

Somewhere in that mosaic of love, rut and hope I had placed George Westcott and Doreen Summers. Bogie and Ingrid might be ending their fiery affair, but we were just embarking on ours — if I had my way, that is. So while the world was in upheaval and my South was irrevocably changing, I dreamed and schemed about George. And tonight in my rented room in Macon I tried to drown out Wendy Clinkscales' whining, cutting voice, a voice now free of British affectation but laced with that lethal Southern mix of self-righteousness and hate that surfaced at times like this.

"He wants to take you to a jazz club where there's nigras? You can't be serious....you'll have to drink from their glasses, you could get syphilis..."

I looked at my storage shoe boxes stuffed with filled-up notebooks. There was no room for my latest: the naval ordnance plant and how gunpowder was turning women's hair and skin a golden yellow.

"You're crazy to do this, Doreen," she said quietly.

"I waited for his call, Wendy, and it took forever and I was giving up, you know that. And this is what he wants to do, why he wants me with him."

"And it doesn't bother you, frighten you? God! Couldn't you have said, 'Sorry, I can't make it, but why not come home to the farm...'"

"No, I couldn't. Look, he doesn't date, he keeps to himself, everybody knows that. This asking me to go to hear some jazz it's like, it's like..."

"Like what?"

"Like I touched him, got through to him somehow, while we were dancing. If it wasn't for our talking about jazz I don't think he would've called me." I groped around for something to add then gave up. It had all been so wonderful at first, after the dance. Feverish delicious nights with Wendy talking about the date with George that was sure to come, and the moment by moment sharing of how it was with him: dancing, his strong hand on my back, the clasp of his hand around mine, the whirl of music and movement. And Wendy's own questions, innocent, the litany of dating: Did he come on to you, hold your hand after dancing, did he stand close? You sure looked good together. Bill Trepick was jealous. You'll have to watch out for him.

And then it had become an agonizing wait, living on recollections of rum flavored tobacco, piano fingers tamping, a crazy smell of soap, and his brown eyes riveting, sometimes lost in hidden thoughts, but always drawing me in. These images swept into my pillow reveries. But with Wendy I had censored out talk about negroes and interracial couples in Greenwich Village, which gave me pause. Were my perceptions selective, just Fred and Ginger? In any case I had to take some blame for how Wendy was now reacting.

"Will you go all the way with him?" she asked bluntly.

I picked up a shoebox, heavy with its load of notebooks, and placed it on a shelf.

"Well?"

"I don't know."

"Landsakes, Doreen."

"Leave me alone, just leave me alone!"

Finally Wendy said, "Are you in love with him?"

"You got it the wrong way round, Wendy. You ask if I'm in love with him, then if I'll go all the way."

"So are you?"

"Am I what?"

"In love with him."

I hesitated. "I only know I've never felt this way before, not about anyone. I want to be with him and spend time with him, no matter what."

"Bill wants to date you again."

I tried to laugh, off hand, bantering. It came out tight. "You know Bill."

"I think he's changed, around you anyway. What you're doing ain't right, Doreen."

"Why? Whites go to colored clubs."

"Not our kind."

"And what's our kind, Wendy? Maidens offering a breast to a clumsy hand?" I let the idea out. "Things are changing, Wendy, times are changing.

"That's war stuff!" Wendy cried, exploding around

her fears. When the war's over things'll get back to normal. Women want to be at home, they want their men folk back home, and coloreds will remember their place."

"Women are flying planes now," I said quietly. "They're operating machines and turning out tanks, I've seen it, written about it."

"But that's war stuff! They don't wanna do that all their lives, that's taking jobs from our men. I swear, Doreen, I don't understand your thinking. Men need those jobs to support their wives and families."

"After the war, I don't think we can go back." I said.

"We will. You'll see.

An unpleasant silence enveloped us.

My head started to ache. "So what's your news?"

"What?" Wendy's face lost its hardness, draining away to a vacant stare.

"You said you'd heard from the FBI."

"Oh, yeah." She reached for her pocket book, found the telegram and offered it. "It's signed by J. Edgar Hoover himself. The guy who got John Dillinger and Pretty Boy Floyd wrote to me. I'm involved in history." She tried to smile around her rehearsed line, but her words were flat. She had come over filled with excitement about her FBI telegram and anticipated talk about George and his phone call. Now we had this tension between us. I tried to reach her. "I'm so glad you heard from the FBI, Wendy."

"Well, it's just about the background check on me, and that could take months, I guess. Do you think they'll find out about that time me and Wally took the pickup truck an'—"

"No."

Wendy's dark eyes were wet. "Do you think there's nigras in the FBI?"

"No."

"What about Washington, if I get there, I mean. Is it segregated?"

"I think so."

"But it's federal, right? Maybe they got northern ways with no respect for our ways."

"You'll just have to wait and see." I rubbed at my temple, the pounding was now more insistent. It always came back to this, the South.

"Have you tried to buy toothpaste yet?" I asked, trying to lighten the mood.

"No, why?"

"You have to hand in your old tube. They need the metal."

"Oh. I'm finding it hard to get metal buttons and zippers."

"I hear they're changing women's fashions now. No pleats, no patch pockets. Billy Odum said girdles are now being made out of bone."

"We don't need girdles, thank the lord."

"No." I felt her eyes steady on me.

"So, what's this jazz club?"

"J.J. Lemon's, near the Magnolia Room on Auburn."

"*Sweet Auburn*, you're supposed to say."

"Stop it, Wendy."

"So who's at this club?"

"Teddy Wilson and Billie Holiday, a singer. I think he plays piano."

"Never heard of 'em."

"I've heard of Billie Holiday, but I've never heard her sing."

"Will you take a drinking glass with you?"

"Wendy…"

"Well, will you?"

"No. I'll get a coke, unopened." My answer appalled me. I was ducking and weaving.

"He'll drink from those glasses. Even northern whites do. I've heard it and I believe it."

"Maybe he will." I was seven, I think, when I watched Daddy answer the respectful knock at the back kitchen door. The colored farm hand had asked for a drink of water. Daddy had poured a generous glassful, adding some ice, then afterwards he had tossed the glass into the garbage. I remember it shattering, but I did not ask why he had thrown it away. "Remember when we were kids, Wendy, and we thought negroes had black blood?"

"So?"

"So maybe we're wrong about drinking glasses."

"Hah! Next you'll be saying it's okay to share toilets and water fountains." She stood up. "I'm going home."

"Wendy..."

"I'm tired, is all. Don't worry, you're not gonna lose one of your few remaining friends." She looked at me as if I were a new girl at the slumber party, someone not quite welcome, someone who shouldn't be privy to talk about the coloreds and their ways, the kind of talk that helped dissipate primal fears in frothy pink bedrooms.

"They're putting Japs in internment camps...is that wrong or doing what's right?"

"Goodnight, Wendy."

"G'night."

I pressed the door closed behind her, and as I did so I heard the familiar sounds of an approaching night flight from Cochran. Three BT's in formation. I knew that power, in ones and twos and threes. They thundered overhead, rattling lamps and ornaments, and I wondered if George was leading them, then they faded and I was left with silence.

Chapter 6

I PARKED THE Nash at Cochran's main gate, winced at the
gas gauge and switched off the engine. It was a beautiful
evening with fine cirrus cloud stained red by a setting
sun, a backdrop for the parked airplanes, barracks and
hangars. Nearby were several family sedans parked in a
row, owners leaning on open doors. At the gate the first
British cadets were spilling out, a tumble of blue RAF
uniforms and some smiling, some uncertain faces. While
I watched for George families and cadets matched up
quickly. I saw Haggis and Archie heading for the
Davidson's car, and there were the cheery inviting cries
on the air, a weekend ritual.

"How y'all like it over here?"

"How about coming home for dinner...real Southern
cookin'?"

"Care to join us tonight? Stay over if you can!"

"Come on, boys, fried chicken tonight!"

Then I saw him and flung my hand around, joining in the
general anticipation. "George! George!" He saw me and
smiled, giving a wave, before talking briefly with a cadet.
Then we were together by the Nash. We did not touch. "I
thought we could use the car to get to the train station."

"Does your editor know?"

"We wangle the gas coupons."

"Ah."

During the car ride and then the train ride to Atlanta we remained rather quiet, as if the scheming and finagling had ended, objective achieved, and we were now retreating into shyness and reserve, contemplating each other and wondering where if anywhere this relationship was going. And I was bracing for a night out at a negro jazz club. If George understood the dilemma he had given me he gave no sign. It was in Atlanta at the train station that we opened up to each other and relaxed. Perhaps it was a sense of freedom and being alone and away from Cochran Field's demands. He took my hand, leading us past the big locomotives. Their hulking sooty presence smacked of exotic places. Negro soldiers occupied the first car of one train, they were leaning out of the windows and smiling. Once inside the station we found it packed with travelers, most in uniform, and there was standing room only. Some slept on the floor propped against duffel bags. Others leaned and talked and smoked their cigarettes. The air was thick with smoke. It was all an odd contrast as this jumble of humanity from far and wide surged under the rather formal cavernous atrium with its choice woods, plants, and carved cherubs. I clung to George's hand.

"Busy place," he said.

"Atlanta's a small town growing big. Lots of history, of course."

"Tell me."

"What, history?" I laughed. "It's different from Hartlepool, I guess. There's the Kimball..."

"What's that?"

"A hotel. Stage coaches stopped there. Stories of ghosts and mysteries. But with the influx of war workers people tend to ridicule it all."

"That's a shame. I believe in traditions."

We stood still as a burly man pushed by with luggage. "Sometimes I think of Atlanta as a favorite aunt showing off her pressed flowers in genteel books, smelling of mothballs and always talking about the future as a way of sustaining the past."

"You're too young to think like that."

"It's the reporter in me."

"Ah."

"Good food though, if you like Southern cooking..."

"I do."

"Like Mammy's Shanty's oyster bisque and corn pudding, and Herren's rainbow trout and sticky buns."

Leaving the train terminal we were stopped by a harried traveler.

"Say, which gate do I need for Chattanooga?"

George smiled. "I'm sorry, I'm not with the railways...British air force."

"Jeezus, sorry, Mac! Stupid mistake, good luck to you!"

"Thank you."

I laughed, clutching at George's arm.

"Second damned time."

"Sorry."

"It does keep me humble."

Outside we stood on the sidewalk, getting bumped, watching taxis and cars. There were fewer cars because of gas rationing.

"It's a nice night. Feel like walking?"

"Fine."

"If you have any questions, let me know. I'll be your guide tonight."

"You've been up here a lot?"

"Not a lot." As we walked I savored the closeness of him, soaking up his touch.

"Isn't that the Loew's where 'Gone With the Wind' played?"

"That's it. Hollywood stars flew in for the premiere. Everything was ablaze with light. They had searchlights you could see for fifty miles."

"Quite a few theaters."

"We go to the movies to escape the heat."

"When we first arrived for training in Americus, some cadets fell asleep in class. Couldn't get used to the muggy heat."

"How about you?"

"I was okay. The army had me in Egypt before the war. Pyramids and camels. After that lot, Americus was fine."

"Is that where you got your tan?"

"Well, only on my face and arms. The rest of me's fishbelly white, your typical Hartlepudlian who goes plodging in the North Sea."

"What's plodging?"

"Oh, just kind of wading about, maybe up to the knees. The North Sea is pretty cold, even in summer."

"Your head and arms tan fits in over here...you could pass as one of us redneck farmers."

"I'll take that as a compliment." He smiled, the crooked tooth rendering him boyish, an English Tom Sawyer. "I never did see 'Gone With The Wind'," he said.

"I hated it."

"Let me guess, you didn't like Scarlett O'Hara."

I hugged his arm. "Simpering witch."

"But she was feisty too, wasn't she?"

"False front. Just noise and petulance."

"Ah. She wore a curtain, I understand."

"George, that's so refreshing. To others around here she's a saint."

"I can see that."

"Did you say it just to please me?"

"Of course."

I was as giddy as a bobby soxer. "There's no time tonight, but we have a fairground here...maybe it's like your Hartlepool carnival."

"Really?" His dark eyes sparked with interest.

"It's very lively, with lights and carousels, and there's a terrific rollercoaster called The Greyhound."

"Who took you on that?"

"Bill Trepick."

He was silent a moment. "Bill's been a bit distant lately. Except for flying talk."

I cursed under my breath and rushed in. "We have a diving mule."

"We have a flea circus."

"And a singing pig."

"We have a flea circus."

"And a walking catfish."

"Did I mention our flea circus?"

And Bill was far away, pushed back.

J.J. Lemon's was a small store front near the Magnolia Room on Auburn Avenue. "This is Auburn," I said, "The locals call it Sweet Auburn. We're nearly there now."

"You know this area?" George asked in surprise. "Sorry, I didn't mean that the way it sounded..."

"I read things, George, that's all. A reporter's instincts, rounding out knowledge." And while I was rounding out knowledge I was all too aware of the colored community around me, the dark faces, some quizzical, some turning away. If George noticed them eyeing his uniform, so foreign to the surroundings, he didn't show it. He was, after all, I reminded myself, a seasoned traveler used to pyramids and camels and hoards of foreigners, whereas I was a stranger in my own country, at least here.

"Look," George said suddenly, stopping to study a billboard. "Duke Ellington's coming to the Biltmore."

I followed his gaze. "That's more uptown, out of this neighborhood. White audiences."

"I wonder if the fans tear his clothes like they did in London."

"I don't think so. Lots of negro musicians go to the Biltmore for white audiences. Count Basie, Louis Armstrong, Lionel Hampton..."

He stopped me and stared into my eyes, all instructor. "What?" I asked.

"How do you know all this?"

I reddened. "A reporter researching."

"Sometimes you make me a bit uncomfortable, Doreen. Like I'm a lab experiment."

My blush deepened. "I'm sorry."

"Is it for a story?"

I took it head on. "No. I just wanted to get closer to your interests, get on the same wavelength."

He smiled, and we began walking again. "I'm flattered."

"Well, don't get a swelled head."

"I shan't."

"Shaaaaan't."

He dug me in the ribs.

As we walked I asked, "George, why me?"

"How do you mean?"

"To come and see the show tonight. "Why choose me, why not go alone?"

He was silent for a long time, and I thought he wasn't going to answer. Then, "I liked being with you at the dance. And talking about music and home. I hadn't done that in a long time." He looked at me: "and you knew when not to push. I'm not much good in some situations."

"You mean Dunkirk, talking about it."

"The Great Miracle."

I was surprised at the bitterness in his voice and I wanted to ask about it, but obviously I held back. Maybe there would be a time, and that was in doubt, but now certainly wasn't it.

"I never did ask you how you felt about being held back as an instructor."

"Yes, the interview. We're not interviewing now, are we?"

"Of course not."

He was quiet a long moment. "I'm no hero, Doreen. I'm pleased to be instructing. I'll do what I have to do, but I'm no hero."

"That's what most soldiers are doing, isn't it?"

He was brooding. "Posthumous decorations for valor are not much help to mothers and widows."

I pressed at his arm, connecting with him, drawing him back. "I'm glad you're here. That's selfish, but I'm glad."

"There's just no equitable way to fight a war." His eyes stayed on me.

"Are we going to win, George? Things look so bad, my parents worry."

"We'll win."

"But your instructing will end one day."

"Yes."

"And when the war is over, what then?"

He brightened at that. "Frankly, I'd like to come back to America. I like the breezy informality here, even if I'm a bit stiff. I like the chance this country offers to do things, make your mark." He hesitated. "I'm not sure about the South. There's so much good here, but…"

I let it go. "And what will you do when you come back here? To make your mark, I mean?"

"I want to fly. I like flying and I'm quite good at it. When this war is over air travel will grow. You can already see it in the heavy bombers and transports crossing the Atlantic."

"Is that why you try to improve your speech, soften your Geordie accent?"

"Yes. It may seem like a small thing, but good diction is an investment no matter what. How about you?"

"I'm trying to smooth out my Southern talk. They'll laugh at me up north."

"Ah."

That's all we said. We walked in silence along Auburn Avenue, and I held tightly to his arm.

Chapter 7

J.J. LEMON'S HAD a red flashing neon sign, but the *m* was out and it looked like Leon's. Dark green paint was chipped and the stairs leading down to the basement were worn and scraped. George pushed open the door and ushered me inside. Warm smoky air buffeted, the interior was dark and cavernous, and lit by small orange table lamps set on white cloths. A stage was a black square of empty space at the far end of the room, but as my eyes grew accustomed to the gloom I made out a grand piano and the gleaming silver stalk of a microphone. Oddly, I took the negroes for granted; they were seated in fours and more, crowded around tables, their faces catching the orange light; but it was the white patrons, a definite minority, who caught my attention. They seemed relaxed. Several white women were smoking, heads back, looking around. There were two white sailors and an army officer. We were looked at boldly. I don't know if it was because we were white or because of George's uniform.

George palmed a five-dollar bill. "Sorry we're a bit late, any chance of a good seat?"

"Ah dig, man."

I watched him pocket the five. He wore a loose fitting

jacket and white T-shirt. We followed him, side stepping by tables. Some perfumes were strong and I didn't recognize their fragrance. Everything was overlaid with cigarette smoke. We got snugged up against a table with two young negro couples. All the tables around us were black, a white couple were some fifteen feet away. George looked around, returning looks, smiling pleasantly. I tried to do the same but felt a little sick in my stomach. I had never been so nervous. Throw away a drinking glass in here, Doreen...And there was no smell of sweat. I caught that thought as it slipped out. Dear God, Doreen, get with it.

A waiter came over, also wearing a jacket over a T-shirt. He slipped easily between the tables.

"What'll you have, Doreen?"

I hesitated. "Just a coke tonight, please."

George turned to the waiter. "A coke for the lady, I'll take a gin and tonic, not too much ice." George pressed my hand and I felt his excitement. "Not bad seats, better than I'd hoped."

"Yes." I looked around, affecting a composure I didn't feel. In my nervousness I hadn't asked for the coke in a bottle. I looked around at other tables and was surprised to find many negroes drinking scotch, a sharp contrast with my notions about moonshine and rotgut. Reporter's curiosity took the edge off my fears. When the drinks came George's was in a glass with a half-empty tonic water on the side. I watched black hands use the opener on my coke bottle. When I looked up I found an impassive face and glistening eyes looking down at me. I thought I caught a look there, some faint amusement, but it could have been the light. "Thank you," I said.

I was saved from that turmoil by the sudden stab of a spotlight hitting the stage. It revealed someone in a tuxedo who had to be Teddy Wilson seating himself at the grand piano. The piano gleamed and applause filled the crowded room. "Teddy Wilson," George breathed, close to my ear. He was lost in it, orange table light glinting off his tunic buttons, his profile was monklike, haloed.

The spotlight moved left and even before Billie Holiday came out the applause went up again, thunderous in that small room. I watched her, fascinated. A negress holding court with authority, blacks and whites alive with excitement at seeing her. She had a languid presence to her, her olive green dress highlighting her skin, her eyes taking in the audience as she touched Teddy Wilson's shoulder then moved to the microphone which was now a dazzling chrome in the spotlight. The raised ebony piano lid was a rich backdrop for her. To my surprise she was quite full jawed, the heavy contour of it caught by the light, even more pronounced than my own. I would never again look at my silver-framed Tennessee forebears in quite the same way. She held the room, controlled it. George squeezed my hand again. A tentative phrasing came from Teddy Wilson's keyboard. Billie smiled and looked around.

"Weeeeelll. I see we got some white chicks here tonight." She looked to her left as laughter and applause quickly died, the crowd hanging on her words, some leaning forward in their seats. Her gaze settled on a table close to the stage. "Hey, girl, this ain't Harlem, swingin' with the cats an truckin' your white ass back to midtown. You on Sweet Auburn, baby. in the Deeeeep South."

Laughter. The negro couples next to us glanced our way, seeing how we were taking it. George was grinning, which aroused in me an irrational anger, a feeling of being deserted. I reddened. The piano strengthened, then offered a lovely descending run.

"You all know Teddy..." Applause. "Me an' Teddy do good things together."

Someone shouted out, a northern accent, "Fine an' Mellow!"

More applause, and Billie spoke over it. "You know it, baby, you cool." She smiled again, continuing to look around. "Yeah, things can be fine an' mellow with cats like Doc Cheatham makin' you look good."

Laughter.

I whispered to George. "What's fine an' mellow mean?"

"A record she cut a couple of years ago with Teddy Wilson. Doc was on trumpet. It's already a classic."

The piano built again, Teddy Wilson gently insinuating his presence, courtly, composed. Then he was moving into a song I knew, but I was never to hear it again the way I got it that night, delivered on a slow beat. Billie pouted into 'Mean to Me', catlike, composing a word picture, by turns droll and simpering for her man. Goose bumps welted up on my arms, and then she left the melody line, my only anchor, and worked with unexpected tones and earthy silences, all of it filled in, answered by Teddy's immaculate phrasing. I knew big bands, of course; and I loved Swing from many hours of listening and dancing, I knew Tex Beneke and his tenor sax, Harry James and his trumpet, but I'd never heard a performance like this. She exuded a street sex, a hunger and hurt that mesmerized the audience into silence with dark visions and sensual undertones. It was an awakening for me, someone who had taken for granted the South's routine censoring of negro artists and cutting scenes from movies, like *Showboat*. Lena Horn's 'Stormy Weather', all of it denied. Not for Southern audiences.

Piano chords closed it out, then lifted into 'Body and

Soul', subduing an audience's applause. Billie brought us back in, another word picture rendered three dimensional on musical phrasing.

"I have the sheet music back at the farm, but I'll never play it again!"

George laughed.

Parts of me were being dismantled this night, I realized. George was lost in it all. I stared at my coke.

There was a break where Billie excused herself, and Teddy Wilson moved into some solo work. And I sat there listening, very much aware of George, his fingers tapping lightly, a second gin and tonic catching the table light. I picked up my coke and took a sip. The coldness of it quenched the dryness in my throat. I gulped it then. When Billie returned she kept Teddy's playful mood, vocalizing to his inventions. It was all light and bright and bouncy and the audience loved it.

But then the mood faded, disappearing down the keyboard under Teddy's gifted hands, and suddenly the mood was blue. Then she made it something more, something I could neither touch nor share. I got very uneasy and I glanced at George, but his face was unreadable. A cool unnerving keyboard, a voice that ached, and their collaboration slipped loose a lyric that horrified me and pinned me to my chair. I retreated under its weight, from George's presence, and clasped my hands between my knees. And when the last beat died, there was no applause. The images and mood permeated the club, touching each of us, forcing each to respond in his own measure.

I had never heard such a song delivered with such power, and I prayed I would never hear it again; but I was glad I heard it once, that one time. The evening went on, of course. Standards from the Thirties impeccably performed. But for me it was anticlimactic. I was drained.

Outside the air was warm, and bright neon washed out the stars. I took deep breaths and welcomed the sights and sounds of the city, anonymous and nonthreatening. George lit his pipe as we walked. "So, what did you think?"

I shook my head. "Right now I don't have a clear hold on it."

"The music, or being in a mixed audience?"

"All of it. Saying it's been a powerful, gutwrenching evening doesn't do it justice."

George said nothing.

I began, "That song..."

"Yes, I know."

"You've heard it before?"

"Only once, but I've read it a few times. It's a poem by Lewis Allen."

"I didn't understand at first, then I realized what 'Strange Fruit' meant. And when I did..."

George shook spittle from his pipe stem. "Powerful stuff."

"George how can you shake that pipe when..."

"Sorry."

I often think back to that moment, with George the foreigner understanding my country better than I did. Too bad Doreen the reporter hadn't diligently checked around, found facts to tuck away in shoeboxes. It had happened twice now. A plane crash had first breeched my world, tearing away a protective gauze. Now a woman had done the same thing with her art. "I've never heard artistry like that before."

"It's American music, Doreen. You can hear it all the time up north. You might even hear it when you don't want to."

"Like in New York."

"Definitely in New York."

"How long have you listened to her?"

"Not long, actually. There was the army, Egypt, then the war, they cut that 'Fine and Mellow' record in '39. A soldier had it at Aldershot...that's a British army post. How he got it I don't know. But Billie goes back to the early Thirties. With Teddy Wilson soon after that, I think."

"He's terrific."

"Yes, he is. Benny Goodman showed courage breaking the color bar like that. Same with Artie Shaw and Billie Holiday."

I stopped walking and looked up at him. "You're losing me here. Teddy Wilson played with Goodman?

"That's right, with his sextet. And Artie Shaw used Billie as the band's singer. It was difficult for her in the South. She had to eat in the band's bus."

I filed it all away, which is what reporters do when they don't want to think. Then I felt George's arm go around my shoulders and he drew me to him and kissed me lightly on my brow.

"Come on," he said. "If we step lively we can make the next train.

Chapter 8

DRIVING FROM THE train station back to Cochran Field we had an air raid warning. I stopped the car by the side of the road and switched off the lights. We sat in the warm cocoon of the Nash. I lowered my window and looked up. "You can see the stars with all the lights off. In Atlanta you couldn't see the stars."

"Perhaps it's dark up there now," George said.

I shook my head. "Just Macon keeping us on our toes."

George leaned back against the seat, reaching for my hand, looking at me. "I like your hair down like that."

"You don't like braids, uh, plaits?"

"They're nice; I just like it down."

"My jawline is a bit heavy. I noticed Billie Holiday's was too."

"You're in good company."

I smiled in the darkness. Only a non-Southerner could say such a thing, with such innocence, so right and yet so paradoxically wrong. "Yes," I said. "Yes, I am."

It was quiet in the car. Insects chirruped in the night, buzzing sounds, aloneness. "Another beautiful moon," I said. "Like at the dance."

"Not a bomber's moon. Too bright."

"George, let's not talk about the war."

"Sorry, I was looking at the blackout, the air raid warning. A natural train of thought."

"Let's talk about other things." I sounded prim.

He squeezed my hand again and leaned into me, his eyes bright in the dark. "I'm glad you came tonight. It wouldn't have been the same without you."

There was a smell of brilliantine and tobacco to him. "You mean that?"

"You know I do. Don't fish for compliments."

He was very close now, I felt the warmth of his skin. "I'm not fishing..."

"Yes you are."

He was smiling. "Listen, I..."

Then he was kissing me, lightly, my cheek, my brow, my eyes, then he found my mouth. I had kissed him in my fantasies a thousand times, and I was always eager, inviting. But now it was my turn to implode, to cave in within his embrace, the strength and sinew of him. "George," I murmured. He kissed me in long searching ways, but never pushing or grabbing; his fingers were an exquisite touching of my hair, ear lobes, cheek, a patient exploring, but I felt myself slowly retreat from my own arousal.

"You're a funny lass," he said softly. "First you're aggressive, pushing your telephone number at me, then you're shy, pulling back."

"I...I have trouble letting go."

"What, because of your upbringing as a southern belle?"

"Fact is, George, we have only two kinds of girl down here. Good girls and white trash. Good girls live by the Southern heritage, they're passive and dependent."

"Oh, that's you all right."

I pinched him. "Done right, you're the perfect mate

for marriage, tennis and mint juleps."

He kissed my cheek, drawing me out, making it easy. Easier.

"I'm not supposed to sweat, smoke or swear. Like a doll, George."

He found my mouth even as I tried to turn away.

"Men give you a hard time?"

"Only those I care about. I'm safe with the others."

"What about Bill?"

I hesitated.

"Go with him long?"

"A couple of months."

George smiled. "Long time, these days."

"Bill's a good man..."

"You don't have to talk about it. I shouldn't have mentioned him."

"It's okay. Just awkward sometimes."

"Like when we were dancing."

"You saw him watching us?"

"Pilots are trained to observe, like reporters. What about me?"

"What."

"I don't know where I fit. I like to think I'm not giving you a hard time, but I don't want to be dismissed as safe, either."

"Oh, dear God, George, I'm lost with you. Just lost. I'm trying to sort it through. But I've never known anyone like you, and I've never cared for anyone the way I care about you. You're with me always, in my thoughts..." I struggled up in the car seat and faced him. "Right now, George. The way we are right now. It's not like riding a bike, is it? It's not, is it?"

"No." His thumb brushed at my tear and his eyes were blacker than the night. Before he kissed me again he said, "When you smile, all things are lovely."

I clung to him.

"Look, sorting things out is okay. I'm sorting things out too."

I lifted my head and looked at him, feeling sick. "You're married, that's it, isn't it? George, no more upheaval tonight, I can't..."

He stopped me, his fingers to my lips. "I'm not married."

It was quiet in the car. When the all-clear sounded, I jumped. Somewhere down the road car lights came back on, probing the night. We stayed in our cacooning warmth.

"We English have a heritage too. We're too reserved." He smiled, but it died aborning.

"It's more than being reserved, George."

"You're right. Things have been bad for me, I've had things happen that I'm trying to forget. They've kept me distanced, out of things."

"I know. I mean, I know you've been dealing with something."

"I'm sorry if it's a wall that ruins our ... relationship." He took my hand again. I liked the way he always found my hand, the simplest and in some ways the most profound of touches. "I'm like you, Doreen. I'm not sure what we have, excepting dancing with you..."

"Suppose you hadn't been held back as an instructor, you'd have gone back to England without ever seeing me...right?"

"Doreen..."

"And if I hadn't pushed you to take my phone number, you'd never have called me?"

"No, that's wrong. I would have come to you."

I punched his arm. "Jesus, George, you took your

own sweet time phoning."

"I wrestled with it, yes. I'd been living on the safety and security of being alone, responsible just for myself." He paused, then said, "You were something that morning when I flew in."

I stared at him in surprise, mouth slack. "What?"

"The way you whaled into me, defending Piggott. 'I don't trade on dead friends, Westcott' you said. You were something. Bill Trepick said if I pursued you, I'd have a tiger by the tail."

"Some tiger I am." I pushed into him, wanting his warmth.

"If you think about it, Doreen, we have the same problem. "You feel threatened about experiencing your emotions. I'm threatened about opening up, sharing with someone."

"Why, why is that?"

He was quiet for a long time. Beyond the car window the insects kept up their chirruping. Cool night air wafted in. "Because I know how cheap life can be. Mine, yours. Anybody's."

"And medals don't help mothers and widows."

"That's it."

There was no way I could deal with that, not tonight anyway. "Just one question, George."

"What?"

"It isn't a woman, is it? I can't fight a memory."

His arms tightened around me. "No. I'm not married and it isn't a woman."

"Then I think we should both shut up. Let things settle."

George exhaled, relieving a tightness in his chest. "Where the hell did all this come from? I just wanted to take you to see Billie Holiday..."

"No, you didn't. We're in this now and I'm glad. For me it's been incubating far too long." I swallowed against a suddenly aching throat and kissed him. "There's nothing I won't do for you, George. Nothing I won't give, with time." I hated the tears, just hated them. Simpering witch. I started the car and switched on the lights, jolting us back. We drove in silence to Cochran. Once there, I looked at the gas gauge and cursed under my breath. "Only half a tank."

"Can you get time off Tuesday?"

I looked at him. "Yes, why?"

"Can you drive down to Ft. Valley, the auxiliary field?"

"George, the gas..."

"Meet me there. I'll fly in and we'll siphon some aviation gas into the car."

"Can we do that?"

"Of course, as long as you don't tell that military police friend of yours."

"Tuesday?"

"Tuesday. About eleven."

"Okay." I was suddenly numb, exhausted.

George understood. I think he knew me better than I realized. "Let things settle."

I nodded.

He kissed me lightly on the cheek, retrieved his RAF hat from the back seat, and got out.

"George?"

He looked in at me.

"Some things got dismantled for me tonight. I don't want any more dismantling, I want what we have to grow."

"So do I. Look, Doreen, fault me all you want, get angry at how I've been dealing with things. You have a right, but don't miss the obvious, which is how much I care about you."

"I'm not missing it, George, but my God, you wear a girl out."

He grinned. "Tuesday. Around eleven."

I watched him stride to Cochran's main gate, returning a sentry's salute, showing I.D. Then I drove back to my rented room. Life, I knew, would not be simple for George and me; and I resented its burden, which right now was larger than its promise. I envied the Wendys and Wallys of this world, and their pickup trucks and joyful rut.

Chapter 9

THE FT. VALLEY auxiliary field was a flat expanse of yellowed grass. It butted against more flat open land offering peach groves and sweet potato fields. Winter had drawn the landscape with her own artistry: the groves were empty, the sweet potato fields stood empty. With the coming of the airfields I had by second nature associated them with crops: Byron for watermelons, Perry for pecans, Ft. Valley for peaches...The airfield was too quiet. There were no airplanes. Today, around eleven o'clock, there was flattened grass, some deep and random tire ruts, and a limp windsock.

I waited for George and the BT-13.

I had trouble deciding what to wear — what do you wear to a gasoline siphoning? I settled on a rough textured gray skirt and a dark blue sweater and my comfortable flats. No one wore slacks, except Katherine Hepburn who was the exception to the rule for many things. The air that morning was crisp, but I was comfortable standing by the Nash, my keys handy to unlock the trunk and grab the gas can and hose. I waited, a farmer's eye tracking Nature's movement. Other creatures of the air abounded. To the west a buzzard circled on outstretched wings looking for carrion. A hawk cruised in, wings motionless, to land on its lookout branch. And while a crow beat heavily into the air, a flurry of Bluejays swept to the ground like broken pieces of sky.

When an engine etched into the quiet, I found only a Stearman biplane making its way south at about three hundred feet. Its wings rocked gently then steadied as it droned from view over a low ridge of bare branches. Then, suddenly, in the unpredictable rhythm of airplane training, several BT-13s were flying at tangents to me, their engines hard abrasive sounds on my ears. But they made no effort to land. They flew on in formations of threes, leaving in their wake a diminishing roar. I wondered about Freddie and Haggis and the others. What if they landed here and saw an instructor and me siphoning gas from an airplane into a car?

A new sound encroached on the quiet. It built quickly, with authority, louder and louder on the crackling stillness. The BT approached the field, turning, yellow wing down and white star bright, as if tethered to me. It arced and swooped gracefully before straightening out, flaring above the airstrip, then settling. The canopy slid open and George waved, his RAF hat pressed to his head by the radio headset. He pointed to the perimeter near a grove of peach trees and I got back in the car and drove over, the grass frosty firm under the tires. He let me get there first, then slowly taxied to within a few feet of the Nash. When he switched off the engine the sounds remained, echoing back into the stillness. The plane stood perched on its wheels and tailwheel, the big engine pointed skyward. Bright blue and yellow paint gleamed in the sun. Hot metal ticked.

"Hi!" I called, as he stepped down. He wore a fleece-lined flight jacket over his RAF blues and it looked nice and warm. He took me by the shoulders and kissed me, lifting me a little as my arms went around his neck, my flats bending around my toes.

"Did you bring the stuff?"

"In the trunk."

"Let's get it then. Some students might decide to put down here." He grabbed the gasoline can and hose while he talked. "Sometimes an instructor will set down to give a student a five minute break. Sometimes they go scrumping."

"Scrumping?"

"Pinching watermelons or pecans. In this case, peaches; but the season's wrong." He laughed. "What a way to prepare for war: scrumping peaches and dodging Farmer Jones!"

I watched him bent on the wing, fitting the hose into the wing tank, then he led the other end of the hose to the gas can. "I can hold the gas can." I said.

"Want to suck on the hose?"

"Are you kidding?"

"Got to start the gravity feed. Here, let me have it."

Gasoline began pouring into the can. I found myself whooping. "Wow!"

"Hey, don't get ideas. We can't do this often."

"It's like finding the end of the rainbow. The pot of gold."

"I've unleashed a monster."

"I promise not to tell."

"Good." He took out the hose, capped the wing tank and we got the can over to the Nash.

"This thing's heavy. I didn't realize how heavy gas is."

"Let me get it into the car."

He had it done in minutes. With the hose and gas can in the trunk he looked me up and down, frowning. "Now what?" I asked.

"Just checking how you're dressed."

"Well! I hope I measure up."

"You'll do fine. Look, we need a cushion, do you have a cushion in the car?"

"Yes, but..."

"I couldn't check out a parachute for you."

"Parachute?"

"Right. They keep records and..."

"George!" My stomach turned uneasily. This was no joke, no Carole Lombard, Clark Gable scene. "George, no..."

"Then at least come and have a look at it." He paused while he grabbed a cushion from the Nash's backseat, one I used on long assignments when I had to catnap. He held the cushion and reached for me with his free hand. "Come on."

"Just to look."

"You have flown before?"

"Only in a Stearman at Souther." I eyed the BT-13. "Not this."

He knew what I was thinking, but he guided me to the wing. "Okay, a leg up here, on the support, then let me get this cushion onto the seat"

He placed the cushion on the rear seat and said, "this-leg in, and stand on the cushion, that's it, then the other leg over and lower yourself in. There..."

I stared around the rear cockpit. It was quite large, with dials and gauges and levers. The slid open canopy allowed me to look out and have an excellent view. The yellow wing was huge, blotting out the grass.

"How does the cushion feel?"

"Okay." I looked at the inverted 'vee' of metal framing the canopy. I knew what it was: a roll bar. For when the plane was in trouble, and landing, and rolling onto its back...

"Doreen."

I looked up at him. His eyes were so dark. Most English boys had blue eyes.

"Just think about it, allow yourself to think about it. Your seat is where Jimmy Peterson was sitting. Your friend John Piggott was up front."

I looked around. The plane had an unusual hot plastic and oil smell. I would learn later that it was a smell peculiar to airplanes and ships, the musk of working machinery under heat and pressure.

"How do you feel?"

"Nervous. A bit frightened."

He didn't say anything. He just waited.

I looked down at the control stick which reared from the cockpit floor. It was bright aluminum with a black rubber grip. It looked like it could turn the whole world. I reached for it, tentatively gripping the rubber.

"Move it to the right." George said.

I moved it right. He stepped back so that I could see both wings. I watched control surfaces move up and down.

"And it goes backward and forward."

The big stick moved.

"Doreen, flying is going to be my life. I want you to fly with me."

With an effort I tried for the light note I had used at the dance. "How come you get the parachute?"

He laughed then, and reached in and kissed me lightly on my brow, but his touch touched something primal inside me and I reached for him, kissing his mouth, compressing my fears against his strength. He gave back, and I knew he would give for as long as I needed, that he understood. I never wanted to lose that strength. Ever. I gently pushed him away, my heart thumping, and took up the loose ends of the seat belt. "Help me with this."

The big engine fired on a chuff of blue smoke and whine of the generator, then the whole airplane was vibrating, needles shivering across dials, the noise buffeting against my helmet. I reached up to pat my leather helmet, to trace the radio intercom lead to something called a jack box. "It's set on intercom," George had grinned at me, "don't knock it over to 'transmit' or the whole world'll be listening to us!" I looked out at the field and everything was shaded yellow from the Plexiglas canopy. The sun beat in, adding more heat. I was in an enclosed womb, cacooned, except that I could see forward through the roll bar at the back of George's head. His RAF hat was pressed down under his headphones. He was constantly looking around, up and down, side to side, eyes squinting in the sun. On a sudden rev of the engine we began to roll forward, taxiing across the grass. I watched the stick and rudder pedals move, in concert with George's movements up front. "Keep off everything, don't touch anything." I watched him as he checked and rechecked, sound and vibration pummeling us. Out to my left the runway stretched away towards a line of trees and peach grove, then we were turning, pivoting, a rudder pedal plunging as I watched it. The noise as George opened the throttle was massive, even with the headphone and helmet protection. The rudder banged behind me like an old tin can, but suddenly it stopped as the tail lifted clear and we were hurtling along, until we lifted free of the ground and were climbing, easing higher into the sky, and I watched my land of farm and crop slide beneath me. The only vibration and noise now came from the airplane itself, but I was getting accustomed to it, and I stared down fascinated at the scene below me. This was no biplane, jaunty and open to the elements. This was the dark prelude to the warbirds in which boys I knew and cared about would fight and perhaps die. I stared at the back of George's head.

"Okay back there?"

His voice was clear in my ears and it startled me. "I'm okay." I saw him looking at me in the small mirror designed for students and instructors.

"Depress the button to talk, I can't hear you."

"I'm okay."

"Great. Try not to shout, just use a firm voice."

I depressed the botton again. "Okay."

"Anywhere special you'd like to go?"

"Not really. But I love looking at the land."

"How about your farm...Camilla."

I looked at him, forgetting the button. "Can we do that?"

"Depress the button."

"Can we do that?"

"Sure. Let's poke around here for a while, then we'll head down there. And watch out for planes, any kind of air traffic. Tell me if you see any at all."

"Okay." I looked around and found I was starting to enjoy myself. The impact of it all was too much to permit a steady fear. I was young, and I was flying as few others had. I stared out at the thin ribbon of the Flint River. It was muddy colored, with a patina of gold from the sun, the flow of it burrowing under the overhanging trees, then flowing free, swirling, glittering...North lay Andersonville, the Civil War graves of Union soldiers, but I kept my thoughts from that prison camp and its dead, and what it all said about wars and those who were forced to fight them.

The land below me was adorned in the browns, pale yellows and pine greens of winter. To my left, looking down and back, I could make out the old cotton rows of the 1920s, before the boll weevil ravaged them. The rows were weathered down, falling back into the earth. An old rusted school bus was embedded in a tangle of undergrowth, a broken window winking back the sun. Other land was robust and rich offering fruit orchards and stands of trees. Pecan trees stood in geometric rows, but vulnerable in these days before chemical spraying. We were climbing now, and everything was changing as it fell away, developing into a new mosaic. I suddenly wanted the height, to climb, to leave the ground. Far to the south the soil became a sandy loam used for tobacco, but I could not see too far through the sunlit whorls of Plexiglas and the blue haze which layered the horizon. As a high school student I had spent summers gathering tobacco. I felt my ears pop and swallowed hard. Then, three black dots shimmered against the blue haze.

"George?"

"What?"

"Are those airplanes off to our right, into the haze?" I watched his head turn quickly.

"BT's. Well done, Doreen. Good pilot's eyes. There are some pilots who can identify stars in daylight. We'll change course a bit. Don't want to hold up the war effort."

As we continued our climb I found myself smirking. Pilot's eyes. Wait till Haggis and Freddie hear that! How perverse is human nature that you can know fear, then fifteen minutes later be smirking. I was completely off guard when George's voice crackled again through my headset.

"Okay, let's have a little flying lesson."

"What!" Fear came back and flooded into me.

"Come on, now. Just listen and watch...okay? We're just going to have a good time, enjoy ourselves. Now, I'm going to make a gentle turn to the right. Don't touch anything, just watch as the stick goes over, like that, until we have a nice gentle bank, then gently bring the stick back and center it again. See how the aircraft maintains its bank? A little on the right rudder and around we go..."

I watched the horizon tilt, the control surfaces on the bright yellow wings. Then we were straight and level again.

"Don't worry about the instruments, I just want you to know the freedom of flight, enjoy it a bit...Okay, same thing for a left turn: bring the stick across to the left, not too far, watch the aircraft respond with its bank to the left, a little left rudder...there we are."

We straightened out again.

"Okay, now let's have you do it, and remember there's nothing you can do to this airplane at this height that I can't get us out of, okay?"

"Okay."

"Take the stick, hold it gently, no need to strangle it, now let's make a gentle right turn." All the time his head was turning, scanning, always scanning the sky.

I gripped the stick and slowly moved it to the right. Immediately the BT responded to my touch. I remembered the rudder, but pushed on it too hard and I felt the tail shimmy.

"Easy on the rudder, we skidded a bit. You're doing fine, keep on bringing us around..."

I leveled us off by bringing the stick to the left, then centering it again. I looked in his rearview mirror and his brown eyes were smiling at me.

"Okay, choose a point off the left wing at ninety

degrees and bring us around."

The BT moved to my touch. Slowly the watertower came around, but then George's head and the big engine cowling cut it off. I leveled out. "I think that's it."

"You used the water tower?"

"Yes."

"Not bad at all. Next time we'll use instruments for turn and bank, compass and so on. Okay, I have the controls, you sit back. I'll show you a loop and a spin, then off to Camilla. Here we go with a loop..."

"George..."

The plane responded to George like a pit bull coming out of a doze in the sun. I sat frozen as we began to dive towards the earth.

"Dive a little to pick up speed, there we are...come up for the climb...keep the stick all the way back, ease up on power as we go over. Here comes Mother Earth again."

Meet it, Doreen, stay ahead of it! Just like The Greyhound rollercoaster at the fairground. Noise, noise, sky, sky. Over, over, tugging at harness, Mother Earth in her winter shawl, pop, pop, swallow hard.

We were straight and level again.

"Okay, we'll do a spin. Are you okay?"

"Fine."

"Feeling sick?"

"Nope. Do the spin."

I felt the nose come up, George and the big engine pulling me behind them.

"Pull nose up smartly into a stall, kick on full rudder, here we go."

I watched the earth spin across the nose of the airplane while my harness caught at my body holding me tight.

"Opposite rudder, stick forward...she's straightening

out now, bring power back on..."

We were climbing again.

"What did you think?"

"I liked the loop, I think. The spin was a bit disorienting."

"Don't worry, you'll get the hang of it." He didn't wait for my answer. "Let's go to Camilla and fly over your farm."

Chapter 10

THE FARM. I wondered if flying there was a good idea. The farm was what had formed me, with its rhythms and seasons. What insights would a bird's eye view offer, what detachment? I knew my farm through Mama's eyes, watching from the kitchen window, hands dusted with flour and gripping Mrs. S.R. Dull's *Southern Cooking*, watching the weather, the bend of branches and lie of grass...and I knew it through Daddy's eyes, the way he looked at horses and negroes...

"Coming up on Camilla."

"So fast? I ..."

"Give me a heading, Doreen, where should we go?"

I looked down at Camilla, the main street and humped roofs of cars; the flat topped buildings and sloping tiles of framed houses. A tractor moved on a back road, a negro bent to the wheel and looking up. At us, I realized.

"Doreen, we're leaving Camilla." Laughter filled my headphones.

"East, we're east about ten miles."

"Okey doke."

"Should we use military commands?"

"Okey doke is fine. Let's enjoy ourselves. Are you?"

"What?"

"Are you enjoying yourself?"

The answer sprang on a depressed mike button. "I am, George, I really am!"

"Good."

"There's the farm!"

"Those red barn buildings?"

"That's it. George..."

"We'll make a pass, see who's awake."

The BT dipped, sideslipped a little, trailing a wing, then leveled out and thundered towards my home. Never had I seen it like this! Shade trees girded the white wood-work; azaleas, camellias, the mimosa trees fending off a future summer heat. There was the dark patch where the barn had burned in the middle of the night and we had had to get the horses out. An image of a crashed BT, of Jimmy Peterson and John Piggott, spangled behind my eyes then was gone.

"Coming around to the left."

"Okay."

"Nice trees."

"You should see them in summer, it's just bursting with color." There was pride in my voice and I felt child-like. "See the cypress pond over to the right?"

"I see it."

"That's where I went frog giggin' with Uncle William."

"Uncle William?"

"A colored hand. I grew up with him in many ways."

"Ah."

George didn't comment on my choice of words, but I felt the sour taste to them. They had come out in the care-less way of a Georgia farm girl, a casual and cruel dimin-ishing of a big man. My prayer was desperately short but filled with need. Below me the cypress pond looked older, wider. Thick tangles and leaning branches explored the scummed water. The pond winked back the sun as we turned, its bright frothy green and dark marble both a mystery and memory.

"I'll come in over the house, not too low. See if anyone comes out."

"Mama should come, she doesn't like loud noises much...there's Melsie Mae!"

"Who?"

"Uncle William's wife, Melsie Mae. Look to the side of the house, the shade trees." I watched as the large negress shaded her eyes and stared up at us, her washpot scrubbed out and upside down on the trestles. Monday had been washday and I laughed, remembering. Some clothes hung on a line, drifting on the breeze.

"Wind's changing," George said.

"Wait until March. The wind really whips around here." We were by Melsie Mae in a blink, even as I waved, bumping my hand against the canopy, but she didn't recognize me. From the corner of my eye I saw the corn crib. When Sadie the settin' hen had died I had buried her in a glade where the morning sun warmed the earth and bathed it in light. The glade vanished beyond whorls of Plexiglas.

"One more time," George said. The BT curved around again, wings gleaming. My farm canted on its side, Melsie Mae tilting with the upended washpot as if she would slide down the earth. She was watching us intently now, her pudgy hand shading her from the sun.

"She doesn't recognize me," I said.

"Okay, carefully now: pull down your goggles and open your canopy."

"It's stuck..."

"Pull down your goggles, I said. You don't want debris coming in on the slipstream and blinding you."

I got my goggles down and twisted the latch. The canopy opened and wind blasted at me, chilling my face around my goggles. But I could wave freely against it.

"That your parents coming out?"

We came in over my home, wings wagging, me waving wildly. Would they recognize this begoggled, helmeted figure? It was Mama who waved, with that timid uncertainty that seemed part of her, then she was waving vigorously at us, her flowered apron cheery bright in the sun. Her hair looked grayer...

Climb, come around.

This time Daddy waved, his hand stiff, cutting, like a salute, or like when he cut off undesirable conversation at dinner. A final wave and we were gone, thundering out across Georgia's farm lands, untidy strings of country roads and matchbox buildings, leaving behind us a farm hand and a mule working the soil.

"Better close the canopy now, Doreen."

"Okay." I dragged it closed and secured it. I shoved back my goggles and blinked around the cockpit. The engine now sounded muted, and my ears were ringing inside the helmet. "That was wonderful."

"Good. Time to go back."

We landed at Ft. Valley auxiliary field just as a BT-13 was taking off.

"C-107. That's Latham," George said, reading the identification numbers.

"Freddie?" I watched him climb, steady and precise.

"Good pilot, flies quite well."

"They're all upperclassmen now. Soon they'll be graduating and going to Advanced."

"Yes. You'll have to help out the new students. Teach

'em how to dance, like me."

I didn't answer, the sudden melancholy of lost friend-ships hitting for the first time. And a different fear, ugly and deep inside, beyond reach. Damn the war!

Chapter 11

GEORGE AND I never looked back after that flight. We grew closer and did what other couples did. We went to the movies and laughed at B-movie heroics and argued about movie stars. Mostly we enjoyed the musicals and their lyrics. We dropped in at the Idle Hour Club and visited homes where instructors and cadets were welcomed, and we went to Atlanta to ride the Greyhound rollercoaster. Jazz artists and their genius permeated our lives, pushing out our boundaries, especially mine of course as I played catch-up. We went to hear Duke Ellington at the Biltmore, but we were not limited to negro artists: Jack Teagarden offered a sweet trombone, subtler than Tommy Dorsey's; and Jerry Mulligan opened up lower register vistas on his baritone sax. And as the weather mellowed on the threshold of Spring, we went to the lake for swimming and picnics and enjoyed its tranquillity. No roar of airplane engines, no frenetic energies from a trumpet section...

But throughout those days and weeks as we grew closer we handled a lot of war tension. Our daily lives were threaded with it. There was the training, the rare but agonizing accidents with the required autopsies at Hawkinsville and interment at Alabama's Oakwood

Cemetery with full military honors. There was the slow rotation of students from Lowerclassmen to Upperclassmen and the seeing off of friends to Advanced training. There were party celebrations for Haggis and Archie. And Freddie, my sweet and sensitive Freddie. Most cadets went to multi-engine flight school and a few to single-engine flight school where they would train as fighter pilots.

By 1942 scuttlebutt was feeding back: from new British cadets just arrived from England who had survived a perilous Atlantic crossing and who now had a first tremor of doubt. And newly returned American boys who had convalesced over cups of tea with wounded RAF boys. Then the prized tidbits of loose talk allegedly overheard by this waiter or that steward at an embassy dinner party. We were planning a Second Front against Hitler, we were winning at Midway, stopping the Pacific advance, the German submarines were destroying whole convoys and Britain could be starved out...We also had the ferry pilots, not only flying the Atlantic but those coming in from the west coast. I always watched George for his reactions, but he was ever the impassive, unreadable flight instructor projecting unwavering confidence. But the war dug around inside us, behind the laughter and dances.

I thanked God for quiet times with George, nurtured sanity in which we grew ever closer. One night, in my room...

"I like the way you have Hartlepool circled on your wall map," George said.

I blushed a little. "I got it out of an old school book. That day in Americus the cadets were arguing about where it was. Some said near Sunderland, some Newcastle."

"Any more iced tea left?"

"Yes, a little. I can make some more."

"Wonder what mum would say about iced tea."

"If I read her right, she would be very polite and not let on one way or the other." I got more tea.

"It's an old town, Doreen, a working town. The people have grit, and a rich heritage going back to the Viking invasions. The Vikings would come over and pillage and burn. But we all get along now." His eyes darkened in amusement.

"A working town?"

"Yes. You can catch the rhythms of it. Just like here in many ways, people contending with hardship, like the Depression."

"The Depression was bad. My parents rarely talk about it."

"Hartlepool kids in darned jerseys and cardboard in their shoes would carry a hot meal to the few fathers who had a job in the shipyard, perhaps a ship in for repairs. If a whale beached, it would be cut up and carted away with not much left." His eyes wandered around my rented room. "Who's the woman stretched out at the top of that skyscraper?"

"Margaret Bourk-White. Super photographer. One of my heroines."

George looked at me thoughtfully. You've the makings of a good newswoman, Doreen."

"What, I'm not already!" I poked at him.

"You'll do well." Outside Bluejays chattered, then were gone.

"I'd like to read some of your work. Do you have a file?"

"Does Sinatra croon?"

"Serious pieces, Doreen."

"Like the struggle with disease, the poverty."

"Right."

"No chic hats and white gloves and perky chatter."

"Right."

While I mentally selected news items I'd written, George talked about the Scots 'fisher lassies' who followed the herring fleet down the bleak coast to ports like Hartlepool and Whitby, there to push baby carriages filled with wet fresh fish. It was always the coastline that summoned his deepest reveries. Old men wading in tidepools, bending into the rocks with their crabbing hooks. Other men and boys collecting seacoal in baskets and sacks or hunting for brass, which they could sell by the pound. And the wrecks, the discharged diesel oil, the dead sea birds in the scummy sea. Wrecks and whales and ancient tales, all to the sound of training plane engines and an occasional air raid drill.

Then came the time when the remaining barriers between George and me were all too stark. I had not invited him to meet my parents and stay at the farm. He had not talked about Dunkirk and what happened to him there. We followed our maxim: let things settle. But we knew we had to confront the barriers to reach a final closeness as lovers.

It would be a vile incident near Hawkinsville that finally knocked everything down. The first trailing edge of the maelstrom to come showed itself in casual conversation one gorgeous weekend in May at the lake. Six of us. Butch Martinelli and Barbara Rucker, one of the reliables for our dances; Bill Trepick and Wendy Clinkscales, home for a long weekend from the FBI's fingerprint department in Washington, and George and me.

I watched Bill, outlined against the far shore and scrub pine, make an excellent swan dive from our raft, then he was swimming back to us using a strong crawl, his deep tan contrasting with water and sky. He came wading out, water glittering down crew cut and torso, his belly muscles taut and thighs as thick as tree trunks. Wendy handed him a towel which he whipped around vigorously, drying off biceps and forearms. Few had a physique like Bill's. "So what're you guys talking about?" he asked.

"Movies," Wendy said. "George likes *Mrs. Miniver*, Doreen likes *Casablanca*."

Bill grinned at me. "Here's looking at you, kid."

"How about you, Bill?" I sipped my coke, watching him run the towel over his crew cut.

"Me? *Pride of the Yankees*. No contest." His quick eyes looked around. "Any pickles left?"

George smiled. "We're down to one Spam sandwich, Bill."

Bill pulled a face. "Okay, I'll settle for a beer. Say, you know something? That scene with Bogie and Bergman in the fog at the end, that twin engine jobbie in the background?"

"What about it?" Wendy asked.

"Midgets."

"What?" I lowered my coke, my enshrined Casablanca scene about to come undone.

"Midgets. Whole thing was done on the back lot at the studio. They used midgets for perspective."

"Who told you that!" I said, color rising in my cheeks.

"Ferry pilot, in from Boeing. He was a stunt pilot in Hollywood. Straight dope, Doreen."

I stared at the sandy earth and pushed away some ants.

"Sorry." Bill lowered the towel self-consciously.

"It's just a movie," I said.

"No, it's not," Barbara said, firmly. "It's a story about two ordinary people swept up on a dangerous world stage, like us."

"You're an incurable romantic," Bill said. "What do you say, George?"

"I still like *Mrs. Miniver*, a touch of home...but also filmed on a back lot," he added, anticipating him. "The backdrops looked fake."

I looked at George and his relaxed easy calm. He sat cross-legged, his face, neck and arms deeply tanned, the rest of him, to use his own words, fishbelly white. He could not have cared less. I always admired that about him. So while Bill was cajoling him and Butch to race out to the raft, George was lighting his pipe, deflecting him, turning aside comments about his 'pinto' suntan with a smile. He was above it all, and it was getting to Bill.

"Taken Doreen for a plane ride yet, George?"

"I'll never tell," George said dryly.

We all laughed. An instructor who had charged civilians five dollars a ride was now doing sentry duty at Turner Field's sewage treatment plant.

"She wouldn't go up with me," Bill said, looking at me. "I thought she didn't like the BT, what with Peterson and Piggott, but I guess it turns out she just likes English guys."

"Then I'm in luck..." George began mildly.

"It wasn't like that," I said, butting in.

"Oh? How was it then?"

"Look, Bill..."

Barbara came in at that point. I missed Wendy now that she was in Washington, but I was liking Barbara more and more. She moved adroitly to head off juvenile comments. "Speaking of luck, did you hear about that

British cadet who cut out some paper wings and pinned them on his uniform? He got washed out three days later. An Upperclassman too."

Butch shook his head. "I heard. Bad thing to do, bad luck for sure. You think so, George?"

"It was a silly thing to do, but I'm not so sure it was connected with washing out."

"He would've washed out anyway?" Butch said.

"I think so, yes."

"You believe in luck, George?" Barbara asked.

"I think there's good fortune and bad. Mostly, I think timing is everything." His strong fingers tamped fresh tobacco into his pipe bowl, and the distinctive aroma lifted on the warm fresh air.

"Do you carry a good luck charm?"

"Not really. But I have a couple of reminders of home: a silver threepenny piece and a small stone I picked up off Parton rocks at low tide. Reminders of where I was born."

"George is from Hartlepool, on the northeast coast of England," I said.

"Pretty bleak up there," Barbara said. "Damp. I read about it in those old novels in English class."

George smiled at her.

"Speaking of damp," Butch said, "I hear guys now based in England can't keep warm. They're sleeping in overcoats...that's Eighth Air Force guys *and* RAF boys."

"Well, it must be warmer now," Wendy said. "It's May, for pete's sake."

"Maybe so," Butch mused. "The scuttlebutt's old."

"Do you believe in luck, Butch?" I asked.

Wordlessly he fingered his Roman Catholic medallion and silver chain.

"That was dumb of me," I said.

"Nah."

Bill sat down cross-legged beside us, exuding tanned good health far removed from overcoats. "A guy at Welleston Air Depot told me some religious nut had written about our bombing efforts. Said we'd lost the moral highground."

Butch gave him a cold look. "Who was it?"

"Bishop of Chichester...or is it pronounced Chister? I have trouble with some of these Limey names."

"Yeah?" Butch said. "Well, he'd better remember Coventry and Rotterdam. What do you say, George?"

I watched George's face shadow. "We're in it. We'll have to see it through."

"And we're going to win," I said, immediately feeling foolish.

Bill sneered. "Got that from George, I bet."

I went beet red.

Barbara tagged Bill's arm and pulled him closer to her. He put his arm around her.

"Doesn't matter who said it, point is it's true." Butch's smile was contagious.

"Damn right." Bill turned to me. "Doreen, you think it's true what you heard the other day, about aircrew smoking on night raids?"

"I don't have reason to doubt it," I said carefully. "But I've only the one source, that British army liaison officer."

"That's better than scuttlebutt any day." Bill picked up the remaining Spam sandwich and washed a bite down with his beer. "Jesus, that tail gunner. Forty cigarettes out to the target and twenty home."

Wendy stared. "Where did he put all the butts?"

I smiled at that. It was what made her endearing, this take she had on the world denied most of us, and her sincere yet haphazard caring.

"Down his flying boots," I said.

Wendy grimaced. "That's disgusting."

Bill changed the subject. As usual it involved himself.

"Had to boot a couple of cadets up to the Commandant of Cadets."

"Why? Barbara asked, putting his arm back around her.

"They glided in over Wesleyan Women's College. The girls were sunbathing nude on a roof. They throttled back, real quiet, enjoyed the show, then gunned it to get out of there. Some girl got the serial numbers."

"I'm pleased to hear that," I said, rather too primly.

"They're just young bucks, feisty."

"It's wrong," I said.

"What, you think those girls don't know about the planes? It's just 'stop it, I love it' stuff."

"I don't want airplanes flying over my naked body," Barbara said.

"Me neither." I glanced at George. He was a little embarrassed, an arch English reserve about such subjects, but none of them knew as I did the hidden passion and supple caress he offered in private — more at ease with himself than I was...

"Nuts," Bill said, his hand making a cutting gesture startlingly like my father's. "You two guys interested in building hours? I'm going over to Welleston and testing airplanes. They're short of pilots. I've already got some hours in B-25s and C-47s. Good for after the war, for the airlines. Lots of guys will be trying for the airlines. Lieutenants and captains'll be a dime a dozen. And I want Pan American." His beer was raised in salute. "Best of the best, see the world."

"I'm not interested," Butch said. "After this, I'm out

of it."

"Yer kidding."

"Nope. Going into the family moving business."

"You mean you don't love to fly?" Bill asked, a bit taken aback.

"It's okay, better than being a dogface in the front-lines."

"You, George?" Bill's eyes found him.

I watched George, his brown eyes reflective. "I'm interested."

I felt a pang of jealousy for the only competition I had: flying.

"Thinking about the airlines after the war?"

"Frankly, yes."

"Like what, Imperial Airways? Fly in that Limey goo and rain?"

"Bill!" Barbara pulled away.

"No. I want to come back to America. I like it here, you can grow here, make your mark."

"You can't do that back in England?" Butch asked.

"Not as easily." George let it go at that.

"Isn't Welleston called Warner Robins now?" Wendy asked.

I nodded.

"And the Army Air Corps is now the Army Air Forces," Barbara added. "Everything's changing. They're building more planes up in Atlanta, they need riveters for the production lines."

"Fingerprint classifying is better than riveting," Wendy said.

"Things are moving quickly," I agreed. "I'm going to do a story on the new dormitories out on the Macon Highway. They should ease the terrible overcrowding."

Barbara said, "Rumor has it they've got sanitation

problems, roaches and things. And the women are wanting house mothers. But the negroes like their apartments. Better than where they lived before, I imagine."

I looked at Barbara, my mind working at it. The story had potential. But then Bill's comment caught me off guard.

"Niggers don't have to live the way they do. They just like it that way, or don't care."

"Please say 'nigras'," Wendy cut in. "Only white trash say 'niggers'."

"Coloreds, then. I'll call 'em coloreds. And they're lazy. Every time you look they're just standing around. Or sitting. They're real good at sitting."

My anger rose up like bile. "That how they talk in the North, in Wisconsin?" I asked. "Nice farm folks?"

"Yeah, it happens. But down here, jeezus. Get on a bus at night and look back there, and nothing but big grins and eyes..."

"Bill!" I yelled at him, looking down at him, surprised to find myself standing.

"Yeah, Bill," Butch said quietly. "Knock it off."

"What, you like the coloreds?"

"That's true about the North," Wendy said, turning to Barbara. "I hear about it all the time in Washington. They're just sneaky about it."

I watched as Butch carefully gathered up picnic wrappings and placed them in the hamper.

"So, Butch," Bill pursued. "You like the coloreds? Even Wendy knows the score."

The hamper lid closed. Butch's voice was very quiet. "You like sports, Bill?"

"You know it."

"Joe Louis, Jesse Owens."

Bill's mouth tightened. "Sure, but there's no contradiction, don't try to…"

"So, you'd like to meet Joe Louis?"

"Damned right."

"How about going a couple of rounds for the fun of it."

"Love it. Never happen, though."

"So he could come into your BOQ?"

"Sure."

"And use the can?"

I watched Bill hesitate. He said nothing.

"How about Skeeter Davis?"

"Don't know him."

Butch pushed a finger between his foot and sandal, scratching at an itch, but his thoughts were elsewhere. "Me and Skeeter grew up together, went to school on Chicago's south side. His dad loaned my folks some money when the Depression was real bad for us. Can you imagine, a negro having money in the Depression and lending it to my folks? It wasn't that much, but back then at that time it was riches, boy, riches."

Bill found a cigarette and lit it, angrily waving out the match. "Okay, I see where you're going…"

"So what I'm saying, Bill, is Skeeter and his mom and dad can take a crap at my house any time they want."

It was a challenge thrown down, and I worried about Butch, but it was Butch who had the vein bulging in his neck and a fist clenched in the earth.

Wendy reprised her whining, cutting voice laced with self-righteousness and hate. "That's disgusting. And all that Joe Louis talk…that's just silly!"

Butch looked at Wendy, skewering her. "I'm a wop, Wendy. I know what it's like to be looked down on."

The small chuckle fell into the ugly silence like the warm blooded bubbling in a pigeon's crop. We all looked at George. We all watched as he tapped out his pipe.

"What," Bill said.

George's smile remained, a small celebration.

Butch got it. I watched his fist relax and the vein pulse down to normal. But none of the rest of us got it. Butch smiled, then laughed, his head going right back in his own celebration of insight.

"And you're not only a wop, Alphonse," George said, "you're ugly too."

The rest of us didn't get it, although in the years to come one of us would. But at that moment, in 1942 at the lake, scared by war, all but George Westcott and Butch Martinelli were far too spoiled and sheltered to understand. Later, when we were packing up things and loading the car, Barbara and I had a quiet moment. We watched Bill at the shoreline skipping stones.

"Barb, thanks for reining in Bill. I don't understand him lately."

"Pulling his arm around me, you mean?" Barbara smiled. "A guy like that needs to look good all the time. Some growing to do, actually. And he's hurting."

"His views are common enough," I said. "But he keeps baiting George and I don't like it."

Barbara smiled. "My putting an arm around him and giving him attention can do only so much, Doreen."

"What do you mean?"

"Come on, don't be naive. He's hurting for you. He's crazy about you." Barbara lowered the trunk lid. "Fancy swan dives, preening and suntans, he-man flyer, and none of it's making a dent in you."

I didn't answer. I didn't know what to say.

Chapter 12

BILL'S INTEREST IN me had finally registered, with Barbara's savvy insights confirming Wendy's gossipy ones. But Bill had not come on to me, he kept his distance. I respected him for that. His views at the picnic had been offensive, but how would I have reacted before George, before Billie Holiday, before coke in a glass?

"Heard from Wendy?" George asked, over coffee.

"Yes. She's enjoying the fingerprint work."

"A bit hard on the eyes."

"It apparently has some fringe benefits. Some girls are looking up heart-throbs like Errol Flynn. If they're caught, though, I think they're fired."

"Can we try for a movie tonight?"

"Love it."

"I thought we could go for a walk afterward, if the weather stays nice."

I looked at him, meeting his brown-black eyes. "Love it."

And I would, knowing that I could be adventurous, exploring and savoring physical needs, but always safe because George would hold back, let me set boundaries, feel them in place.

That night after the movie, nestled on a grass embankment, I felt so free and newborn under starry heavens and feeling the warm breath of our murmurings about who we were and where we were going...

"That's the Big Dipper. In England we call it The Plough."

We looked starward at pinpoints of light against a cavernous black void. I felt the night air on my cheek and against my blouse and legs and over my shoeless feet. Blood coursed through me, hot and bright, and a musky sweat clung to my underclothes. Nothing was undone, no loosened buttons, but my blouse had pulled loose on eager stretching arms. Memories of George's touch, his mouth, his breath, were imprinted on me, ghost echoes of exquisite points in timelessness, all feeling and no thought. His strong hands had moved over me, over cloth and silk, never intrusive but aware, so aware, of the touchstones of my release. I found his hand, entwined my fingers with his and gazed at the stars, feeling a hot glow under my skin. I cast around for something neutral to say, something to move me from a tremorous desire.

"When will we travel to the stars, George?"

"Not sure. The moon first. When, I don't know. Maybe by the year 2000. Flying I'm more sure about. People will fly everywhere after the war. Costs will come down as more people fly. Could be like buses and trains one day."

I squeezed his hand. "You'll get mistaken for a train conductor again."

He laughed, easing his arm under my head.

"Is your arm cramping?"

"No. I'm fine." We were quiet a moment, then "Doreen?"

"What?"

"Mind if we drive down to Hawkinsville this week-end?"

I looked at him. Hawkinsville was where they had taken John Piggott and Jimmy Peterson. And while George and I had grown closer, our blood pumping, cadets had died and been taken there. I said nothing. I waited.

"I want to see how things are handled. What care is taken." The haunting look faded and the dark eyes showed only concern.

"I'm sure they do a good job," I said. The haunting look bothered me. It was haunting, not haunted; not a chasing of terrors. It was something I couldn't define.

"Then we can drive around a bit, go to a yard sale or something."

I grinned. "I'd like that. By the way, how's the plane testing?"

"Good, very good. Bill was right about that. I'm building hours and fattening up my log book."

"How is Bill?"

"Fine, I guess. There's a bit of a wall between us. It's okay if we stick to planes and flying..."

"Am I the wall?"

"Yes."

"I can't help it George," I said, turning to him in the starlight. "I want to be with you, I need to be with you."

He kissed me then, slow and sensual. When I had a grip on myself I said, "I couldn't believe all that racial stuff at the picnic. It just spewed out. He's never talked like that before. It was as if he wanted to provoke us..."

"Not us, you. Well, okay, perhaps me too." I watched George smile as he looked at the stars, his strong profile shaded by the night. "Butch was something. I hadn't expected it."

"But you room with him. Don't you both share things?"

"Well, since the picnic we have. But before that we were just cordial, each of us busy." He turned to me then. "Bill's a good man, Doreen. He's just going through that stage when a man has to prove things, usually to himself, not others."

"You never have that need. You're so in control all the time."

"I have my moments."

The silence grew, a cushioning of our revelations.

"You were like Bill?"

George laughed. "Look, Doreen, I can't sit here in judgment on a friend and fellow pilot..."

"How were you like Bill?"

"Well, it's not that I was like Bill, it's that boys growing up..."

"Tell me something you did, as a boy growing up."

"Oh, Christ. An interview. How did we get onto this?"

"Tell me."

"Well, I can remember being a skinny tall kid. I shoved handkerchiefs up my jersey sleeves to make my shoulders look broader."

"You did?"

"Trouble was, it only worked in the winter when I wore jerseys. My shoulders broadened and narrowed by the seasons. Then I got barbells. I was in pretty good nick when I joined the army."

I smiled, pushing my face into his chest. "Girls put tissues in their bras to look bigger."

"Ah."

I propped myself up on an elbow. "Don't say *ah*, don't give me that *ah*! You know about women, I suspect." I pinched him. "What are Hartlepool girls like?"

"Very different from the Egyptians."

"George!" I went to pinch him again but he rolled me over, gently pulling my hair back, running his mouth and tongue up and down my neck. I shuddered uncontrollably. He pulled back.

"It's all right," he said.

I clung to him, heart thumping. "No. Wait a minute." I fingered my blouse buttons and released my bra hooks, then I was under his exploring mouth and swirling tongue. "No padding, George," I managed, "No..." He took a breast and I cried out against the cooling night air honing once hidden flesh, the warmth of his touch, the exquisite arch as he gathered me up into his arms. "George," I said. "George." That was all that came out. Only Mama's imposing image detracted. 'You must remain pure, Doreen, chaste...'

That Saturday we drove down Highway 129 to Hawkinsville under a slate gray sky. Perhaps the sky was appropriate for a trip to a mortuary, but George kept the conversation light. He was not, as he put it, 'going off the deep end.' Quite the contrary. He was a man who knew how cheap life could be, so certain things mattered to him. It followed that a flag and ceremony by the military was not enough; in fact, he viewed them with suspicion. Privacy and the care of the dead revealed more than public pomp. And I could see it. He was a man who loved deeply the beaches visible from the room in which he was born. And he had stood on a Dunkirk beach among teeming thousands of men wearing the tattered garments of war, and watched the sea stain red. Somewhere in all of it was the key to George's haunting look.

I glanced across at him. His RAF uniform was immaculate, his shoes highly polished. His hat, as usual, was on the back seat. Brown eyes were soft and reflective as he looked out at Georgia's farmland and May's greening crops. He reminded me of John Piggott and our drive, but I pushed that remembrance back.

"I wish my mother could see all this and enjoy the warm climate," he said. "Barbara Rucker was right about the northeast coast. It's damp."

"Like in those old novels?"

"Right. The bitter cold and damp get through jerseys and blankets, and when you gather close to a blazing fire you get chilblains."

"Sounds nasty."

"Mum has had rheumatism from the cold. Her knuckles swell up with it and her wedding ring hurts her. But she won't take it off."

"What does your father say about it?"

"I lost my dad. He was crippled very young with arthritis. He spent a life with his feet propped high on the mantelpiece to ease the pain. You could watch the seasons change against the sea and Dad's propped up legs. As a boy I'd go out back and get the coal and bring it in for the fire. But on warm summer days he'd go through the alley on his crutches and watch us play cricket on the common."

"He sounds like a nice man."

"He was. Wiser than me by a long chalk. I remember one time he was perched on his crutches helping Mum do the dishes in the sink. I made some smart mouthed comment about dishes being woman's work."

I glanced across at him. "What did he say?"

"He said manhood didn't wash off in dishwater."

"Ouch."

"A good man"

"Tell me more."

"What, about my family?"

"Yes. I know about your mother and sister playing the piano, and now your dad. Tell me more."

"You've not talked about your family."

"Daddy is rigid, Mama is pliant."

George took out his pipe and tobacco pouch. "Oh? Or should it be Daddy is strong and Mama's supportive?"

"No," I said coldly. "I've got it right."

"That why I've never been invited to the farm?"

"Partly. I'm working things through."

"I see." Blue, rum flavored smoke trailed out the open car window.

"Please talk to me, George." I felt his eyes on me, gauging my tension.

"Okay. What about? Flying?"

"No. Something else. How about explaining the English class system."

George laughed, full timbred in the car's confines. "You've been hanging around the cadets too long."

"No, seriously. Haggis is just plain bitter about it. Archie is more easy going but it's there, you can see it's there."

George bit down on the pipe stem and stared out through the windshield.

"George?" When he spoke I was given a careful, deflected answer.

He shrugged. "There's class structure everywhere. Here, Boston, New York. Everywhere. People tend to sort themselves out. People like to be comfortable with each other. It's hard to enjoy dinner when one of you is figuring out which fork to use."

"That's it, that's your answer?"

"I've failed miserably."

"What were you thinking when you were looking straight ahead?"

"I don't understand."

"You were thinking, but it wasn't about which fork to use."

"Don't be crackers." He smiled engagingly, and I knew I would never get through. "Look, here's a couple of things that I find useful. One, everybody wants to be equal with those above them, not those below them. That should tell you something. Two, I've found that the working classes don't have a monopoly on all that is good and decent, and that the so-called upper classes have no shortage of kind, hard working people in their ranks. I'd take Haggis with a grain of salt if I were you."

"Somebody named Higginbotham sneered at his pigeons."

"Well, that would do it. A man's pigeons are sacred."

"George?"

"What?"

"Are you pulling my leg?"

"Me? Heavens, no."

"Yes, you are." I reached over and pinched him.

"Hey!" Sparks flew out the window.

"You know what Haggis says about it?"

"What?"

"'Every man for himself,' said the elephant as he danced amongst the chickens. The class structure means it's not a level playing field."

"Ah."

"What ah?"

"The secret to life. We are chickens aspiring to be elephants. You can bet the upper classes, the privileged school boys, will make the transformation to elephants look easy."

"Why?"

"Because that is the God given rule of an elitist, privileged education. It's a sin to make any endeavor look difficult."

"What about you?"

"Me? I worked damned hard and I don't care who knows it."

"Ah," I echoed, letting in John Piggott and his egg sandwiches and the London Science Museum. "George?"

He let out an exaggerated sigh and gestured with his pipe at the scenery. "Doreen, can't we just relax and enjoy the ride and..."

"No."

"Why not?"

I looked at him. "Because I don't get to see you as much as I want to, need to. You're with Bill at the Air Depot when you're not instructing, it gobbles up our time..."

"Oh, I see. Bill took my plane, by the way. Time in a B-25 Mitchell. I gave it up to be with you."

"Don't do me any favors, George. I can handle it. But when I've got you in my clutches I want us to talk."

"Okay." He was silent for a long moment, then he reached for my hand. "I need our time too, Doreen. I need to be with you. Don't ever think you're just a fill in."

"No, I don't think that."

"How are we doing?"

"Doing...you and me?"

He said nothing. He just held my hand and looked at me.

"I think we get tense sometimes," I said slowly.

"Tense with private worries that we haven't shared."

"Sometimes things are best not shared."

"I suppose so. I guess it's a matter of deciding what to say." I looked at him again. "But just for the record, George Westcott, losing you would rip me apart, and you'll never know how hard it is for a Georgia girl to say that." I felt my hand gathered up in his.

"Doreen, how do you think a news reporter's career and a pilot's career would work together?"

My mouth went dry. "Are you proposing to me?"

"I don't quite know what I'm doing, except sharing thoughts. I've had this particular thought for some time."

I stared down Highway 129. A tractor hauling an empty wagon chugged along, and an airplane was turning low against the slate gray cloud. I took the Nash around the tractor. "It's a nice thought, George. A good thought."

"And?"

"And I think it could work, the pilot and the reporter could work."

"Shall we leave it at that for now? Let things settle?"

I nodded, numbed by my feelings.

"Of course, there could be an unsettling interlude."

"What? Why?" My stomach flip flopped as I turned to him. He pointed with his pipe stem, his calm brown eyes staring straight ahead, and I followed his gaze. The B-25 Mitchell bomber was coming at us, its twin engines roaring, skimming telephone lines, barreling true down the highway. I screamed as it flashed over the car with a sound like tearing silk, then thunder, and we buffeted in its slipstream. Bill made two more passes, enough for me to gather my wits and curse at him.

In the settling quiet George said, "He's pretty good. But I'm better."

Chapter 13

SHE WAS A small woman in her fifties, sturdy, with quiet eyes that had seen too much. Her face was pale and bore the smooth planes of a religious. A superficial reading would conclude a blind acceptance of nature's onslaughts, but that would miss the tireless patience of a guided life. If she were here in this place, I thought, then it was a good place. I kept a little behind George, a Southern deference. When he spoke he was the flight instructor, the Royal Air Force officer and gentleman, his diction precise and his manner cordial but reserved. The little boy who carried coal for a crippled father was not in evidence.

"Good morning, madam. My name is Pilot Officer Westcott, and this is Miss Summers. I'm an instructor at Cochran Field."

"Yes. I am Miss Scruggs." She glanced at his tunic and RAF wings. "You are with the Royal Air Force?"

"Yes, madam. We have lots of RAF cadets training at Cochran."

The quiet eyes stayed on George. I think she had some sense of why we were there. She had spent a life standing on the threshold of the hereafter, helping people cope with worries and concerns about the dead. With the exception of Uncle William I had not been close to death and its rituals. And the military ceremonies for Jimmy Peterson and John Piggott had been just that. Military. I had spent that day of reporting with Billy Odum at the office, by turns crying and typing, until Billy gently turned me from the keyboard and pulled me to him. I wondered what this composed woman would think about Uncle William's grave, and the service. The small negro church had been packed, with Daddy, Mama and me in prominent seats in the front pew. The colored children had continuously wafted us with large hand held fans to keep us cool.

"Is this in connection with Cadet Fowler, sir?"

"Fowler? No madam, not at all. Except in the sense that I am wondering if you could tell me...us...a little about this funeral home."

"All the boys."

George's voice softened. "Yes. All the boys."

She stepped back and turned, a practiced pirouette. "We always welcome visitors, please come this way. Here, of course, is the chapel..."

Of it all I remember the stark and the odd things. The stark bright room of tables and jars and sinks, of glittering chrome and hospital smells. The odd fact, slipped into the conversation, that the entire house which the funeral parlor occupied had been sent from a Sears and Roebuck catalog. There were no nails used in its construction. The stairway was orange and quite lovely. And for always I would remember the record ledgers.

"You may look through the ledgers, sir. I ask only that you respect the privacy of others. The records are not for the public, but you are serving with our own air force, and we are contracted to them." She paused. "I think it would be helpful to you to see them."

"Thank you." George and I sat down at a table.

They were heavy green books with cloth covers and maroon bindings. Entries were in pen and black ink, a graceful calligraphy, a respectful marking of life and its passing. There were entries for farmers in their seventies, children under ten, and military cadets, both USAAF and RAF, who were nineteen and twenty. The juxtaposition of entries was heartbreaking. Joshua Mobley, farmer, white, born June 10, 1871 died December 12, 1941. As did Clive Hammersmith, #1233980, RAF, white, born April 12, 1921...

George closed the ledger gently. "About ready?"

"Yes."

We stopped by the chapel and then went to find Mrs. Scruggs.

"I hope you found this time worthwhile," she said.

"It has been very helpful."

Mrs. Scruggs hesitated. "It's not easy for us."

George nodded. "I know. Thank you."

Outside the slate gray of the morning was lifting. We stood on the funeral parlor steps and looked up and down Commerce Street. George was very quiet.

"Anything you want to say?" I asked.

George shook his head. "No, except seventy five dollars for a casket is little to show for a life cut off so young. And these British boys are so very far from home."

"After the war some parents will come over here to see where their boys are buried. Oakwood Cemetery is a worthy place."

"Yes, yes it is. What's over there, across the street?"

"Statues from another war."

"Let's have a look, then I'll take you to some yard sales."

He took my hand as we crossed the street which was alive with noise and traffic. I knew a secret gladness to be there, caught up in life, heart beating. We stood before the monument. "A Confederate monument, of course. It's unusual in having two statues, Robert E. Lee and Stonewall Jackson. Usually it's only one, and when possible he faces north."

The magnolia tree was in early bloom, delicate in color and scent.

"And this building?"

"That's the court house. Interesting point, George. Back in the nineteenth century itinerant architects traveled around the country selling plans for court houses. The country was growing so quickly every new community sooner or later needed a court house. They had four basic plans. That's why wherever you go in America the court houses all have the same look."

"It's not bad."

"It's plug ugly."

George laughed as he stepped over to a historic marker. "The Slosheye Trail..."

"The Trail of Tears. Indians were shifted from Florida and Georgia up to the Indian reservations. Commerce Street is where Indians once walked." I got defensive. "It's not exactly Vikings and the Crusades."

"It's history," George said simply. "Not America at its best, but history. In any case, Hartlepool wasn't all Crusades and Vikings. We're also famous because we hung the monkey."

"You hung a monkey?"

"Another time, Doreen. Come on, garage sales are beckoning."

"You hung a monkey?"

"Yes, we thought it was French."

"George!"

The yard sales were enjoyable with their treasures turned bric-a-brac loaded awkwardly onto immaculate front lawns, with people drifting through, men in old pants and women in large sun hats, occasionally stooping to examine something. Comments were pure Americana: 'How much is this?' and 'what is it exactly?'

We listened and smiled. But there was one sale where I pulled us up short. "Look, George."

It was a glossy enameled box with ornate gilt scroll work. It looked oriental. A man came over, his white shirt crisp for the occasion, his face deeply tanned and leathery. "I can give you a good price on it."

"What is it exactly, a sewing box?" I tried to open it.

"No ma'am. It's a puzzle box with all kinds of compartments for you to keep good stuff in. See, you hit it here, on the side, while at the same time you press here." Lids and drawers slid open in odd directions. I loved it. "George, can you lend me..."

"No, this is on me, I want you to have it. Besides, I get to spend some of my instructor increase in wages."

"A gift?" I said.

"Yes. From me."

"Then I'll buy you a gift. Not here, not now. Later."

"Okay, if you insist. But it's not..."

"I'll take it," I said, cradling it in my arms. "I love it."

"Well, miss, it's fine with me, but you're supposed to horsetrade a little, not just take my first price."

"We'll take it," George said, smiling.

"Okay, son." He looked George up and down. "Say, ain't you one of those English flyboys?"

"Yes, sir."

"Always wanted to fly. I was in the first war, you know. But I was a blacksmith, shoein' horses for the old cavalry."

"Important work," George said.

"I guess. You folks have a nice day now."

I hugged my puzzle box and smiled at George.

"Wonder where he got it."

"I don't know, and I don't want to know. That's part of its mystery."

"Okay, come on."

It should have ended there. It should have ended with banter about monkeys and nice old men who shoed horses. Instead we chose to drive into the countryside, with me offering odds and ends about where we were traveling.

"I'm glad we went to Hawkinsville," George said, lighting his pipe.

"Me too. Next time I'll show you where they keep the harness racing horses."

"Harness racing?"

"They race them up north but bring them down here in the off season. It's a good climate for boarding and the rains run off real quick." I smiled at him. "We're not just peaches and mushrooms, you know."

"I know."

I glanced out the car window and scanned the sky. "Think Bill's out there waiting to pounce?"

George laughed. "Not with the gas consumption on a Mitchell."

I felt his eyes on me, studying me. "What?" I said.

"I was thinking that for someone wanting to get away to New York you talk rather proudly about Georgia."

"Ah," I said.

"What ah?"

"I guess I want you to like it. It's important to me that you like it here. I suppose that doesn't make much sense."

"No, I understand."

We drove in silence after that, not realizing the bitter irony to our words. We came to a small town whose name is burned into my memory but I will not share it.

"Let's walk around here," George said, tapping out his pipe.

"Okay."

It was a nice town square draped in early flowers, the buildings painted and cared for. Grass expanses offered quiet. There were benches and the lively call of birds. Signs saying 'Whites Only' were neatly done. It is difficult to understand that there is always violence hidden away in these tranquil scenes. My South is shaped by its landscapes of sultry beauty and the beguiling formalities of manners and traditions, but it is shot through with violence. And this violence has nothing to do with stylized duels for the honor of a lady, or the bark of musketry, or the roar of cannon and bloody gray tunics. It is a random, senseless, bestial thing, the cruelty of which was borne in those days by negroes and 'nigger lovers.'

"It's peaceful here," George said, looking around. "Away from those BT engines."

"Like to sit down?"

"I'd rather walk if you don't mind. Stretch the old legs."

We walked.

Lots of people were out, white and colored. An easing slate gray sky offered a pleasant Saturday morning. I saw what was happening before George did. I watched as a tall and very thin negro lifted his little girl up to the Whites Only water fountain. She cradled on his forearm and drank urgently, slaking a child's thirst. The negro was not quick enough, not on a Saturday morning peopled with citizens.

"George, I think we should go now..."

"What? We've just got here."

I watched the policeman. He was full bellied, his gunbelt low slung under it. His face was gross with outrage and he moved quickly. There was no warning. The billy came down on the negro's head. He dropped his daughter, pushing her away. The billy was relentless. You could hear it strike over the bull-like roar of the policeman.

George was already moving forward. "What the bloody hell...!"

I grabbed at him, holding him back. "George. No! No!"

George was strong, so strong. My grip fell down his body and I clung to his legs. The policeman turned, watching George. He turned full front, the billy bloody, the negro down on the ground, the child screaming, a horrible keening sound. I clung desperately. The policeman came towards us.

"You look like you're getting ready to interfere with the law."

"What in God's name are you doing to that man!" George's voice was held down, but his muscles were taut, he was a hair away from unleashing a trembling coiled anger. I struggled to my feet, getting a better grip on his arm. I would not let go. No matter what, I would not let go.

"George, George...please!"

The policeman's gaze settled on me. "Better listen to the little lady, flyboy."

"You have no right to hit that man, you need to be reported."

"George." It was litany, a cringing, a stark terror. "George, he can destroy you, your flying, us...everything."

"You want to report me, Limey? Go ahead. Right after I arrest you for interfering with a law officer carrying out his duties. And after that you can pack your bags." He took a step forward. "Just who in hell do you think you are? Coming over here while American boys fight your war for you, messing in our ways."

I clung to him. I clung.

Suddenly George went slack.

"That's more like it."

I loosened my grip on George's arm and we just stood there.

"Mind if I give him a handkerchief?" George said.

The policeman looked back at the negro. Blood trickled from his temple spattering his shirt. The child screamed. "Sure, why not?

George slowly took my hand from his arm and went over to him. He took out his handkerchief and pressed it to the man's temple. He said something and the man took the handkerchief, holding it to his head. George went to the little girl and took her hand. He didn't gather her up into his arms. He held her hand, and I knew that touch. He talked to her and her crying subsided, but I couldn't catch his words. I moved forward. The policeman stepped back. His feelings for me were clear: one of their own gone bad, no respect for Southern ways, causing unpleasantness, messing with foreigners who didn't 'unnerstan.' I watched as George got something small and shining from his pocket. Her father got up and comforted her. George held out his finger on which balanced a coin.

"Know what this is, chook? This is a silver threepenny piece. Back where I come from mothers put them in Christmas cakes for good luck. I'd like you to have it. Would you like it?" From her father's arms she reached out. "There you are, chook. Don't cry now. Your daddy's all right."

Back at the car we ignored each other, each taking stock of the ravaging not only of the little girl and her father, but of us. My broken nails were bloody. I looked across at him. There was blood on his tunic. I didn't know if it was negro blood or mine.

"Dear God," he said.

I managed to turn the key in the ignition and start the engine, but we drove only about a hundred yards before I pulled over and wept. I couldn't stop. I cried for me and I cried for my South, where our lives moved forward on a gracious moment, with exquisite floral tapestries, and family gatherings on summer porches, and lazy talk about weather, hunting dogs, and cotton. But now, all too clear, was the strange fruit hanging from sturdy branches, a silent harvest that knew no season; and the Jack Daniel's poured straight under soft amber light, and guns oiled, and robes and hoods kept ready.

"Talk to me George," I said, wiping at my face. "Please talk."

"How did that filthy animal get a policeman's uniform!"

I shook my head.

"Leave the South, Doreen. Get away from here."

"And what about us? There is an 'us'..."

"Yes, but not down here."

"So I leave and then what? We write letters? George, I need to be with you, I thought you needed to be with me."

"I do."

"Then I can't go, at least not yet! God, this country's full of couples loving each other, finding each other, and they're being forced apart by war across thousands of miles. We can be together, we have each other at least for now."

"Is this why I can't meet your father?"

"What?"

"Is it?"

"Daddy holds strong Southern views, it's a heritage..."

"You call this obscenity a heritage?"

I cowered over the steering wheel. We were losing each other, losing each other. "George."

"What?"

"I don't want us to talk any more. I want you to promise me something."

"What?"

"That you'll come and meet my editor, Billy Odum."

"Why?"

"Because you must."

He stared ahead, his eyes lost to some distant horizon.

Chapter 14

SUNDAY MORNING THE *Macon Dispatch* office was locked up and closed. I opened the door and ushered George inside then closed the door after us. Things were very tense between George and me, and I felt sick to my stomach. A strong smell of coffee wafted over the silent typewriters and telephones.

"That you, Doreen?"

"Me and George, Billy."

"Okay. Be right there. Want some coffee?"

I looked at George. He shook his head. "No thanks," I said.

"Be right there."

Billy came out of his office carrying a cup. In many ways Billy was the *Dispatch*. Small in stature, bald, smooth featured and with a bright sometimes unpleasant gaze, he had biceps knotted like small apples against his short sleeved shirts. Usually he had a newspaper open before him, some membrane slice of our ways and traditions. And he fit. He fit, bellied up to the potbellied stove on a cool Fall day, or staring at his heirloom brass spittoon (once used by Doc Holiday, he swore, before he headed West). The hard blue eyes looked at me. "This is not my idea of a Sunday, Doreen."

"I know. Thanks for coming." I made the introductions.

"Come on back to my office."

We settled into the two chairs facing Billy's desk. Countless people had sat there. People wanting favors and news coverage. Politicians, salesmen, ministers. I had too, listening to writing critiques, learning from Billy the difference between writing thin and writing lean. On the wall behind him were some of our stories, nicely framed and positioned but dusty and neglected, along with a photo of President Roosevelt at Warm Springs wearing a swimsuit, smiling, holding a girl with braces on her legs. Billy's Doc Holiday spittoon gleamed in the morning sun. I watched him light up a cigarette.

"So, George. I hear you bumped into some of our Southern ways yesterday."

"That's right. I don't think there's anything to say, Billy. What happened, happened. It was brutal and disgusting."

"You want to tell me about it anyhow?"

"Doreen wants me to talk."

"Oh? And what does that mean exactly, that you don't want to, that your own mind is made up and we're a bunch of brutal, disgusting bastards?"

I stirred uneasily. I had gone to Billy desperate for his help, but this was not what I expected. I watched George hesitate.

"I usually work things out for myself," he said slowly. "Think things through for myself."

"Only this you can't."

"No, I can't."

"You're jammed up. You've been living here for some time, you've met some Southerners, made friends, been made welcome into their homes, you've liked their kindness, their caring, and now you're jammed up. How can this ugliness happen?" Blue smoke curled, disappearing into the slants of sunlight, reappearing again, wafting upward. "Well, Doreen's upset and I won't get a lick of work out of her until we get some things straightened out, clear the air."

George moved angrily in his chair, yesterday's rage still carrying its momentum. "Surely you're not excusing..."

"Nobody's excusing anything," Billy said sharply. "But you're a reflective man and you've had time to reflect. So let's take a look at what happened. Why don't you ask your questions?"

"Very well. But understand this: I traveled with the army before the war, the Middle East. I've seen ugliness. I've seen hands cut off for stealing. But those laws applied to everyone of every social cast and ethnic makeup. I'm just saying, Billy, I'm not naive, I'm not stupid. I see things here that are grossly unjust, and I just keep quiet and try to follow RAF rules. We're guests in this country, and so forth, but when it explodes in front of you, the violence and obscenity of it..." His voice trailed off.

Billy smoked his cigarette, exhaling at the floor. "And your question for me is what?"

"How can a policeman beat up a negro because he got his daughter a drink of water? So segregation applies to water fountains, why didn't the officer just move them along? God, he assaulted the man, beat him bloody, and he got away with it!"

"He got away with it because he's a bad cop hired under segregation laws which tolerate it. There are many like him, and many other sadistic whites who thrive on segregation. Tell me, were other people around?"

"Yes. It was a nice day, people were out walking."

"And you're saying that these nice people just stood there and let this cop beat up a negro in front of his little girl?"

"That's right, that's what happened."

"Or could it have been, George, that your own actions precipitated a totally unpredictable, totally unusual situation, in which some of those people couldn't act?"

"What!"

"Hear me out, George. You're fair minded. Do you think decent white Georgians would have let this assault pass, just gone on their way, enjoying the nice day?"

"What are you saying?"

"I'm saying that for all the ugliness and brutality of segregation, there are checks and balances. Brutal things happen, yes. But this is a society, a culture, and it must sustain itself to survive. So there are unwritten codes, way to influence, tacit understandings, signaled messages that help in these situations."

"What in God's name are you talking about, Billy!"

"Well, I'm going to tell you, but I have only an hour or so to explain a couple of hundred years of evolved culture. So bear with me, okay?"

"You're saying I'm to blame, that the man was beaten up because of me?"

"I'm saying that had you not jumped in the way you did, that somebody and probably more than one somebody, would have done his best to stop the cop. And it would not have been a challenge to his dubious manhood, the way you went at him. It would have been something like, 'Hey, he's not bothering you,' signaling that this negro is off limits for abuse. There are phrases used to make wishes known. Also, these locals knew that cop, they would know his family. They would know about certain skeletons in the closet, or maybe someone went to school with him and knows about him. A couple of words and pressure can be brought to bear. But no one had a chance to do this because you got in the cop's face and backed him into a corner in front of folks he grew up with, went to school with, and would go on living with. No one was going to talk about *him* and this Limey fly-boy down at the hardware store, no sir." Billy smoked his cigarette, staring at the floor. "And you must remember these whites must guard against going over the line, being perceived as 'nigger lovers.' That wouldn't happen here, the situation was clear cut ugly and could've been stopped. But there are other situations which are not so clear cut..."

I glanced at George, not wanting him to meet my gaze, but he was totally absorbed in listening to Billy.

"See, down here George, we suffer from the fears of segregation; we're caught in our own trap. We fear the negro will rise up, so we keep him down. And in our paranoia we spin stories: like our fear of syphilis and our fear of white women being raped. Separate drinking glasses, separate water fountains. There's a deep-seated fear of disease, and we use the negro to personify it, to focus our fears."

George looked at his hands, twisting them. "Tell me more about these ways of getting along."

"Sure. You went to a jazz club in Atlanta, didn't you...? J.J. Lemon's, Billie Holiday?"

"Yes."

"Did you tip?"

I watched George's face. It was guarded.

"Yes, of course. For a good seat. Billie is world famous, and..."

"So how much did you tip, for a good seat?"

"Five dollars."

"Five bucks? For a seat?"

"Yes."

"Well, you see George, in our more rural way of life if a man paid a colored more than two dollars a day for any kind of work, then he would be condemned as a nigger lover. And a nigger lover is the lowest life on earth. If you think about it you can see how this sick segregated culture is kept whole, you can see why things are...If this white man persisted in paying too much — that is, pay a fair wage for long labor — then things would start to happen. For paying over two dollars he'd first be ostracized. Not only by whites, but by coloreds too, who would be frightened of retaliation from angry whites. At the worst, his farm would have to be sold off because no one would work his crops, provide for marketing and transportation. Lawyers and bankers wouldn't give him the time of day, because they're caught up in the web too, and a similar fate would befall them. So this white man would have to move, leave the area. And keep in mind his family might have been there for generations."

"And how long has your family been here?" George asked.

Billy smiled, but there was pain in it. "You're quick on the pick-up, George. My family's been here for five generations. They fought at Bull Run and Manassas and on the Western Front. I have a boy right now up on the Great Lakes for Navy training."

"And your newspaper, if you embarked on crusade against this...?"

"I'd be shut down or burned out within two months. Only one newspaper editor is courageous enough, and his newspaper strong enough, and that's Ralph McGill with the Atlanta Constitution. He's under constant death threats, late night hate calls."

I thought about that. Ralph McGill was fighting in his editorials against segregation, and he would one day win the Pulitzer, while I looked for ways to escape.

Billy stared at his spittoon, gathering his words, trying to explain the unexplainable. "There are good people here, people of good will and wisdom, black and white, and they struggle with segregation and the way it diminishes all of us. You have whites saying, 'Goddamn slavery and the system it spawned,' and 'how in God's name do we get out of it?' And the negroes say, 'The boss man knows it's wrong, knows it ain't right. And I know he'd be there for me if I got sick, needed help; and I'd be there for him. And he'll be there when they put me in the ground, just as I'll pay my respects to him the same way.' But..."

George reached slowly for his pipe and tobacco.

"Sure you don't want some coffee?"

George hesitated.

"Doreen, fix him some coffee will you?"

They let me bustle through.

"Suppose a white man wants a negro friend over for supper," Billy said. "Know how it's done?"

"No."

"Well, if a negro eats at a white man's home, they all have to eat out on the porch, not inside. But if the white man goes to a negro friend's home, he can sit at the table. There's no problem; that's accepted."

George said nothing. I handed him his coffee but he did not look up.

"And the negro understands, George. Understands that his white friend could be burned out if he were to sit at a white man's table inside a white man's house."

"So negroes go into a white man's house only to

work, like as a domestic?"

"Generally that's so. Some kind of work bringing them into the home. But he or she can never sit down. Sometimes, like when a white man dies and there's a viewing, what we call 'sitting up with the dead,' negroes are made welcome to pay their respects, but they can't sit down. They pay their respects to a white man they cared about, then leave."

George glanced at me and I looked away. I was finding it all very hard to take, a mix of shame and fear.

"What else?" George asked.

"Okay, lessee. A couple of weeks back in a small town near here, we heard that some white boys about sixteen or seventeen years old were going into the colored part of town and tying cat's tails together and slinging them over a clothesline to fight it out. Then they'd throw bricks at the colored's homes. We heard they tossed a dog down the well. The white community responded immediately. They disciplined those boys. Why? Because what the boys were doing was something you just do not do. It got stopped quick.

"Here's something for you. There's an old colored woman living in my home town, my last newspaper job. Big woman, sassy and lovable, she knew how to walk that line. Like that big colored woman in 'Gone With The Wind' who won the Academy Award. Doreen...?"

"Hattie McDaniel."

"Right. Well, everybody had an affection for her in that town. Anyway, this woman stole silverware. She stole it from people she cleaned for...but the white folks let her do it. Why? Because she took exactly one piece of a dinner service, one knife or one fork, until she had herself an entire set. Nothing matched, of course. And here she was in her shack, with newspapers mushed into paste to seal out the cold, using fancy silverware. Folks talked about it at tea socials, lauded each other on how they had sacrificed, really enjoying the game. She got tacit support. But anybody else..."

I got myself some coffee and thought about Billy's story. It was a common practice for negro domestics to leave at the end of the day with a folded newspaper hiding some sugar or something else. Daddy and Mama ignored it.

"Doreen, get me the Jack Daniels, will you? This is turning into a Jack Daniels sort of day." He turned his attention back to George. "I interviewed a colored man one time at his home, a shack really. Anybody driving by could see it was a shack. Anyway, it looked the way it was supposed to look. But inside, inside, that man had decorated with taste and culture. He had these framed pictures on the wall, art illustrations he got out of some book or other, illustrations from the Renaissance, some Moderns. God knows where he got them. Rembrandt's 'Man in Armor,' Van Gogh's 'Self Portrait.' Damned if he didn't have my favorite picture up there. Mercel Duchamp's 'Nude Descending a Staircase', a brilliant piece...not that I know much about art. Where is it, Doreen, at New York's Metropolitan?"

"I don't know." I watched the hefty pouring of bourbon.

"Doreen's going to New York. Getting away from all this. She's reading up on New York attractions. Say, where are all those books you had?"

"Returned them to the library." Anger arose in me. "But I've checkout out others."

Billy lit up another cigarette. "Point is, if I told anybody, his place would've been torched. A nigger with ideas is uppity, dangerous. He risks lynching. But this man trusted me with his secret, all he possessed, perhaps his life." Billy shook his head. "I don't have that kind of guts."

"Tell me about lynching." George said.

Chapter 15

"WELL, THE HANGING of negroes isn't considered much of a topic for newspapers, so you won't read much about it. The talk would be on street corners, like this." (Billy's voice filled the office, malevolent and cruel.) "He smarted off at a white woman, Sarah Dunhill?" (Voice rising in a Southern inflection.) "God's truth, it was Fred Dunhill's daughter. Salt of the earth, that gal. Yes sir, salt of the earth. That coon like to scared her to death, so we took care of that uppity nigger real quick, took him up behind that land old Wilbur Tilly keeps trying to unload."

Billy looked at George. The bourbon was opening him up and the anguish showed through the hard planes of his face. I retreated under the weight of his words, the way I had with Billie Holiday's lyrics.

"There are dangerous niggers who don't know their place, you see." Billy went on in a quiet voice. "They undermine the security of our way of life, our civilization with its white columns and lush flowers and calls to Honor. And a nigger lover is the flip side to that coin. He's also seen as a threat to the natural order of things. Sometimes a nigger lover is tolerated if he is seen as deranged, 'a might touched in the head', eccentric and harmless." Billy's grin was ugly. "After all, we're not animals."

I went to the window. The sun beat warm against it, and there were dead flies and dust on the sill. I made a mental note to clean it off on Monday. Outside several well polished cars moved, using saved rations of gas as they carried their families to church.

"The trick," Billy was saying, "is to keep them down. So we strip them of their dignity. Like we say, 'the colored people,' or 'that colored man who works for Mr. so and so.' All these phrases are used in polite society. You've surely come across them at air force socials, or in public relations with the locals. Then there's field talk, yard talk, that you may not hear: 'You Yancy's nigger?' There's never an identity, an equality. Separate but equal is a lie." Billy stubbed out his second cigarette and lit another one.

"What else, Billy?"

"What else, Billy?" Billy said, as if casting around for some lodestone that would explain everything, simply, quickly. He held up the Jack Daniels. "Want some?"

"No thanks," George said. "Coffee's fine."

"Well, put it in your coffee then." Billy poured a liberal shot of bourbon into George's coffee cup. "You have to understand, in the South there's a concept of fair play, of honor and self respect as a working man; so in the days when things are bad and there's little food or money, a farmer will show you what he has to barter, and when he sees what you're interested in, say onions or mushrooms, he'll load you up generously, because he doesn't want to cheat you, and he'll say, 'I wanna please yuh.'" Billy smiled, the bourbon bottle steady. "I wanna please yuh."

"Thank you," George said, lifting his cup for a second shot.

"You learn quick, George. You sure as hell do."

I watched my editor lean back in his chair and clasp his hands behind his head. The biceps twitched, knotted gristle. "Where did you do your Advanced, George?"

"What?" George looked startled, his pipe out.

"Did you go single or multi-engine?" He smiled. "See, I know this stuff from Doreen. She keeps an old fud like me updated."

"I was multi-engine at Moody Field."

"Near Valdosta?"

"Right."

"I see. Do you know how turpentine's made?"

My stomach turned as I watched George's face, a mixture of bafflement and intelligence as he grappled with the fast moving Billy. "No," he said.

"No, Billy, not this one," I said.

"You settle, Doreen." His eyes watched me to see if I would come back at him. "Anyway, over near your Advanced training field we've got pine trees used for making turpentine, and about five years ago..."

"Billy!"

The eyes cut at me. "He wants it all, Doreen. Don't you, George?"

"Yes."

"Okay." Billy spoke into the silence. "About five years ago I was out hiking and camping. It's good to get away from the desk, focus better, get perspective. And I camped near a turpentine still, or distillery, if you wish. Want to know how to really keep the negro down? You work him on a turpentine still. The owner of the still is white, of course, and he owns everything. The pine timber, the commissary, the negro quarters, everything. The trick is to keep the coloreds in your debt. So you lend them money for work clothes and food from your commissary, charging outrageous prices and interest, and you put everything on the negro's tab. Then you own him. He's never out of your debt."

"He can't work it off?" George asked.

"Nope. He's in the hole so deep he never gets out."

I began to worry as Billy poured more bourbon into his cup.

"So when another white distillery owner wants men, he sends over a pickup truck and pays off the debt to the current white owner, then hauls the negroes away. He owns them now. Anyway, that night I heard the talley-men calling."

"Talleymen?" The dead pipe turned in George's hands.

The bourbon poured.

"Billy," I said.

"It's okay, Doreen. Just reminiscing is all. See, George, on a turpentine still you got workers who rake the pinestraw some three feet from each tree, so the burning off won't set the tree on fire. Then you have the talleymen who keep records of trees cleared. Each talleyman has a distinctive call, you see, which is recognized as his as he registers the number of trees worked by each worker." Billy brought his hands down and rested his forearms on his desk. "All night long, rich and melodious, these beautiful voices calling out against the night sounds of insects and birds and animals." The hard eyes found George. "Know what happens if a worker tries to cheat on the number of trees he's cleared?"

George didn't speak, he just waited.

"There's a white overseer or outrider on horseback. He checks. If a worker is caught cheating, they tie him to a tree and whip him. Your night flights have gone over some colored man tied to a tree."

"That's enough, Billy," I said, reaching for the bottle.

He didn't stop me from taking it.

George twisted his pipe. After a moment he said, "It's hard to take it all in."

"Yeah, well remember that whites and negroes of good will live with it and hate it and are sick with it. But they look to tomorrow, because it will change, George." Billy leaned across the desk. "Don't ever give up on my South." I watched his intensity wash back. "Things are chipping away, George. True, we have a town with a yellow line down the sidewalk, where the negroes must walk closest to the gutter, and keep three paces behind a white man. But we also have Rich's Department Store in Atlanta, which gives credit to negroes. That's how one gifted concert pianist got her start. She performs up north, of course," Billy said dryly. "Not here."

George finished his spiked coffee.

I stood by the window that day, looking out at that peaceful Sunday morning. I would remember it years later when the first indictment of a white man for beating and lynching a negro was handed down in 1952. George, Billy and me, with the Jack Daniels and spiked coffee.

"See, George, it's not just that whites are changing their views on negroes since the Depression, it's that negroes are changing their views about themselves." Fingers tapped on the desk top. "And with that comes a sense of identity, and with that there can be no stopping equality."

"Tell me about the Klan," George said.

"The Klan." Billy pinched the bridge of his nose. "Well, the Klan is like an enforcement arm. They try to dress it up with stuff about Southern heritage and states rights, but basically they're in the enforcement business. It's members are everywhere: lawyers, barbers, doctors, accountants. They serve as mayors, police chiefs, county commissioners. You've talked to Klan folks and never known it. See, in a system like ours politicians and wealthy businessmen need a big stick to make things run, get certain unpleasant tasks done. For instance, suppose I hire a negro to work here at the paper. A clerk job, I mean. Not cleaning toilets and sweeping up. I'd get a visit from a well dressed man who would remind me of the natural order of things, and the consequences of not abiding by that order. It would be polite, no robes or hoods. I'd be perceived at first as misguided, a bit weak, influenced by that northern liberal talk, not a nigger lover. I would just need reminding." Billy's smile came back, not bitter but playful, the kind a kid would have playing hooky. "It'll please you to know that the KKK is short of robes because of the cloth shortage."

I poured him some coffee but he just let it sit in front of him.

"What else you got for us, George?"

"When Doreen and I were in Atlanta," he began slowly, "I noticed negro soldiers in the very first carriage of a train. In England the first carriages are all designated first class, then second, then third."

Billy laughed. "This guy would make a reporter, Doreen. But you see, George, there's no rhyme nor reason to segregation. Like how can negroes take care of white babies, and fix food for whites...sticking their fingers in it...but they can't drink from the same glass? Anyway, to answer your question, soot."

"Soot?"

"Yup. First cars, at least on our trains, get covered in soot and grit from the locomotive. So coloreds sit up front. Fact is, there's soot and grime everywhere in Atlanta. Monday mornings law clerks and secretaries routinely clean it off law books and typewriters."

"That's interesting. In Hartlepool, where I'm from, there is coal dust. Housewives clean it off sideboards and tables."

"Small world," Billy said. "I understand you're from a coastal town. Do you like the sea?"

"Yes."

"Well then, you can appreciate the sea's moods, good and bad, and how they shape the community. Same thing here, with the land and the seasons."

George asked quietly, "Is it true about the negro paratroopers?"

"Is what true?"

I waited on that one. George was ahead of me.

"That in Atlanta, if they wore their airborne insignia and bloused their pants over jump boots as paratroopers do, they went to jail?"

"Yes, that's true. They're not good enough to make airborne, you see. So we pretend they didn't. You're talking about the 555th, the Triple Nickle. You should also know that German prisoners of war can go into white military establishments while negroes fighting and dying for our country's ideals are not admitted."

George leaned back. "Christ."

"Don't look for coherence, consistency, George." Billy said softly. "It ain't there. You're dealing with prejudice and fear." Billy gave a weary smile. "Don't you want to go out in the sunshine, take this lovely girl with you?"

George stood up. "Thanks, Billy. I got a lot out of this."

"Don't go slugging cops."

"No."

"Take a look at our writers sometime, see why we're

the way we are. But don't give up on my South, George. Time will prove us worthy. Doreen?"

"What?"

"Take this guy to our beaches. Go to St. Simon's or Savannah. Show him our sea."

"The beaches are covered in barbed wire."

"Go anyway. It's important to him." His eyes found George's and this time they were a humorous blue. "I understand you have a unique way of getting gasoline."

"I'll never tell," George said.

"And Doreen, take him home to meet your folks."

As we left and I locked the door behind us, I watched Billy get up and retrieve the Jack Daniels.

Chapter 16

THE BT-13 BLASTED over the Alma light beacon against a backdrop of stars, all sound and exhaust flame, red and green navigation lights, blue and yellow paint work. I sat on the wing of George's parked BT and watched the trainer thunder away, disappearing into the night, lights winking. George squatted on the wing a few feet from me, next to the open cockpit, working the radio. More planes were due along the light line, and it was a special time, the final exercise for Freddie, Haggis and Archie before they moved on to Advanced. I had heard rumors that Haggis had a piece of chalk which he used to make a mark on his instrument panel for each beacon in the light line he passed over. "Then I simply erase them one by one, and when the last one is erased! I'm back home!" Only coin juggling Haggis would think of that. But they were all about to move on, and I wanted to be here tonight.

"That was Peters, Doreen. Your friend Watkins is coming over next. Archie, is it? Want to talk to him?"

"Can I? Wow!"

"Very short, now. It'll go out over the air."

"Okay." I scrambled up the wing to George and the radio headset, my coke bottle clanking on the wing.

"Archie, you there?"

"Good lord, who's this?"

"Doreen. I'm at the Alma check point."

"Doreen! That's wizard! With luck I'm at Alma too."

"You are. Dance with me Friday night?"

"Once around the garden, as they say."

George took back the headset, his head shaking in bemusement, then he was all business. He spoke quickly, serial numbers and professional exchanges, his radio procedures so fast I couldn't follow them.

"Here he comes," George said.

Archie's BT swooped in over the beacon, thundering at the stars, his wings rocking.

"That's for you," George yelled above the racket.

"He was surprised to hear me." I tried to imitate Archie the Yorkshireman. "Gud lawd, who's this?"

"You'd better stick to smoothing out your Southern accent," George said dryly, looking at the roster. "Only two more."

"Who?"

"Latham...that's your Freddie, of course...and Trowsdale."

"Good old Freddie."

"The dancer."

"He really is good, George."

"Hey George!" Bill Trepick yelled from the nearby hangar. "Where was your coke bottled?"

"Oh blast," George said, tilting his coke to look at the glass base. "Newnan."

"How about Doreen's?"

George looked at my coke. "Statesboro."

"Hah! You lose, George. Pay up. And we're buying for the kids too."

George waved, but he was muttering to himself.

"Never won yet."

"What's going on, some kind of game?" I asked.

"Oh. We figure out which bottle was bottled farthest away from us. Whoever has it, buys the next round."

I looked at the night sky, its gathering cloud edged in a honeyglow of moonlight. I loved the night, the way it summoned private thoughts and opened them up for sharing. The passing planes, the banter, the night-cushioned insights.

I watched Bill over at the hangar as he hoisted a colored boy into a plane cockpit, pointing, explaining. "Look at that," I said.

"Bark's worse than his bite." George slid lower on the wing, cradling the headset. "Good talking to Billy."

"Yes."

"Did you know Northcountrymen marched on London and the Houses of Parliament?"

"What were they marching for?"

"Jobs, food. Help with sickness and disease."

"Were they successful?"

"I think so. Lorries, that is trucks, took supplies north. Those men had walked south for over two hundred and fifty miles. At the end of it they were too tired to smile or cheer themselves on. There was only the sound of loose shoe soles flapping and slapping as they walked. Someone said it was the most frightening sound he'd ever heard."

"It sounds very frightening."

"Politics are different in England, but not by much."

"You're not dealing with segregation."

"True, but..."

The radio chattered on a burst of static. George answered with that fluency too hard for me to follow, then he turned to me. "What we have is a class structure,

Doreen, and you know about it from the cadets...it's impossible for you not to. Class permeates everything. It helps or holds you back depending on where you are in the pecking order."

"The elephant story?"

"Yes."

"John Piggott said the English pigeon hole you as soon as you open your gob."

George smiled. "Gob?"

"See!" I said.

The smile bloomed into a laugh. "Got me." Then he grew serious in the penumbral light. "Dad had a favorite observation. He'd listen to some aristocrat during an election, some patrician type say, 'Vote for me, I understand your needs...' And Dad would say, 'He wants to be Prime Minister and he says he knows my needs, this chap who reads the Classics in their original Latin or Greek, who has an aperitif before a dinner provided by shotguns and hunting dogs on a generous land which he owns. How can he possibly know what I need?'"

"George?"

"What?"

"No more serious politics talk, American or British. Let's talk about us." I waited, expecting him to say, 'Let's go to see that new film at...'" Instead he shook my world under those magnificent stars.

"You look lovely tonight. I'm sorry I can't get you alone."

"You have plans?"

"Definitely."

I squeezed his hand and released it, looking across at the airmen and kids. Bill was lobbing a ball to them. "How are we doing, George?"

"I'd say very well." The headset swung on his hand,

faster now.

"That's too British. How are we doing?"

The headset stopped in mid-swing and I watched George lower it to the wing. It dangled on its wiring. "I love you, Doreen. I'm in love with you."

I looked at him stunned, my heart lurching a beat. "George..."

"What, too British?"

"George..."

The radio let out its static screech.

"It's Latham. Freddie. Want to talk to him?"

I shook my head, numbed, looking at George who was in love with me.

"I say, is Doreen still there?" Freddie called.

"Off the bloody radio Latham, she's indisposed."

The BT hauled away into the dark, wing lights glowing.

"I've recommended Latham for single engine, Advanced. Had him up for a check flight. His flying skills are excellent. He'll make a good fighter pilot."

George's eyes were glistening, an intense black. I just stared at him.

"Doreen?"

"I...I didn't expect that," I managed.

"It's all right."

"I can't answer yet."

"It's all right. I guess I jumped the gun a bit."

"No, no." My tears were scalding. "I'm glad to know, need to know. You rock me, George, you just rock me. But why me?"

"Oh, lord, she's fishing again."

"Tell me. Because nobody likes me, George," I challenged. "I have Wendy and now Barbara. I'm not too likable. You know those heroines in women's love stories, the kind you root for? Well, they're not me."

"I'm not in love with a story book girl. I want you. Why? Because I admire your grit." His voice was gentle. Plane exhaust fumes wafted, phantom engines echoed. "And I see the girl inside," he said, "and I want your dreams and mine together...like we said, the reporter and the pilot."

"Billy wants me to come back to Georgia."

"I can understand that, after talking with him."

"Could you live here? Not that I see it happening," I added quickly. "But supposing..."

"Yes, I can see myself here. Now. And Atlanta's Candler Field will grow. I could try for Delta. We could work it. The South is changing and we'd fit in."

I pinched him.

"Hey!"

"One spiked coffee and now you're saving the South!"

He laughed, open to the night, like that time at the dance when his shirt smelled of Lifebuoy.

I touched his arm. "Just give me time, George. Not much. Just a little."

He nodded, then looked past me at Bill who was leaning against our wing. I jumped.

"Okay, George," Bill said. "Cough up. Let me have all that loose change you keep hiding."

"There you are." George hefted the coins. "Want another coke, Doreen?"

"No, no thanks." I stared at the ground below my dangling feet.

George said, "Buy extra for the kids."

I glanced at Bill then, meeting his intelligent eyes which were giving us the once over. His A-2 jacket looked black in the dark.

"Something going on here?"

"No," I said.

George said nothing.

Bill let it go. "What about that weather front, George?"

We all looked to the south, the cloud against the horizon edged in moonlight. But there were no ominous anvil clouds or hammerheads towering up. A weather front like that had destroyed twin-engined trainers out of Moody Field, and Gunter Field had lost two BT-13s. "We're fine," George said. "Only Trowsdale left."

"Agreed." Bill waved a casual hand. "Catch you later."

When he had gone George pulled something from his tunic pocket. "I want you to have these."

I looked at the silver USAAF wings and RAF wings.

"I'm not using them, and the RAF ones are a spare." He hesitated. "I want you to keep them, find a safe place for them.

My hand closed over them. "I know just the place."

"Where?"

"My Chinese puzzlebox."

George winced. "Symbol of my stand against Southern wickedness."

"Symbol of you smoking your pipe, casually pointing with it at Bill coming at us in the Mitchell; symbol of your caring at the mortuary. That Mrs. Scruggs saw it in you, you know."

"Saw what, that I cared about how airmen were treated?"

"It was more than that. She divined why you cared, something I've yet to learn." I added hastily, "Of course you care, George, but this is something different. I think it goes back to Dunkirk." I watched him retreat, but gently this time. "Anyway, everything meaningful to me will go into my Chinese puzzlebox. My secret treasures."

"Do I get to look in it?

"No."

"What's in it now?"

"George..."

"What's in it?"

"Okay, I'll share one thing. There's a photo of you and me at the lake with Barbara and Butch, not that earlier time when Bill was obnoxious." I cleared my throat. "I'm going home now."

George looked at me in surprise. "You are, why?"

"Because I'm happy and I want to savor things. Anything else tonight will be anticlimax. I want to be alone."

"That's Garbo, not Lombard."

I pinched him. "And savor, I said."

"Okay."

"You'll have to meet my parents now."

"I've always wanted to meet them, Doreen."

"Yes, well..."

"At least it's easier now, with the Chrysler."

"True." Butch, Bill and George had gone together on the purchase of an old Chrysler. It lacked a hub cap and part of its chrome grill, but it ran well. "Let me talk to my mother. It'll be a Saturday, though. And we'll eat around noon."

George grinned. He made no attempt to kiss me: he always knew, he always let me breathe at times like this, when we grew so intensely close; he let me move around my own heart and gut, knowing I'd share it when I was in his arms. Back at the Nash I was startled to see Bill leaning against a fender, smoking.

"Hi, Summers."

"Hi." I stood still, waiting. Something was coming. It was in Bill's eyes.

"You and George. I guess it's pretty serious."

"Yes."

"The Madame Butterfly stuff."

"More than that, Bill," I said softly.

He stubbed out his cigarette. "I've been keeping in the background."

"I've noticed. Thank you."

"And that negro stuff at the lake? I was just trying to get at George. Stupid, I know."

"I saw you lift a colored boy into a plane's cockpit tonight. I know you, Bill Trepick...and I never want to hurt you."

"Forget it. Do you love him?"

"Yes."

He winced. "Does he know?"

"Probably. You know George. But I haven't told him yet."

A baseball caromed off the side of the hangar. I watched a boy chase it into the night.

"I blew it," Bill said. "Came on too strong, too quick with the hands. Didn't realize what I had."

"Only the timing was wrong."

"And you can't call back time."

"Goodnight, Bill."

"Night. Say, Doreen?"

I turned.

"You sure he loves you?"

"Yes."

"How can you tell with an Englishman?" The smile was forced.

"There are ways."

"I don't want to hear about it." He rapped his knuckles on the hood. "Need gas? It's a long ride back."

"I'm okay." I wanted to leave but I sensed Bill needed to talk, some words of transition as he left important things behind him. We hung on this long beat, this fast fading rhythm. "You were something in that Mitchell, Bill. I thought you were going to mow the grass."

He laughed, brightening. "George is good, but I have the edge in the air. Say, you'll be having him over to your folks' farm now. He's told me he's never been down there."

I gave him a mock frown. "Don't you guys dare compare notes on me!"

"Oh, I would, for sure. Unfortunately, George is a gentleman."

"Goodnight, Bill."

"'Night. Have your mom fix that Lane cake jobbie, with the raisins and pecans. He'll love it. Better still, you make it."

I laughed. "I haven't helped Mama cook for years. We don't get along too good."

Bill shrugged, his big shoulders filling out the A-2 jacket. "Maybe now is a good time to fix things."

I drove away with Bill's words settling into my brain where I knew they would trouble me until I had them resolved. They would be set against an array of golden days and nights wrought from the Hawkinsville day crucible. Wonderful times, with Bob Hope and Bing Crosby's latest, 'Road to Morocco,' and George's digs about Egypt; and that first visit to my rented room, its door open under my landlady's unblinking eyes and George looking at my map of the British Isles with Hartlepool circled on it; and visits to caring, fine Southern folks' homes, relishing the warmth and friendship. And now George loved me, and Bill loved me. And there was dinner at the farm, and Daddy. And Mama and me in the kitchen making a cake. Timing is everything.

Chapter 17

THAT SATURDAY MORNING I sat in a favorite window bay watching the curve of driveway down to the gate. I would need to get dressed soon and offer more help to Mama and Melsie Mae in the kitchen. But the Lane cake was ready, waiting to be placed decorously on the sideboard in the dining room. Beyond the window Spring offered a parade of color. Late pear tree blossoms billowed; dense azaleas, forsythia, magnolias and wisteria drenched the gardens and farmhouse. Fence posts were well tended, marching away in precision towards Melsie Mae's wash house. Insects buzzed and hummed beyond the screens.

With an effort I turned my attention back to the page in my typewriter. It read:

The proud state of Georgia gives vitally to the war effort not only in the patriotic response of her young men to the armed services and her women to the factories and timberlands, but in the rich offering of its minerals, mica, asbestos, and manganese. She also provides pyrite, copper, talc and bauxite. And her clays make good fire bricks for marine boilers...

I crossed out 'The proud state of' and changed 'its minerals' to 'her minerals.' Then I sighed heavily and leaned back in my chair wondering how the day would go. That Saturday morning had begun earlier in a uniquely air force manner with the sound of a BT-13 basic trainer.

"Some more airplanes," Mama called from the kitchen, bustling with Melsie Mae over vegetables and chicken.

"Only one BT, Mama. It's George," I said smiling.

"How do you know, dear?" Mama came from the kitchen with hands gripped around a dish cloth. "Doreen, you're remembering our talks?"

"Of course, Mama."

"In my day we didn't kiss until we had that engagement ring. One didn't damage the merchandise." She laughed nervously.

The BT grew louder.

"Doreen, dear, my ears can't stand it."

I ran outside. George had the canopy open, he was waving and smiling, his hat as usual crushed under the radio headset. He made one more circuit then he was coming across the lower grassed acres behind the house, wings rocking. I watched the small object drop, a dark rectangle in the sun, then the BT whipped away and steadied into a climb. I ran out onto the grass, past Mama's victory garden of carrots, turnips and peas, and picked up the tobacco tin. It was St. Bruno Flake, with 'a touch of rum.' Inside was a note:

How goes the savoring?

I watched the BT slowly disappear towards Cochran Field until it became a black dot, then it disappeared into the sun's bright veil. "Until noon, George," I murmured. "And for heaven's sake, don't be late. And the savoring is desperately, deliciously good, so good."

"What is it, Doreen?" Mama asked, as I came back into the cool of the house.

"Nothing, Mama. Just George saying hello."

"It's a tin of tobacco."

I laughed and put my arm around her and squeezed. "Empty. But there was a nice romantic note inside."

She looked into my eyes, her own blue and sometimes gray eyes offering worry tempered with hope. The war was almost too much for her, I thought. An inundation of foreign ways onto the Southern cultural flood plains; harsh, abrasive, and a menacing harbinger of things to come. How maternal I was at that moment, how self-satisfied. And totally wrong. My arm was still around her. Her gray hair, perked on curlers and an earlier permanent, shone in the shaft of sunlight.

"Do you love him, Doreen?"

"Yes, Mama, I do."

"Then today will be very special for me as well as you."

"I want it to be," I said.

"Will you tell your father?"

I smiled. How in control I was, how smug. "I'll see how it goes. I want George and Daddy to get along."

"You know how he can be."

"I know how you both can be." Mama blushed and turned shy. I kissed her brow the way George kissed mine. "I was thinking we could make a Lane cake."

"You mean together?"

"I'll even shell the pecans. You get raves on your Lane cake, Mama. Bill Trepick loves 'em."

"Bill's a fine boy, a farm boy. He understands our ways."

"That's true." Some things you can't fight.

"You know, I had hopes for you and Bill. To take over the farm, I mean. After Daddy and me are gone."

"You're going to be around a long time," I said crisply, heading off ailment talk. "And Bill's folks probably hope he'll farm their place in Wisconsin."

"Oh. I forgot that. It's true, they'll want their boy."

And so will Pan American Airlines. Truth be told, Bill had made it clear in our talks about picturesque red barns and cows that his younger brother would be running the farm. "How's dinner coming along?" I asked.

A frown lined her brow then cleared. "Daddy wants turnip greens the country way, with roots cut off and diced with hamhock. You know, greens and roots served together? I thought George might not like them, but your Daddy said he would, that other cadets had liked them."

"I'm sure he will, Mama."

"It's good to have you home, Doreen."

"It's good to be home."

"You'll be showing him around the farm, of course."

The silence vibrated.

"Yes, I'd like to do that. Personal things mostly, about growing up. The corn crib, the smokehouse, Uncle William's grave which I need to tend this trip."

Mama was about to say something but held back. "What will you be wearing to dinner?"

"I'm not sure. Why don't we decide together, have some girl talk?"

Mama nodded, her eyes smiling.

I heaved a sigh and stared again at the page in my typewriter. I pulled it out and tore it up, then picked up my tobacco tin. I was still savoring when Mama called, "Will you come and sit with me while I get dressed, dear?

Then you'll need to get ready, of course. We don't have that much time."

My parents' bedroom was a pretty, feminine room dominated by delicately patterned curtains and prints on the walls; there was a silver framed photo of Tennessee relatives. The bed was large but self-effacing in pastels. Daddy's heavy, uncompromising dresser was littered with cigar packets, ashtrays, and a few letters in need of careful responses. All the bills, invoices and farm paperwork were to be found bulging carelessly in the rolltop desk beside the oil lamp in the parlor. As a child growing up, I had spent time here with my mother talking about 'life' and a Southern woman's place in it.

"I see you've cut your nails, dear," Mama said, as her fingers explored a drawer of silk slips and satin step-ins.

"Yes, I kept breaking them. A shame, really. I loved Carole Lombard's nails."

"I know, dear. Such a shame, her dying in that horrible plane crash. Clark Gable was destroyed, just destroyed."

"Hardly destroyed, Mama, but devastated for sure." It was childish of me to moderate it down, this palpable moment of a woman's hold over a man, but there was anger in me.

"I think that's why he joined the air force," Mama said.

"I think so too. Tyrone Power and James Cagney have just signed up. I think Power is in the Marines."

"Mercy's sakes! There'll be no one left to make films."

I laughed then, and Mama returned my laugh with a smile. There was a moment of calm and caring that I think we both enjoyed. I had been fortunate in my upbringing, I realized. Going to school I had a lunch box loaded with a successful farm's riches: a pear, an apple, wedges of cheese, carefully cut and dainty sandwiches. Wendy Clinkscales had not been so fortunate. Her conversations in those early adolescent years had been filled with ugly talk about fights and empty bottles, and money problems and fearful blasphemy against the Baptist faith. And her lunchbox, in our 'everything is appearances' culture, was often a twice used greasy paper bag.

I felt around me on the bed. I got the package and showed it to her. "I got this for George...in return for those lovely air force wings he gave me."

"Why, Doreen, how precious." Her hand closed over the neat wrapping. "What is it?"

"Go ahead and open it. I'll rewrap it."

Accomplished fingers moved about a familiar task, not too fast to be unseemly, not to slow to be uncaring. "Why, it's a cigarette lighter."

"I got it for his pipe. Some of the girls are buying identification bracelets, but I thought George would like this better."

"And there's a ship on it. Where's my glasses..."

"It's a fishing boat, Mama. A drifter. I looked it up in the library. They're used on the northeast coast of England. The engraving didn't cost much extra."

"Goodness. I'm afraid I don't know anything about the sea..." her voice trailed off, then rallied. "But it's lovely, dear. I know he will just love it."

"I think so."

"Well, now we'd better be getting ready, we're falling behind."

Chapter 18

I WATCHED THE old Chrysler turn in through the gate, display a missing hubcap, and come up the driveway, its gap-toothed grill winking in the sun. I ran out to meet him. "He's here, Mama!" I yelled. At the car I kissed George through the window. "Mama's watching. Daddy's pretending he's not interested."

"I understand."

I looked at him in his summer khakis, his RAF wings lustrous white and new. As he reached for his cap I said, "Be advised Mama doesn't like the noise from low flying planes."

"Okay." The brown eyes looked me up and down. "You look lovely. Is that a new skirt?"

I linked arms with him. "No. Part of the wardrobe I keep at home. I don't wear it much."

"You should."

My parents stepped out then, coming to welcome us, haloed in sunlight against the porch shadows. I'll always remember them freeze-framed there: Daddy in a blue shirt and tie he hated to wear, his weathered face with its lean look from extracted back teeth, the calm gray eyes. And Mama in her favorite dress, the flowered design with white collar and pocket trim. The sun caught her lovely eyes, and I realized I maneuvered as she did, a lesson learned unconsciously through osmosis.

"It's so good to have you here, George," Mama said. "Doreen has told us so much about you. I want to hear about these drifter fishing boats."

I kept smiling.

"Come in, son." Daddy said. "Let Christine have your hat there."

"Doreen has told me about flying too low, Mrs. Summers," George said. "I do apologize. Those engines..."

"Nonsense. You fly over any time. My, I do like your uniform, George. The cadets are wearing them too."

"Summer dress, Mrs. Summers."

"So very nice, and so different to our own boys."

"Well, actually, our cadets' hats are different, the RAF forage cap with the white flash on it."

"Yes, of course," Mama said vaguely. "Do come in now."

We walked into the cool of the house with its angular shadows and high ceilings.

"Now, George, why don't you and Francis go sit in the parlor while Doreen and I take care of a few things."

"Thank you."

"You'll find big ashtrays there. I know you enjoy a pipe. Francis did at one time, but now he likes cigars. King Edward cigars."

I watched them go into the parlor, overhearing Daddy's calm 'company's here' voice. "Take that chair, George, it's more comfortable."

"Thank you, sir."

And then I was cut off, unable to monitor what was being said. But the parlor looked good, with its polished furniture and everything dominated by the piano. I wondered if it was still in tune since I had left.

"Do a last check of the dining table, dear," Mama said, "and tell Melsie Mae to put out the bowls, the Lane, and rice pudd'n."

"Of course." While Mama bustled I looked over the dinner table. It was the perfect Southern offering, embellished by victory gardens and constrained by ration books. Family silverware gleamed. Its origins went back to Tennessee and a Knoxville silversmith before the Civil War, but we were not its first owners. I smiled at the extra spoon for George for dessert, English style. Mama had remembered; I hadn't.

Fried chicken, fresh made biscuits, turnip greens and diced roots served together; macaroni and cheese, sweet potato soufflé with marshmallows on top; Lane cake and rice pudd'n on the sideboard. Sweet iced tea with mint from Mama's garden, or lemon. I wasn't sure about the mint. A bit early in the year. Melsie Mae came into the parlor with large serving bowls and spoons. She ignored me, having ripped into me earlier about not coming home to my folks. Dear Melsie Mae, another carefully remembered image. Uncle William's wife was named Melissa Mae, but we all called her Melsie. Now, after the talk with Billy at the office, I wondered if we had asked her permission to shorten her name. Probably not. Melsie Mae was a sturdy negress, her countenance forever neutral while she took in everything around her. If you were lucky, if you piqued her intelligence or wicked sense of humor, you were rewarded with a smile that transformed her. She brought in the big bowls, her forearms fat and powerful from years of washing clothes regardless of the weather. I remember the heavy sodden clothes she lifted on a stick from the wash pot in chill winter winds, steam billowing, cradled in those powerful arms.

"Miz Doreen, would you check the tea for me? I don't want it to get too strong."

"Okay."

"It's nice to have Mistuh George here."

"Yes, it is."

"The folks talk about him. They've been wondering when he was coming."

"What did they say?"

"Oh, you know. Teaching flying to those other boys. Jazz stuff."

"Jazz stuff?"

"Mister Bill says you like jazz now."

"When was Mister Bill here?"

"Your mama had him down for some cooking."

"Oh."

"Your mama likes Mister Bill."

"So do I."

"Yessum."

"I'll check the tea for you."

"Yessum."

"Melsie Mae?"

"Huh?"

"Don't handle me today. I don't want to be handled with the yessum stuff."

"No, Miz Doreen."

I gave up.

Dinner began with George and Daddy walking into the dining room on a waft of cigar and pipe smoke. They were easy with each other, they had that comfort that I tried for in interviews. I wondered what had transpired between them and made a mental note to quiz George.

"Sit there, George," Daddy said. "Christine's put out a dessert spoon for you, English style."

"Thank you, Mrs. Summers."

I watched Mama beam and I suddenly felt out of things. Like when I was at J.J. Lemon's and George was laughing at inside jokes. Mama said, "Please say the blessing, Francis..."

"So, George, did Doreen tell you she's a good pecan shaker?" Bowls were passed around. "Grab a biscuit now. They're Melsie Mae's own. And we eat chicken with our fingers, remember. Don't go doing that knife and fork, horse'n'buggy thing."

"Francis, please! You leave George be. He may eat as he wishes."

Daddy grinned at her.

"I didn't know Doreen was a pecan shaker," George said, making it sound like a profession.

"She's born to the farm, but she's a good reporter too, I'll give her that. I've read some of her articles. She's heading north, though."

"Daddy," I said.

"Well, it's true. It's not like you keep it a secret, girl." His gray eyes took in George. "She's changing her ways, our ways. Like she says, 'negro,' instead of 'nigra.' Nigra's a perfectly good word." Daddy waved a chicken leg. "It's just high fallutin' talk from up north."

"Francis," Mama began, then faded.

"You're right, Christine. Too serious, I guess. But George is easy company, so serious stuff comes out."

George smiled. He bit into his piece of chicken, apparently quite relaxed.

"We have lots of RAF boys here, George. Christine will tell you. Nice nights playing cards or someone on the piano. That Archie Watkins is some piano player."

"He certainly is," I said.

"Good pilot, too," George said.

"And that guy, Haggis. You seen him roll that coin

across his knuckles? Real slick." I watched as Daddy helped himself to turnip greens and a hefty spoonful of macaroni and cheese. "Tell me, George, what do you want to do after the war?"

"You're confident too, Mr. Summers? We'll win the war?"

"We'll win, what with American mass production, material, good fighting men. Your guys too, of course."

George smiled and put down his chicken. "Anyway, after the war I want to fly, if I can get with an airline. Delta would be good."

"Come back here, you mean?"

"Yes, sir. I want to come back to America."

"How come? I mean, I'm glad you like our country, son, but why in particular?"

"Well, it's like I tell Doreen. I like the freedom here, the openness, the willingness to try things, not be hide bound."

I waited for Daddy to pounce on 'freedom' and the negroes, but he was biding his time.

"You don't get that back home?" Daddy asked.

"No sir, not really. In my country people are kept in their place by how they speak, which schools they can go to. But I think after the war things will start to change. This war has brought a certain sophistication, a thirst for knowledge, boundaries are coming down. Look at British cadets over here…how many would be in America if not for the war? Think of the ideas they'll take back home."

"Yeah, I can see that. Doreen?"

I took the macaroni and cheese from him. It was hot in my hands.

"Doreen wants to be a big newspaperwoman."

"Not big, necessarily, Daddy," I tempered. "Just do good news reporting."

"So when are you going?"

I was ready. I had thought long and hard and I was ready. "If and when George is called back to England for flying duties, then I'll go." I was aware of George's steady gaze. In fact, everybody was looking at me. Melsie Mae poked at the bowls.

"Got any money?" Daddy asked.

"I...I saved some," I said.

"Where will you live?"

"Greenwich Village." Straight ahead, Doreen. Ruin dinner.

Mama took a breath behind her napkin.

"I've heard about that place," Daddy said. "Strange folks, strange ideas. And all mixed in together, nigras and whites."

I pushed at my macaroni and cheese.

George said, "Could I have some more turnip greens, please?"

"You like 'em?" Daddy asked.

"Yes, sir. Very much."

You are lying your pants off, George Westcott, but thanks for stepping in.

"See, Christine, I told you. Just like that Cockney boy, what's his name?"

"John Piggott," I said.

"Yeah. We got real upset when John died. He was a nice fellow. I had trouble understanding him with the Cockney accent and all, but a nice fellow. He told me once he was scared of washing out."

"That's a common concern," George said.

"Concern, yes, but it shouldn't be a fear. You've got to overcome fear." Daddy looked at George. "Look at you...soon you're going to get into the war..."

"George was at Dunkirk," I said, keeping my anger

down. "He's been in the war." I felt George's eyes on me and looked at him. His eyes were darkened to near black. Not anger, more a weariness.

"Why, that's right," Daddy said. "Your mama told me. Dunkirk! Now there was a miracle. Got everybody out right from under Hitler's nose."

"Not everybody," George said lightly. He looked at Mama, smiling. "This is a lovely dinner, Mrs. Summers."

"Why, thank you, George. It's so nice to see you enjoying it."

"So you've got this class thing in England?" Daddy said.

"Yes, sir. I'm an RAF officer, but I got in the back door. The English believe only gentlemen can be officers.

"You sound bitter," Daddy said bluntly.

"I was, at one time. But I've been lucky. Luckier than some." He put down his knife and fork. "Things can happen, events change you, you mature."

"How? What events?"

"If you don't mind, sir, could we..."

"Oh, sure. Sure. I understand." Daddy leaned back expansively. "You know, my family is from England...a few generations back, of course. Doreen's heritage is Tennessee mountain folks and English settlers in Georgia." He smiled at me. "Kind of explains her temperament a little."

"I'll take that as a compliment, Daddy," I said.

Daddy spooned out more macaroni and cheese. "Melsie Mae, more macaroni next time."

"Yessuh, Mistuh Summers."

"You for integration, George?"

"With respect, sir, yes I am."

I waited for Daddy to explode, but it didn't happen. Whatever chemistry existed between my father and

George bridged any animosity and put in place a genuine reaching out. And George had been tutored by Bill, thank God. A cultural separation of thousands of miles across the Atlantic paradoxically brought them together. George was a foreigner, at least for now; not involved, an outsider. Of course, in Georgia, without three or more generations in the land he would still be a foreigner.

"I don't see it, son," Daddy was saying, "I just don't see it. As far as problems with segregation go, well, the fleas come with the dog."

"It'll be generations, sir, not overnight."

"Not at all, more like. Bill Trepick was over for dinner a while back. He said you and Doreen went to some Atlanta jazz club where coloreds go. Bill wasn't talking out of turn, you understand. It's just Doreen doesn't get home much so we try to get what's going on by talking with friends."

Daddy's voice was tart, almost gossipy, and I found myself hiding a smile. A far cry from being sick to my stomach, which is what I had feared.

"You really like that nigra music?"

"Yes, Mr. Summers. I view it as American music. You've got arrangers like Billy Strahorne, and singers like Ella Fitzgerald and Billie Holiday...vocalists, I should say, because they are musicians, using their voices as their instrument. And musicians like Coleman Hawkins, Lester Young, Teddy Wilson, Louis Armstrong. The history of jazz is American history. Billy Strahorne..."

"The arranger?"

George smiled. "Yes, sir. Strahorne worked with Duke Ellington on some variations on Chopin's etudes, and Jelly Roll Morton was influenced by French classical music in New Orleans. And so on."

I watched George hesitate, carefully choosing his

words. "Truth be told, Mr. Summers, without the negro's contribution to music my world would be smaller, I would be diminished."

Melsie Mae took Daddy's plate and I watched her intently. For an instant I saw something in her eyes, like with the waiter who had brought me the unopened coke bottle, then it was gone.

"Diminished," Daddy said, like someone had just explained to him why he played the wrong card at poker.

George smiled.

"Well, I don't agree, but let it ride. What about white musicians? Benny Goodman and Artie Shaw? Doreen has loads of records upstairs."

"They are fine accomplished musicians, I agree. But swing peaked in 1938-39 at Carnegie Hall. Now swing is just popular music and there's nothing wrong with that, of course. But real jazz innovation, the exploring and experimenting, well that lies with small groups and Bebop and men like Dizzy Gillespie."

"Dizzy?" Mama said.

"Like Dizzy in baseball," Daddy said, eyes still on George.

"Oh." She returned her gaze to George and so did I.

George's face was animated, engaged like a boy, the way cadets look when they've had a good flight. Oddly, George was never excited about flying; he wanted me to enjoy it, but there was always with him a clinical detachment. Melsie Mae put a generous portion of Lane cake in front of Daddy while Mama bustled.

"Miz Doreen helped make the Lane cake, Mistuh Summers."

"Looks good," Daddy said. But his thoughts were far away.

I think, looking back, that the silence that ensued was

good for all of us. When Daddy asked about the English class system, I listened to George talk about his father, his observation that an aristocrat running for Prime Minister could not understand a working man's needs. The aperitif, the Classics in their original Greek and Latin.

"How can that man know what my needs are?" George finished.

Daddy smiled, shoving aside his empty cake plate. "Sorry, son, that dog don't hunt!"

Surprise held George's eyes. "Pardon?"

"Well, look at President Roosevelt. There is a true patrician. Those so-called good northern schools like Groton and Princeton. We know that stuff, we're not stupid down here...and loads of money. He's pretty much on record as a man who knows what the little guy needs. Think your dad would quibble with that?"

"Well, no."

"Want some more rice pudd'n?"

"No thank you, sir. The cake was grand and I've had sufficient. A fine dinner, Mrs. Summers."

"Why, I'm just so glad you liked it, George. But, like Melsie Mae says, Doreen made the Lane cake. She's such a good cook," Mama said, putting me on the auction block with my cooking skills. "Now I suggest we go into the parlor so these gentlemen can enjoy a good cigar and pipe. I'm sorry about the mint for the tea, George; it's a bit early in the season."

"Lemon was very nice, Mrs. Summers. Actually, the mint brought back some memories. We would use it with New Zealand lamb when we had the extra money for lamb. Before the war, of course. Dad would cut up the mint really fine and add vinegar for a sauce."

"Why, I've heard of that. I think it's in Mrs. Dull's cook book."

"Mrs. Dull?"

"Oh, I mustn't take your time on that, George..."

"Say, George," Daddy said, butting in, "do any fishing?"

"Some off the Hartlepool pier, sir. Pretty slim pickings, some flatties..."

"Flatties?"

"Flatfish, bottom fish."

They were walking away, leaving me, just like when Bill and George walked way that morning at Cochran Field.

"You'll just have to come fishing with me. See, I hitch up the boat, drive down to St. Mark's on the Florida Panhandle. I'm a goof I suppose, but I'm up at two in the morning, driving in the rain to the coast, get the boat in the water, go to St. Marks or the Ocilla River, get near those rocks at the river mouth. Ever seen redfish or speckled trout? I tell you..."

I stared at Melsie Mae.

"I wish my William was here," she said.

Chapter 19

"...TAKE THAT SAME chair, George. Anyway, you get down off those rocks and you can hook 'em at high tide, low tide, or when she's turning. Makes no nevermind, and you know what? I swear that moon affects everything. Not just the fish, but the wildlife around you. You look along the shoreline and see dozens of deer, eyes glowing. There is nothing like it, George."

"It sounds great."

"We gotta do it, gotta do it. Christine, I forgot brandy. George, loosen your tie. I hate these things..."

"Coming, Francis. George, I do hope you like this brandy."

"I'm sure I shall, Mrs. Summers."

I sat down in the parlor on the end of the couch, the end with the broken spring.

"George," Daddy said, "until you open your mouth and talk, people could take you for one of us rednecks."

I smiled at that unintentional irony and watched George. He was so relaxed, just so relaxed. And I wasn't.

"I spent some time in Egypt. A pretty hot sun."

"Just your arms and face?"

"Yes."

"How about your neck?"

"An embarrassing circle, sir, at the collar line."

"See, a farmer has a 'vee' neck undershirt, he goes red in a 'vee', then it's all white."

George laughed.

I sat there trying to pinpoint my resentment, because it was resentment. George was supposed to be bearing up, putting up with, scalded by the racial prejudice of my insular parents, and it wasn't happening. And Daddy had pretty much dismissed my newspaper dreams, dwelling instead on George. And Mama now moved like a Southern belle, reveling in it all. This wasn't my script. Damn it, it just wasn't my script for this long postponed day. "Care for another brandy, Daddy? George?"

"None for me, thanks," George said.

"Top 'er up," Daddy said.

While I was topping, Mama came into the parlor with her cook book.

"George, dear, don't let me intrude, but..."

"Is that your cookery book?"

"Yes. You say 'cookery,' don't you? Some of the cadets say cookery." A finger pointed at a well-thumbed page. "Here, you see, mint. And if you enjoyed the Lane cake, I'm sure you would enjoy our ambrosia and heavenly hash. Lots of oranges, cherries, coconut, pecans, whipped cream, all kinds of delicious wonders."

"It all sounds grand, Mrs. Summers. You know what we have in Hartlepool that I think you'd like?"

"What's that, dear?"

"Spotted Dick."

Only George could have gotten away with that. I watched Mama reel, her face recapitulating every Southern belle's emotion since Pickett's Charge.

"It's a popular dessert," George went on. "Vanilla sponge cake, currants or raisins or sultanas. I like sultanas...and you use a deep baking tray and serve it with hot custard."

"A sponge cake?" Mama said.

"Yes. You need self-raising flour, shredded suet, a teaspoon of baking soda, a large egg and some milk, not too much. You give it a good beating and it mustn't be too runny. Then you place it in a bread tin and steam under grease proof paper." George stopped, suddenly embarrassed. "Sorry, I'm going on and on."

"No, dear. In fact, I'd like the recipe."

"Well, it's the only one I know, to be honest, Mrs. Summers. I used to make it for Mum when she was poorly. Dad and I made it together, actually."

"I want the recipe," Mama said firmly.

"Okay."

Mama returned triumphantly to the kitchen. I watched George fiddle with his pipe over the large glass ashtray. "Here, George, let me." I took his pipe, its bowl warm, and tapped out its contents. "Give me your pouch." I began preparing George's pipe, looking all the while into his bemused dark eyes. "And don't forget," I said. "With me you also get Lane cake."

"I'll remember," he murmured, so only I could hear. "And with me you get Spotted Dick."

"Doreen used to fix my pipe all the time," Daddy said, "back when I took it. Now I like a cigar. These are King Edward."

"I'm using St. Bruno Flake. Rum flavored."

"Nice aroma to it." Daddy leaned forward, his voice low, not unlike Mama's *soto voce* parlor asides. "George, ask Christine to play the piano."

"Oh, Daddy!" I said, finally unleashing it. "There's just no need for..."

"You mind your manners, girl. I mean it." His face

was flushed dark with blood. "And while we're on the subject, you get off of that high horse of yours. You come home and act so damn superior. I tell you, girl, you ain't! And quit acting so superior around your mother. You tear her down with that snide way you picked up some place, you pull at her life, her beliefs. Well, listen here: don't tear down you mother's life unless you've got something better to replace it with...and from where I'm sitting, you ain't got it. When you're half the woman your Mama is, you'll be okay in my book."

I sat stunned, throat constricted, cheeks hot. In all my years my father had never loosed such a tongue lashing on me. Tears welled up hot. And all in front of George. I was too frightened to look at him. I didn't want a freeze-frame remembrance of this. When my throat loosened around its burning ache I said, "I'm sorry, Daddy. I truly am."

Daddy waved his hand in that cutting dismissal motion. I thought it was for me, concern for me. But he wanted me to get myself together because Mama was back. She obviously felt our tension, the room was charged with it. And she would know intuitively it concerned her.

"Doreen, how nice," she said quietly. I haven't seen you fix a pipe since Daddy's."

"I know, Mama. I thought it would be nice for George."

"It is, dear, it is." She hesitated. "That little object we looked at this morning..."

"No, Mama..."

"I think now would be a good time, dear."

I managed a smile. "Okay. Back in a minute." I ran to the bathroom and splashed cold water on my face, then dabbed it dry with a towel. I was blotched, a mess. Puffy eyed. I used a facecloth as a compress over my eyes. I stood in the cooling dark of the compress and thought about what Daddy had said. Not half the woman. And then Mama had gotten me out of there, pride intact, saving face by running an errand, getting to the bathroom. I suddenly felt very tired and ugly. I got myself together and retrieved the rewrapped package for George. When I returned to the parlor I went straight to George and offered him my gift. "I want you to have this."

"What is it?"

"Open it and see."

We all waited. I sat down on the couch, my rear end on the broken spring. I mustered the thought that perhaps a pain in the ass was symbolic.

George looked at the Ronson lighter, turning it over in his strong brown hands. It shone silver chrome in the afternoon sunlight.

"I had the drifter engraved and your initials, of course," I said. "The library had a reference book. There was a drifter photographed at Whitby."

"Whitby is not far from Hartlepool." George got up and walked over to me and kissed my cheek, gently, taking his time, his lips soft. "Is this for those wings in your Chinese puzzle box?"

"Yes."

"You couldn't have gotten me anything better."

I sat there now, having the attention but uncomfortable, my face hot.

"Like to see it, Mrs. Summers?"

"Oh, yes, George. Why it's lovely. The drifter has such a small sail."

"That's for drifting, engine shut down. It catches the breeze."

"I see."

George sat down and looked at me. I'll remember that look always, the darkened down eyes bathing over mine. "Thank you," he said. But it was more than a thank you. It was a rescue, it was 'I love you,' it was 'everything's okay.' "Mama," I said quietly, "How about playing the piano for us? 'Für Elise,' perhaps."

"Aw hell, Doreen," Daddy said. "Your Mama is way beyond that."

"What?"

"She's been studying. It's been kind of quiet with you gone."

"Let me see," Christine said. "I have some things here." She rummaged in the piano bench, setting aside some of my popular pieces, including 'Body and Soul,' the piece I swore I would never play again after hearing Teddy Wilson's and Billie Holiday's work on it.

"How come your stuff ain't on top?" Daddy said impatiently.

"Oh, I was looking through to see if there were some pieces Doreen might like to play again. Here, here we are."

I watched my mother seat herself at the piano, sweeping her lovely hands against her dress, smoothing it, settling herself at the keyboard, reaching forward to adjust the sheet music. "This is a piece I rather enjoy. Mr. Billings at the church has been giving me lessons. He's most kind and so accomplished."

Suddenly the parlor was alive with Mozart, brilliant prancing phrases at Mama's fingertips. Her hands were vigorous, controlled, summoning Mozart's genius and enlivening the very air we breathed. She took my breath away. When she finished the Rondo, Daddy beamed.

"Better than that nigra music, George."

"Wonderful, Mrs. Summers," George said. "Very fine

indeed."

Later, when she played a Scarlatti sonata, I had to look at the sheet music selection to know how to spell his name. I told Mama that. She just smiled.

Chapter 20

WE WERE WALKING on the back acreage, admiring the flowers and Mama's victory garden. The sun was pleasantly warm as it began a long arc to the horizon. "I guess I got my comeuppance," I said.

"I witnessed history." George grinned.

I pinched him. "You did well with Daddy, you didn't back down."

"No, and neither did he. I owe a lot to Billy Odum, he taught me a lot."

"When we left Billy that Sunday I saw him get the Jack Daniels."

"I did too. I was hoping you'd missed it. I learned much about pain and obligation in that one act."

"Have you ever gotten drunk, George, to numb the pain of something?"

"Only once."

"And one day you'll tell me?"

"Yes."

"I was thinking this morning, George. Technically, we've known each other a year this month."

"Technically?"

"Well, you disappeared on me. George the loner. Americus, the gray suits and black ties."

"And bloody silly elastic belts to keep our pants up. Boy Scout belts, I think they were. I remember you getting out of the Nash and pulling at your dress."

"I was sweating and...hey! You noticed me? You saw that? You were watching me?"

"I'm not a eunuch, Doreen."

I said nothing, just looked at the blaze of flowers, awash in my celebration of womanhood.

"What's Melsie Mae doing?"

"What?" I followed his gaze down to the wash house. "Oh. Doing a quick check before Monday. Monday's wash day."

"Let's go and see her."

"George..."

"Come on."

I had to catch up. There he was, striding down towards the wash house, his tie loose and no cap. "Melsie Mae!" he called, as we approached.

"Yessuh, Mistuh George."

"Would you mind if I talked to you a bit?"

"No, suh." She clutched the lightered sticks in a big hand, her eyes wary.

"Thank you, I really appreciate your time."

"Yessuh."

"Miss Doreen just told me you're getting ready for the wash, Monday."

"Yessuh. Just checking. I'm ready. Needed some lightered sticks is all."

"For the wash tub?"

"The wash pot, yessuh."

"You know, Melsie Mae, you're bringing back a lot of memories for me. Times at home in the north of England. Monday was our wash day."

"Sho' nuff?"

"Yes, indeed." George stepped back. "See, this is how we do our clothes in Hartlepool."

"Ha'lpul."

"Yes. The women wash the clothes in a big pot over an open fire, or in what's called a set pot. We don't have lightered sticks. What are they?"

"The heart part of a pine tree," I said, "or stump knots. They keep the fire going."

"Ah. Well, what we have is sea coal. It washes up on the beach, all smooth and round from the sea's movement. People go along the sands collecting it in sacks. Sometimes they have an old bike and balance the heavy coal sack on the crossbar."

"Ah ain't never seen the sea, Mistuh George."

"Well, I hope one day you do, Melsie Mae. It's beautiful and it's always changing in color, grays and blues, just like Miss Doreen's eyes." He smiled at me.

"And like her mother's eyes," Melsie Mae said.

"Yes, indeed. And Mrs. Summer's eyes." George looked at me long and deep. "See," he went on, turning his attention back to Melsie Mae, "we have a large strong table, like your trestles here, and we use it for scrubbing clothes. Then we transfer the clothes to a tub and pound it with a poss stick. A poss stick is huge and heavy and spotlessly clean. You just hold onto the handles and pound it up and down on the clothes in the water."

"How do you dry it?"

"Well, sometimes in the early days, we'd lay things out on sandstone rocks with stones at each corner to prevent them from blowing away."

"Uh, huh. I've a line."

George ran his fingers along the wire between the two posts and looked at the bag of wooden clothes pegs. "We don't use wire, we use a clothesline made of rope. So you light a fire under your wash pot with the lightered sticks?"

"Yessuh. Sometimes it's hard to keep the smoke out of your eyes."

"I can believe that!"

"So I put my clothes in my wash pot, then I use my washboard. I use Octago-an soap."

"You like Octagon best?"

"Yessuh. Best there is."

"We use loose soda crystals and sometimes Fairy soap. After the wash was done, my Mum would say, 'Off with those clothes, George, and hop in. Clean yourself up!'"

Melsie Mae snorted, her highest praise when she was amused. It meant all effort at decorum was lost, and the snort would turn to a laugh and her face would be transformed. She was lovely. "Anyway, Mistuh George, then I rinse them in my rinse tub." A powerful arm gestured along the trestles. "Lots of steam, especially in cold days when that wind just whips everywhere."

"Then you use your clothes line?"

"Yessuh."

George shook his head as he looked around. "There's one for the book. Virtually the same way we do it in the north of England. Must've come over with English emigrants."

I just looked at him, smiling. "So you went skinny dipping in the laundry water."

Melsie Mae snorted.

"I was having my bath, and enough said on that subject. I'm sorry I brought it up." He turned to Melsie Mae, smiling. "Thank you, thanks so much for showing me things."

"Yessuh, Mistuh George."

"That woman will kill for you," I said, as we resumed our walk.

"It's amazing. I felt right at home there."

"No poss stick."

"I could make her one. She'd like it."

"You did the wash George, didn't you, because your father was crippled and your mother had arthritis in her hands."

"Terrific exercise. I was in good nick for the army. And the barbells...I used the barbells."

I squeezed his hand.

"That wash house took me back to when I was a bairn."

"A bairn?"

"Scottish word. It means small child. Lots of Scottish words came over the border into northern England. Other words too, and names. Like those Norsemen who sailed across the North Sea to raid English coastal towns. One man named Svenson took a shine to England and he hid in the woods when the Viking long ships sailed back. Later he came out and married a fisher lass from a village near Whitby. When they married he Anglicized his name to Stevenson."

"Interesting," I said. "You know, when I was looking up the fishing boats for your cigarette lighter, I also looked up our names."

"Oh?"

"Guess what George means?"

"Haven't a clue."

"Tiller of the soil, a land worker. When you come back you should be a farmer, George. Thrill my parents."

George laughed. "No offense to your parents, but no thanks. How about Doreen, what's that?"

I took a breath. "It's Irish for sullen, but the word

usage means serious about life. Also, devoted heart."

"Have I won your heart?" George asked. "You still haven't told me."

I squeezed his arm. "Some say Doreen is from Oscar Wilde's Dorian, but it's more likely to have come from a woman writer in the last century. She wrote popular fiction. Anyway, Mama heard it and liked it."

"Me too."

I bit my lip, remembering.

"What is it?" he asked.

"Oh, it's nothing..."

"What?" He stopped our walking and gently lifted my chin until I was looking into his eyes.

"A dance we had," I said. All the fellows, Freddie, Archie, Haggis..."

"Yes?"

"Well, you know Freddie and his Keats. He called me 'the beautiful lady without pity.'"

"That's a quote, of course."

"Yes, I don't know from where."

"Sounds like he'd had one too many. What were you doing at the time?"

I swallowed around the ache in my throat. "I think we were talking about Mama."

"Ah."

"What ah?"

"Something to work through, perhaps. And after today I'd say you and your mother are starting to enjoy each other."

"Bill said it was something to work through."

"He did?"

"Well, actually, he said make a cake, but it's the same thing."

George chuckled, moving us forward on our walk

among the gentle slopes of grass and singing birds. "Bill has a practical bent. Anyway, after today, things are different for you." He looked at me. "I'm very happy for you, Doreen."

"I am too."

"And forget Freddie Latham. Whatever he said is ancient history."

"I can give, I can do things."

"Yes, you can. You're a fine talent. Just remember, it doesn't have to be either this or that. To go to the North doesn't mean jettisoning the South, your heritage. Look at Billy: 'Don't give up on my South', he said."

"Yes."

"And speaking of New York, I understand what you said at dinner. That if I'm called to active duty in England, you'll be heading there. I understand. But we'll need to figure out some codes, if and when I go."

"George," I clutched at his arm, "you haven't heard something..."

"No, not at all. I'll tell you. But with a simple code or two we can communicate through the censors in our letters."

"Is that legal?"

"I'll never tell. What's that building over there?"

"That is where Uncle William told stories."

"Show me."

The corn crib offered its warm shadows and dusty shafts of sunlight. The smell of corn was musky and strong. For a moment I was a girl again, listening to Sadie clucking in the cool corner and listening to Uncle William.

"You okay?"

I nodded. I looked for the old box Uncle William had sat on to shuck corn, but I knew it wasn't there. I had destroyed it because it was so empty, so incomplete, without him. "And out here, just over here, is where I buried Sadie, our settin' hen. We've come at a nice time. See how the sun bathes the glade and surrounding bushes?"

"It's nice, Doreen, very nice." He kissed my brow, his arm around my shoulders. "Want to go back to the house?"

"In a while. I've got to visit Uncle William, say a few words, tidy things up a bit."

"Okay."

The last lesson of the day, this day of carefully held remembrances, was for me. And I could barely stand it. The gravesite was neatly bordered in stone with an immaculate headstone that read:

CORNELIUS WILLIAM HORTON
Loyal and Faithful Worker
1873-1928

I stood quite still, taking it all in.

"Looks like someone has been keeping things tidy," George said gently. "The flowers are lovely."

"Pansies," I said, smiling. "He loved pansies. He liked all things small and delicate and lovely." I hesitated. "It's more than just keeping things tidy, George. In a while I've got to talk with Melsie Mae."

George nodded.

"I just about worshipped this man when I was a little girl. He was such a big man, he could blot out the sun as I looked up at him. Daddy always spoke respectfully of William as his finest colored worker. When he died, he received a good piece of land for his resting place."

"Yes, indeed." George looked around at the sloping land.

From here you could see the tree blossoms, the azaleas and crepe myrtle.

I hesitated.

"What?"

"With graves for colored people we let the grass grow over, the weeds grow over. After that the casket rots out, the small wooden cross collapses, and then there is nothing but a delve in the ground."

"Doreen..."

"I swore that would never happen to this man. I worried about leaving and who would take care of it."

George kissed my cheek. "I'll see you in a bit, give you some time."

I looked at this place, this quiet meld of man's labor and Nature's girding of petal and leaf. There were things I needed to say to Uncle William: some of them were from earlier visits, a ritual of remembrance with my hands patting at the soft earth, and my words carried low amid the cries of birds and insects. Deep, deep words from a young girl's heart. But now there were questions chiseled into granite and I needed answers. I started back to the wash house. Melsie Mae was waiting for me. I didn't hesitate, I went straight into her solid warmth and felt her arms take me in. "Who did it, Melsie Mae, I'm so glad for you and Uncle William, but who did it?"

"Why, your daddy did it, child. He did it for me. I ain't strong like I used to be, and I told him, with you gone..."

"And you and Daddy keep it nice, you do it?"

"We try. And your mother does her victory garden and then she helps. But Mistuh Summers, he always gets a field hand to look out for William."

"I'm sorry to let you down, Melsie Mae, so very sorry."

"You didn't, child. You've got things going on, big things."

"But with me gone..."

"He was my William, but I knew how much it meant to you to tend him. Then you left, Miss Doreen. I'd watch for you, but time went by, it surely did, and I talk to Mistuh Summers."

I kissed her cheek and wiped my eyes against her strong bosom. "Thank you."

"Uh hummm." She was stroking my hair.

"His name was Cornelius?"

"Yes, child: Cornelius William Horton."

"Horton?"

"It's on his papers, his birth papers."

I had to ask. "Did he call you Melsie Mae or Melissa Mae?"

"Just Melissa, but oh, how he said it. There were nights, girl, there were nights...I'd give anything to hear him say my name just one more time."

I held her. Beyond the wash house I could see George sitting on the grass. His pipe and pouch were beside him, and he was looking at the sky.

Chapter 21

LAUGHTER AND RAISED voices came from the patio work area: George, Daddy, Mama and Melsie Mae. I stood in the small half-bathroom Daddy had built so he wouldn't have to tramp through the house after working outside. There were chewed cigar butts, old copies of Life and fishing magazines, and photos of fish on the walls, including Daddy's big catch, a wahoo he caught while trolling off Destin. The mounted wahoo gathered dust in a closet, along with a stack of old fishing rods and a bait bucket. I was struggling into an old shirt and a pair of Daddy's cast-off pants. The hip boots were dried out and cracked, but I managed to haul one over my foot and up my leg. I opened the bathroom door to have more room and Mama's words traveled clearly.

"A monkey hanger, you say? Landsakes..."

"Hey!" I yelled, hopping on one foot and hauling at the other hip boot. "Don't let him tell that monkey hanger story till I get there!" I clumped down the hallway.

"Hurry, Doreen," Daddy called. "Come see this guy."

I had by now figured out George and Mama. He always startled her with words, totally ignoring Southern traditions of the soft, demure female. He came at her hearty, impishly, piquing her emotions, and she reveled in it. When I got to the patio there he was, wearing a pair of Daddy's pants, a baggy shirt, and a spare pair of hip boots. Melsie Mae was fitting him out with a newly cut croker sack. She was kneeling, tucking the sack, running her big hand along the halter. I was at some Mad Hatter's version of 'Gone With The Wind,' Scarlett and a seamstress getting ready for the ball. "Oh, my." I grinned. "Where's my intrepid airman?"

"Or even a train driver," George said. "What do you think?"

"Great, George, you're all set. Melsie Mae, can I help you with the other sack?"

"I'm okay, Miss Doreen."

A croker sack, simply put, is a sack, usually a two hundred pound fertilizer sack, that is cut in half. The top half is fashioned into a halter arrangement and it holds the bottom sack-half at a person's waist. That's where the frogs are put. And to get the frogs you have your giggin' stick, or croker stick. For the life of me I don't know how we ended up readying ourselves to go frog giggin', but there we were.

"So, how come you're a monkey hanger, George?" Daddy asked.

"Well, it's an old story from the Napoleonic Wars. Hartlepool had a shipwreck during one of the many bad storms, and the locals were down on the sands looking for survivors. Unfortunately, the crew drowned. The only survivor was a monkey which was hanging onto a wooden plank."

All eyes watched him, there in the Deep South, as he spun this bizarre tale of storms and wrecks and crashing seas. Now he stood there will his giggin' stick and croker sack like King Neptune holding court, and I realized I was spinning literary allusions off him as if he were some touchstone. But I knew why I was doing it. I was totally, indescribably in love with him, and my too cerebral ways of dealing with things were coming undone. George, my darling George, you stand wingless and you shine.

"Anyway, the monkey comes ashore on his plank and stands there, chattering." George's eyes took us all in, they were alive with humor. "Well, these were simple fisher folk, of course, who had only heard by word of mouth that England was at war with France. They called it Frenchland."

The silence hung while George fiddled with his sack. "How many frogs can I get in this? Will they jump out?"

"George!" I said.

"Come on, George," Daddy said.

"Oh, so they hung it," George finished, matter of factly. "They thought it could be a French spy since they couldn't understand its chattering. Better safe than sorry."

"Ah'll be," Mama murmured.

"Is it true or just story?" I asked.

"Well, back in those days people were uneducated and they were very superstitious. It's possible they did hang it. I know down south...*our south*...in Oxford, some villagers tried to sweep the moon's reflection from a local pond."

"And they're supposed to be smart in Oxford," Daddy said, deadpan.

"So, anyway, if you're from Hartlepool people call you a monkey hanger."

"Ah'll be," Mama said again.

"We got things, too," Melsie Mae said.

"Oh?" George looked at her.

"Never put a hat on a bed. You get bad luck. Never pass a child through a window, because you'll stop him growing. Other things..."

"You must tell me more about Georgia's superstitions when I bring the frogs back."

"Okay."

George coming home frogless never entered her mind, I thought. In a matter of hours she had become devoted to him.

"Okay, folks," Daddy said, taking charge. "About tonight. It's a pretty good time to go, you shouldn't get bit too much. August and September are real bad months, George. We got yellow flies. They're kind of like horseflies but yellowish brown. If one gets you, then in half an hour you'll welt up and itch and it won't quit. But you should be good tonight." I watched Daddy look at me and smile. It was a good smile coming from our recovered trust. "William always took care of you frog giggin', Doreen."

"He sure did." When I had found Daddy after the walk and my talk with Melsie Mae, I had run to him and kissed him. I can count on one hand the number of times I'd seen Daddy embarrassed. That was one of them.

"Remember how William caught 'em? He's use his fingers, real expert..."

"My William was the best," Melsie Mae said.

"...stab with that big hand of his, get that index finger and middle finger between body and legs and pin 'em, then pop his head against a log."

George looked startled. "Really?"

"You bet, George. Yessir, William was quite a swamper." Daddy looked at me again. "Gonna use a light and battery or a flambeau?"

"Flambeau."

"Good girl. Ain't nothing like tradition!"

"What's a flambeau?" George asked.

"It's a rag dipped in oil," I said, "then wrapped around a stick. It'll burn for an hour easy if you do it right."

"Like Huckleberry Finn, or was it Tom Sawyer?"

Mama's eyes were bright. "This'll be part of your training for citizenship, George. You must know about frog giggin'."

George laughed.

"Do they hunt frogs in England?" Daddy asked.

"I don't think so, sir. Closest I can think of is going sprattin'."

"Sprattin'?"

"Yes. At low tide we'd go out on the rocks and hunt sprats and conger eels. They would be stranded in rock pools until the tide came back in."

"Do you eat them?"

"No. It was just something we did as kids."

"How'd you catch them?"

I was starting to itch. We needed to be out and about, but George and Daddy had this bond, and so did Mama and George, and so did I.

"Well," George was saying, "we'd get an old hacksaw blade and grind it sharp. Then we would chop at 'em while they swam. If you got really good, that hacksaw blade made no splash at all, just, *chung!*"

"Hey, we got something like that!" Daddy was shifting from one foot to the other in excitement. "We do something like that after heavy rains. We get flooded grassy ditches beside the road? They're about six or ten feet wide and fish get trapped there. As kids we'd get an old car spring and grind it sharp, like a machete. We called it 'strikin' fish.'"

"Francis," Mama said. "I believe we should let them leave..."

Daddy smiled. "You're right, Christine. I'm holding up the show."

"Not at all," George began.

"Nope, I am. Now, George, don't forget. Don't hit him in the leg with your stick because the prongs will mess up the meat. Go for the back of the head."

"Okay."

"And that's out of the water, like if you see him on a log or lilly pad. Under water you've got to allow for refraction of light..."

"Like deflection shots in gunnery," George said.

"Well, I don't know anything about deflection shots and flying, but aim back of him if he's underwater."

"Okay."

"We're relying on you to bring home the family meal, George. Pioneer style. Lessee, there's five of us, so you've got to catch a bunch. Better catch forty. That's forty pairs of legs. Then Christine and Doreen can show you how to fix 'em. Like first, you cut the kick out."

"Sorry."

"Cut the ligament behind the legs or they'll jump around in the pan, and fat and grease will splash all over you. We serve them deep fried, you see."

"Yes, sir."

"And we skin them, of course."

"Right."

I started to laugh, I couldn't help it. There was George, grappling with Daddy's admonitions, this flight instructor so cool and calm in the air, so fine looking in pressed summer khakis with the lustrous pair of RAF wings, now decked out in old pants and boots and a sack.

"Now, Doreen," Mama began, then she too couldn't keep it in, and she was laughing too. "George, we do apologize, we don't mean..."

"They'll always be an England!" George beamed, brandishing his stick. "And up the Hartlepool Rovers!"

Daddy smiled at him. "You go get 'em, George."

The moon was high and luminous, casting a blue tinged veil on the land, bathing low grassy plains and stands of scrub pine. It was warm as we set out, clumping in our boots.

"Got the matches?" George asked.

"I have some, but I thought we'd use your new lighter."

"Okay, that's nice. A great line-shoot for when I'm with the lads. I'll offer the lighter and say, "By the way, did I tell you about the night I went giggin' for frogs?"

"You haven't done it yet, you don't know what's in store."

"I'll catch twenty, you catch twenty."

"Kiss me, George." He didn't hesitate. He gathered me up in his arms and we kicked each others' boots and he just drank me in and I cried out.

"I love you, Doreen."

"Oh, God, George. I love you. You're every part of me, I'm so damned hungry for you." We clung under the moon on a grassy glade. Only our hot-breathed effort pushed us apart.

"We really need to talk, now," George said softly, kissing my brow. "The pilot and the reporter."

I nodded, my breath warm against his shirt. He found my mouth and gently gathered me up, but holding back, banking the fires. "How the hell are we going to catch frogs now?" he said.

I laughed into his shoulder, running my hands up and down his back.

"Tell me again," he said.

I looked up into those dark glistening eyes caught by moonlight and shadow. "I love you, darling, and I think I've loved you since the day I first met you." I pulled him towards me. "I'm glad you looked at me in Americus, when I was pulling at my dress."

"God, you're beautiful." He buried his mouth in my neck.

"And I'm glad you're not a eunuch."

"You'll never know how difficult it is..."

I kissed him, tasting the first salt sweat of a primordial night. We began to walk, trying to keep our arms around each other, but croker sticks and flambeaus got in our way, almost tripping us up, and we laughed and parted.

"I guess your parents'll want a church wedding."

"I guess."

Not much of a proposal for some but right, so perfectly right, for George and me.

The cypress pond stood like an oasis in the rolling grass. The moon broke against silver cypress trunks and meandering branches. The water was still and dark, but so very different from the view I had flying over in the BT-13. From the air the pond had offered a bright marble and mystery on a brilliant blue day. Now, the softness of night and carefully draped veils of life's beginnings held sway against the cry of an owl and the incessant noise of frogs. George stood beside me and we just looked.

"How deep is it?" he asked.

"Cypress ponds are just depressions in the earth," I murmured. "Sometimes four feet deep or so. This one is knee deep; it hasn't changed much since I came here as a girl with Uncle William." I pointed with my stick. "We always waded in over there."

"We can do that, too."

"There's an old limb you've got to watch out for or it'll trip you up. Listen to it all, George. Catch the life here. It's like the beginning of the world, down in the muck and ooze of prehistoric life." A possum shuffled on the far side of the pond, shifting and gripping at fallen, waterlogged branches, its eyes golden orbs gathering in moonbeams as it looked at us.

"Listen to the frogs," George said. "I've never heard such a racket."

I felt for his hand and held it. "Catch the different calls, George? There's two calls, really. Hear that chirrupy call?" I watched his profile, sharp edged in the night.

"The chirruping one. Yes, I hear it."

"That's a tree frog. He goes chirrup, chirrup. Now listen again, that lower call..."

"I hear it."

"That's a bull frog. He goes ribbit, ribbit."

"I've got him." He squeezed my hand and looked at me. "Now you, Doreen. Look at the branches. What do you hear?"

"Hear?" I stared at the cypress branches, the meandering of them, their entwining, their crackling broken members spread across water and embedded in mud. "I don't hear anything, there's no breeze to rustle..."

"Catch the music," George insisted. "Look at the movement of the limbs and think of sounds, of composers, like Bach."

"Bark?" I burst out laughing. "A Freddie Latham pun?"

He grabbed me then and tickled me, and I doubled over, giggling. "You wretched woman..."

I dropped my stick and flambeau.

"Listen, Doreen, be serious and really listen. Watch the shape of the branches, see their rhythms as they sculpt out space for themselves. A Bach etude...and look at that one!"

I followed George's gesture. A silver barked branch dipped and wandered. "Who?"

"Who do you feel it is?"

"I don't know...Scarlatti?"

"Feel Doreen. Don't think, feel."

I watched the branch amid the ribbits and chirrups of frogs, and suddenly, beguilingly, I heard it. "Chopin."

"Yes. Maybe Sibelius. Or perhaps Ella or Billie improvising on 'Sophisticated Lady.'"

I pinched him. "You know what we do with cypress limbs?"

"What?"

"We skin 'em and make water resistant fence posts."

"Ah. Wagner!"

"George..." We rolled and rolled across the soggy ground, starting to smell as primordial as the myriad forms of life venting around us. "Frogs, George," I managed, "gotta catch frogs."

He kissed me, holding me down, and I fell endlessly through a velvet black abyss. Soft kisses on my eyes and cheeks and mouth brought me back.

"I think the flambeaus are wet," he said.

"God, George, you know what you do to me?"

"I know."

I struggled up. "Give me the lighter."

As I held the lighter to the oil soaked rag, flame curled and swelled, and the drifter sailed against my palm on a gleaming chrome sea. The flambeau lit up the cypress pond, casting grotesque flickering shadows across the scummy surface, the lily pads and exposed logs. The water was dark, a tea color, from dye exuding from dead leaves. And there were frogs, much to George's delight. They sat on stumps, eyes bright, fat bodies heaving and slimy; they swam, heads above water, swirling eddies beyond their strong kicking legs; they sat on wet grass and croaked, luminous eyes bulging, throats ballooning.

George lunged with his giggin' stick, only to see the frog leap in a graceful yellow green trajectory, its mouth in a wide gaping grip. "Blast! The little booger hopped off."

"Lead, George, lead."

"Lead the blighters, right?"

I watched him swirl the marble waters around his hip boots, holding his flambeau high, pitching shadows at the night. His face was all concentration now, just another test of his resources, like a barrel roll or sideslip.

"Gotcha!" The giggin' stick struck, catching the frog as it flexed to leap, unfortunately bursting its fat innards in the surreal light. "Good grief!"

"We only use the legs, George."

"This is disgusting."

"What about chopping sprats in half?"

"That was different, I was just a bairn. What do I do now?"

"Put him in your croker sack."

"What, goo as well?"

"Goo as well."

"What happens to all the goo?"

"We feed it to the hogs."

"Ah."

"Nineteen more, please George."

"I don't think I'd make a good pioneer."

"Gotta know how to gig for frogs to win my hand,

George."

The stick lunged, points bright. "Down to eighteen."

"Terrific."

"You haven't caught any yet."

Pilot and reporter, extraordinaire.

Chapter 22

WE WERE FLYING at four thousand feet, south of Statesboro. Occasional wisps of cloud streamed over our bright yellow wings as condensation touched off rainbow dances. I brought us around to 097 degrees and gently leveled us off.

George's voice came through my headset. "Nicely done."

Ahead I could see the sea, a bright dark blue, with a gray hulled warship driving a wedge of wake towards the horizon. The city of Savannah offered a church-spired silhouette, lush with skirts of trees and magnolias and palms. Smoke belched from factories on the river and the shipyards offered skeletal shapes destined to become ships in convoy across a hostile Atlantic. I stared at my engagement ring as part of my instrument sweep. It sparkled in the sunlight refracted through the Plexiglas canopy. It had cost too much, but George had insisted.

"I have the controls," George said.

"You have the controls."

"P-40s at two o'clock low and coming up."

I watched them: warbirds in Army Air Forces camouflage, six of them in precise formation. They were flying fast and true, but because of our own airspeed and course the fighters appeared to be sliding sideways, crabbing across the sky, sunlight winking from cockpits. A couple of pilots looked at us, their oxygen masks hanging loose. I could see the guns in the wings and they frightened me. George had recommended Freddie Latham for Advanced — Single Engine, and one day Freddie would fly a fighter, perhaps a P-40, perhaps a British plane, a Spitfire or Hurricane.

I felt frightened for our BT-13, our brightly plumed bird, and I was suddenly frightened for George. I looked at the back of his head, a view that had grown loving and familiar as we had flown together, sneaking lessons for me. No log book entries, of course, but I could follow instruments in a rudimentary way, and I was pretty good at keeping the needle and ball centered. I watched the constant turning of George's head. He missed nothing. The roll bar angled between us and over my dual instrument panel. Strangely, but perhaps not, my fear of the 'Flying Coffin' had gone away. I loved the airplane because it meant sharing with George, and sharing something that was terribly important to him. The control stick eased under a ghostly hand between my legs. I kept my hands and feet well clear of the stick and rudder bars. We were close to Hunter Field now and I watched the sky for more traffic...The P-40s meant war and death. Not accidental death, not Stearman death, or BT-13 death, but deliberate kill or be killed. I shuddered, rubbing my engagement ring, my lodestone of luck and timing.

If my attitude towards the BT trainer had changed, so had other, deeper and happier things. I was closer to Mama and Daddy and Melsie Mae. There were sunlit days when Mama and I pored over cookbooks with flour dusted hands; and I was close to Daddy as ambiguity towards the South and my irrational anger abated. I could leave without giving up my home. Other things, other things...like Billy Odum praising my writing...more heart now, he said. And George held it all together. I had these quick takes of him forever in my mind: George readying the boat to go fishing at St. Mark's, working out with Daddy the gas coupons and dash of aviation fuel; George feeling out Chopin's famous nocturne on the piano, forgetting the next few bars and lightly gesturing with his strong hands, his eyes bemused, and smiling that crooked toothed grin. And George becoming a good dancer, surprising me with new moves.

"Am I as good as Freddie yet?"

"You're getting there."

"I've got to outshine that cadet!"

"Don't be so competitive."

"Pilots are competitive."

"Am I as sexy a dancer as Trepick yet?"

"George!"

"He's got some good maneuvers."

"So do you, and we'll say no more about it." I hesitated. "By the way, how are things with Bill?"

"Much better. He's a good man."

And always the jazz, a downbeat in our lives; a rim shot and flatted fifth for zing. We had heard Duke Ellington twice, gotten caught up in 'Satin Doll' and 'Take the A Train', but when the orchestra moved into 'Sophisticated Lady' all we could think about were trees and frogs!

George's voice came through my headset. "There's supposed to be a jeep. If not, we'll try for a taxi."

"Okay."

"Got your PRO badge?"

"Yup."

"What's your subject again?"

"Shipbuilding for the war effort. But I've got all the research from before, a story I never wrote. The time is ours, George. We can go straight to the beach."

"The sea looks good, but the beaches are a mess."

I looked forward and out, beyond the leading edge of our wing. Below us barbed wire coiled like ugly snakes. Military vehicles had left parallel gouges in the sand. The sea would wash them away, leaving nothing.

"I want to buy your Mum something in Savannah."

"Okay."

Our jeep tore at the sand, digging in, then surging forward. The view from the plane had been kinder. Here the beach revealed the ugly residue of sunken ships. Shards of metal, curled and blackened by fire; splintered wood from shattered lifeboats and dinghies. Bodies, I knew, washed ashore under a scorching sun or moonlit caress, while at sea the rumble of explosions and the flash of detonations continued. Most of the bodies wore civilian clothes. They were merchant seamen, whose paychecks stopped the moment their ships sank, and their widows and children were left to make do. Bodies were taken in by local mortuaries.

And oil, oil. It clung to the sand, it choked sea birds, burning out their crops and coating their wings. Oil, bits of lifeboats, feathers and bodies. German submarines had brought havoc to Georgia's coast in early 1942. January, February, and March saw increasing numbers of ships, especially oil tankers, blown up off its coast. To our shame, fast boats ran out to sea with gasoline and food for the Germans. The enemy paid well, and they paid in U.S. dollars. Not our most heroic episode in American history. And Germans came ashore as spies and saboteurs. German sympathizers were alive and well, especially before Pearl Harbor, when personnel working with the British flight cadets were screened for anti-British, pro-German feelings. And now, along the curve of beach, shipyards toiled for victory, with three shipyard workers to a room on rotation. And with women now in the yards, the inevitable condoms were found behind machines and in alcoves, along with bits of orange peel and half eaten sandwiches.

The jeep slowed to a halt. George got out his pipe and tobacco pouch.

"I'll do it." I said.

"'s'okay."

Strong fingers tamped at the tobacco. The Ronson flamed and smoke drifted away on a touch of rum. I waited.

"Children should be here," he said. "They should be playing with sand buckets and little shovels. They should be shouting as waves come up against the sandcastles. Ever seen that, Doreen?"

"No.

"The tide comes in and waves lap at your carefully made fort. You've used stones and cork and bits of driftwood to strengthen it; and when the sea starts to lap you scamper around and dig little ditches to channel the water away. 'It's getting in over here, Malcolm, I'll fix it! Man the barricades!'"

"Who's Malcolm?"

"A playmate, when we were just bairns. He's in the Royal Navy somewhere. Probably on convoy duty, trying to prevent all this." The pipe bowl gestured at the sea. "Oh, almost forgot." George smiled, brightening his mood, fumbling in his tunic pocket. "Letters from Mum."

"Oh, George!"

"Thought you'd like to read 'em."

"I'd love to. And I want to write her..."

"Writing's a bit iffy of course. If the ship is lost, so is the mail. But so far I've been lucky. Just takes forever, that's all. They're in order, but about a month old."

I opened one of the letters and began to read.

Well, I'm sitting at the kitchen table with a nice cup of tea and I thought I'd get a letter off to you. We are all thinking of you, George, and I know it's selfish but we're glad you're safe in America. You did your bit in the Army is our way of looking at it. Marian wants to know if she can play your early jazz records, the 1920 ones. She promises to be careful with them. She's also protecting your collection from the bombing by putting newspapers between them and boxing them up.

You might want to write and thank her, dear. Oh, and she has good news. She passed her examinations, theory and performance, and she now has her letters: A.L.C.M. (Associate of the London College of Music.) When all this war business is over, it will certainly help her teaching career...

I'm sorry to say we got bombed the other night. H.E.? It landed down the street from us, but no one was killed.

"What's H.E.?" I asked.

"High explosive."

Anyway the air raid sirens are going off every night but mostly it's false alarms, not like those poor souls in London...However, a big bomb did land on Hilda Street and several people were killed. Some poor bairns were found without shoes, running around in their bare feet. Their names were taken and fortunately they were matched up with some relatives.

I don't wish to sound 'down', dear. Things are not
that bad, really. One funny thing, Joe and Mabel next
door are the laugh of our street right now. During an
air raid everybody went to the shelters, but Joe went
back to the house. Mabel said, 'Where you going?' and
Joe said, 'I forgot my teeth,' and Mabel said, 'What do
you think they're dropping tonight, sandwiches?' We
all had a good laugh, but Joe's sulking because he
thinks Mabel made him look daft...

I held the letters in my lap. "She's lovely, George, just
lovely."

"Yes, she is. And Marian's a grand sister."

"Going to let her play your records?"

"Oh, sure. But I'll remind her that she used to steal
my desserts if I got in late from a soccer match. Mum
would make stewed apple and custard and set it in the
larder. Guess what budding pianist took it?"

"This Joe and Mabel are something. You could make
a comic strip out of them." It would be many years
before Hartlepool characters would inspire the comic
strip, 'Andy Capp', and see it syndicated around the
world.

"Hartlepool's full of characters, my family too. I
remember Granddad coming home tiddly one night with
his drunken friend, 'Kipper' Sykes, a window cleaner
blessed with two little fingers on each hand, and a great
voice for opera. They both were wearing prize winning
carnations they had seen fit to pick from a neighbor's garden. Our families are still not speaking and it's been
years." He tapped out his pipe. "I just have this marvelous memory of Granddad banging out 'Hear My
Song', with Kipper harmonizing, and these gorgeous carnations in their lapels."

I laughed and looked out to sea. I did not want to
change the mood, but I had to. "George?"

"What."

"Your mother refers to the army, your time there."

"Yes?"

"I...I want you to tell me about Dunkirk. I know you say you'll tell me," I added quickly, "but I want to know now. If you will."

He got out of the jeep and leaned against the windshield. "Why now?"

"Because we're on a beach sullied by death and war, and I can't get it out of my mind. Talk to me now, while I have the sea and beaches in my senses to help me understand. I know whatever it is, George, it's been bad for you."

"Frankly, it's not that bad. Now. I've done the weeping. The one night drunk is over with."

I reached for his arm on the windshield. "George, once in a while, when we talk about the war and sometimes other things, you get a haunting look in your eyes, not haunted, I don't mean that...But haunting, a deep melancholy."

"I see."

I took a breath. "I don't want us to take that look into our marriage. If it turns out that we can't eradicate it, then we share it. Support each other."

George watched the sea, his eyes sweeping up and down the coastline, then up at the sky. He studied the broken sand. "The sea was calm, like this," he said, "but the upheaval, the abandoned vehicles, the hundreds of men..." his voice trailed off then picked up, stronger. "And the dive bombers strafing, of course; the Heinkels and Stukas. God, I hated those Stukas. They also bombed the rescue ships. There were burning hulks, pillars of smoke, like up there at the factories, but dirtier. A couple of ships ran aground. And the hundreds of men wading out in an endless line towards the ships, with civilians and naval ratings getting the army on board. Not just British troops, either. French military, too, and French civilians hoping to get to England and join the Free French." He smiled at me. "I guess you'd better have a look at this."

He startled me by undoing his pants. Before I could say anything he had pulled at his underpants. Two ugly indentations, each the size of a dime, puckered the flesh at his groin. "Couldn't see this at the lake picnics, my swimsuit covered it."

"What...?"

"They're bullet holes. Nothing romantic, Doreen, no derring-do. No one picked me out as I went about my valiant occasions. Just machine gun fire, some over there, some over here. Two inches this way and I'd have no plumbing." He pulled his pants back up and stared out to sea.

I had been right about the sea. It helped. It was where he gathered and replayed his memories and found his solace. I wanted to reach out, grasp his hand in that magical way his hand could grip mine, or a terrified child's. But I knew I must not.

"I was a sergeant, a regular, with the 2nd King's Royal Rifles. We were in retreat, backing up to the beaches. The captain and major were both dead, and leadership fell upon the youthful shoulders of a subaltern, Second Lieutenant Clive Tyne-Harding. As if things weren't bad enough, we had Tyne-Harding. He was something of a joke in the ranks. He was nineteen, and had a smooth face devoid of experience, and slightly bulging blue eyes that constantly sought approval. To look a bit older and more seasoned, he took up smoking a pipe, but then he looked like a kid with a pipe stuck in his face. It was desperately important to him to be a good officer. He had gone to good schools, he came from a fine family and talked with a plummy accent. He was just so damned earnest. Somebody walked in on him one time and found him reading Thucydides and the Peloponnesian Wars, a dog-eared pocket version."

His laugh was quick and ugly.

"Our units got separated, we fended for ourselves, with Tyne-Harding, me as sergeant, and some of the lads, about a dozen of us. It was a rough count that changed from hour to hour, day to day, as soldiers joined up with us and others died. We ended up cut off at Calais, with Tyne-Harding issuing endless unnecessary commands, his eyes bulging in his dirty face. I had the impression he sensed this could be the defining moment of his career; if he could just figure out what to do. At Calais we ended up with a few hundred French troops. They held an old citadel while French marines diddled around with some very old coastal guns. I don't think they got them into action. The Stukas came that morning. I was a regular soldier but I'd never been through a strafing and bombing like that. Tyne-Harding ordered us into a cellar where we kept company with an old lady and her terrified cat. After it was all over, we got outside. Everything was rubble. Just shattered glass, bricks, bits of buildings... We retreated to the harbor, Tyne-Harding exhorting us all the way. At the harbor isolated units kept fighting, including us, but soon men began surrendering, breaking up their rifles so Jerry couldn't use them. Later a German waved a pistol at them and told them to pack it in."

"What about you?" I asked.

"Me? We didn't surrender, and we dodged the Jerries. After a few hours we were down to seven men. Tyne-Harding got us to the east breakwater where he'd seen a Red Cross-boat. We helped get some wounded onto the boat and got it safely away. Then the Germans began closing in and we got marooned out on the breakwater. We hid in the pilings, water up to our chests. God, the sea was cold!"

A low hard drone reached our jeep and we looked up. A U.S. Navy blimp ballooned its way overhead, bright starred, bright silvered. George watched it drone up the coast towards the belching smokestacks and shipyards.

"Anyway, we clung to those pilings and somebody said a swastika flag had gone up on the jetty. Then two British destroyers hove in and began shelling. That was when Tyne-Harding said we'd swim for the far end of the breakwater where he could see some other soldiers. So off we went...we got about thirty yards out when some machine gun rounds hit the sea...and me. I remember the spouts of water coming towards me, then the pain. White hot pain in a fearfully cold sea. I doubled over, my head going underwater. I couldn't straighten up. Then here he is, Tyne-Harding, getting me onto my side, twisting my head, holding my mouth above the waves to suck in air. 'All right, sergeant, I've got you. I've got you.' And he began swimming us to the far end of the breakwater, it was a helluva distance, I was coming out of the shock, and I saw how far we had to go, but my damned legs wouldn't work. Tyne-Harding wouldn't let go. 'Soon be there, Westcott. Hang on to me. Soon be there...'"

I watched him, and saw the wet coating on his eyes.

"Soon be there," George said again. "I managed to look over at the breakwater, at the other soldiers, and I made the decision that I was going to make it, by Christ, get back with the lads. But I was bleeding and losing a lot of blood, and there was Tyne-Harding, his blue eyes inches from my face. 'Nearly there, son, nearly there.'" George looked at me. "He was easily five years younger than me, but he was calling me son. I raged at him. And as I felt myself getting weaker, I got greedier and greedier for his support, and I rested on his arm and let him carry me forward. Then we were there, thank Christ. Hands were reaching out for us. I found myself looking at regimental badges and insignia, perversely identifying who was getting me out of that horribly cold sea. Somebody from the Territorials, somebody from the 1st Rifle Brigade, another from the 2nd Queen Victoria's Rifles...Then Tyne-Harding started up again. 'Smartly now, sergeant, look lively there'. He gave me a final shove and hands hauled me up onto some rocks. I can still smell the seaweed where my face fell against it. They got me undressed because I was shivering so much, and they all pressed around me to keep me warm. Some of it was crackers, just insane. Me naked but still wearing my helmet. When they crowded close, our helmets clanged together and they worried the Germans would hear us." George smiled, a very tired smile from somewhere deep within. "A naval yacht found us and got us out. The heavy, overcast helped. The divebombers couldn't get at us."

I watched him. He was fearfully tense, his eyes anguished. "What is it, George?" My voice jarred him. He looked again at the sea.

"When I could get it all together, covered in blankets, I said to a sailor, 'Where's the subaltern, Tyne-Harding? I need to thank him.' Nobby Clarke overheard me. Nobby and I had been together since before the war. It turned out that Subaltern Tyne-Harding was dead. Nobby said he had given me a final push up to the breakwater, then he had floated away, his face like a sleeping baby's. He'd just floated away. Then he rolled over and they saw the bullet holes." George reached into his pocket and took out his lucky stone from the beach at Hartlepool. "He had to make it look easy, you see. Bullets in the back, wounds that would take his life, and there he was, moving me forward to the breakwater. And I had clung to him. He came from a fine family inculcated with fine values and traditions. So it had to look easy..." The smile he gave me was far too bright. He held up the stone. "A little bit of Hartlepool for my future adopted country."

I watched him walk out onto the sand and carefully place his stone.

The BT-13 roared into the air and through a darkening sky. Instrument panel lights glowed, and a simmering red sun at the horizon stained our cockpit a rosy pink. As we climbed away from Hunter Field the sea below us offered a gentle tide and phosphorus edge. I watched George, his head now in shadows beyond the roll bar. It was my first chance to be alone, and I let out the ache, the tightness in my throat, and I cried into a balled up handkerchief. Sooner or later he would catch me in the rearview mirror, ever the instructor, so I kept it brief and struggled back. When his voice crackled through my headset, sounding louder in the gloom, I jumped.

"Doreen?"

"Yes?" There was only silence, a fuzz of static, and I thought something was wrong with the radio, then...

"About today, at the beach. The way it turned out. Was it a good idea?"

"It was a necessary day...for us."

"Yes, that's it. That's about right. Doreen?"

"Yes?"

"I might still get that look."

"It's okay now. I know what's going on."

"Mind if I do the flying back to Cochran?"

"No."

The BT roared into the gathering night, the setting sun a fiery cauldron.

Chapter 23

"PEACHES ARE LANCASTERS, pecans are Halifaxes, and Stirlings are watermelons. Okay?"

"Okay." I clutched my couch cushion against my chest and waited. We were in my rented room in Macon with its tableau of New York posters, the door propped open with library books. Being engaged to be married in two weeks did not get us privacy from my landlady, Mrs. Wiggs. Her unblinking eyes would peer in at us.

"Okay," George said. "Try this. 'Things are going well here, but I miss the peaches.'"

"You didn't get Lancasters."

"Good. Now this. 'They have nice pecans over here and I'm enjoying them.'"

"You got Halifaxes."

"Right." He grinned at me. "Probably none of this is necessary, but just in case. And in Billy Odum's words, you catch on quick, you surely do.'"

I smiled, fighting back remembered talk at the picnics. The scuttlebutt, fragmented and distorted, delivered on sneers and whispers, fears and hopes. Air gunners smearing lanolin on their necks against twisting and turning in subzero cold, looking for nightfighters. And the odds against a bomber crew finishing a tour of operations.

"George?" I squeezed my cushion.

"What."

"I know why we're doing this. You want to get me used to the fact that you'll be leaving for England."

"It's not definite, Doreen," he said softly. "I've not received orders. But it's likely. Rumor has it that they need twin engine instructors in Canada. Maybe I'll be sent there."

"But you're expecting word soon."

He hesitated. "Yes, yes I am."

"If it's England, I could go. Good stories."

"No, I don't want you to."

"Why not?"

"Well, there's the risk, the bad risk of the Atlantic crossing. When some cadets came over the Bismark was loose. She's sunk now, but there's the U-boats. It's too much risk, Doreen."

"But...?"

"I want you safe. If I'm flying on ops over Germany, I at least will know you're safe. Please go along with me on this one."

I watched him. "I guess if you put it that way, I don't have much choice."

"Anyway, like I say, it could be Canada."

A seam was coming loose in my cushion. I'd need to stitch it. "What if you receive word before our wedding day, then what?"

"Well, we're having a small wedding anyway, so perhaps we could bump it up a little."

"Mama's working on her wedding dress for me. She wants me to wear it."

"I know," he said slowly. "We could end up in the Justice of the Peace's office."

"What about Haggis, and Freddie, and Archie?"

"They probably couldn't make it, they'll be finishing up advanced training. But we'd have Butch as best man, and Bill, and Billy Odum."

"Yes, we could get that, I think. And your parents and Melsie Mae, of course. It could still be nice."

I managed a smile. "Let's hope the wedding day goes as planned. And," I said, by way of concession, "I'm lucky to have had you this long. Luckier than most girls."

"I'm lucky to have you, Doreen."

"Mama's going to wear the cross you bought her in Savannah."

"That's nice. Guess what?"

"What."

"Butch got hold of a fancy bottle of champagne. He says it's for our wedding night."

"That's very thoughtful of him," I said, in deliberate, measured tones.

"Nervous about it?"

"George..."

"Nervous?"

"A little."

"Excited?"

"That too."

He wiggled his eyebrows at me. So help me, he wiggled his eyebrows!

"George!"

"What."

"Don't do that."

"What."

"That Groucho Marx thing, that eyebrow thing."

He did it again, and I flung the cushion at him, then I had him by the feet, yanking him from the chair to the floor, where we tussled and rolled over and over, laughing hysterically.

Unblinking eyes peered through the open doorway.

"Everything all right in there?" Mrs. Wiggs asked.

"Everything's fine," George said, not letting me loose. We were entangled on the floor looking up at her.

"It's after ten, Mr. Westcott."

"I'm just about on my way Mrs. Wiggs," George said solemnly.

"I'll say goodnight, then."

"Goodnight."

George and I looked at each other, holding in our laughter, rolling over and over. "George, only you could've gotten away with that. Just like with Mama."

"English charm."

"It was right out of a Carole Lombard movie. Zany, and flaunting convention."

"Then I'm Cary Grant, right? After all, he's English."

"Then who's Mrs. Wiggs?"

He kissed me. "Be kind now."

"I can't think of anyone."

We got up.

"Now," I said formally. "I've a surprise."

"What."

I retrieved the letter. "Billy gave me this today."

"What is it?"

"Read it."

Dear Mr.Odum,

I've now had a chance to read Doreen Summers' writing samples you kindly sent me. I agree she's a talent. Still, she's a bit rough, but the makings are there. I particularly liked her piece on the coastal rice fields and the slave-built canals. Good restraint on disease and challenges they worked against. Not a piece we can use, but well done. If she comes to New York we can give her freelance work but no advances. If she can

support herself for a few weeks and works hard, she should do well. Solid work could see us taking her on as a stringer. I hope this letter encourages her, and thanks for getting in touch.
Cordially,

Sam Rowland, Editor
The Village Opinion.

"Wow." George murmured.

"I was all over Billy, hugging him, kissing him. I think I embarrassed him."

"Don't worry, he loved it. You're the daughter he never had, and you're his protégé."

"I'll go to New York when and if you get your transfer orders."

"Good."

"I'm scared, George."

"You'll do well, you're a fine writer."

"I mean us."

He took me in his arms.

"We'll make it through, Doreen. Just don't ask me to be a farmer when I come back."

"How about a train conductor?"

"No."

"After the war you might have a better chance getting a flying job in New York."

"It's possible. There might be red tape problems with my RAF qualifications. Transferring them into American aviation, I mean."

"I don't think so. Remember what you said you like about America, George. We're free and easy, not so hidebound."

George smiled. "I might get put to the test on that one. Hundreds of ex-service pilots trying for the airlines."

I kissed him as we stood in the doorway. Ostentatious banging came from downstairs. "She's reminding us that she's still the boss," I said. "Look, if I am in New York, I'll cover the jazz scene for you. I've a lot to learn, but I want it."

"I'd love that. Anyway, no one's going anywhere yet, and it might not happen for some time. Depends on supply and demand for British and American pilots. But one day they'll turn off the tap." He hugged me then. "How do you feel about the Georgia mountains for our honeymoon?"

"I like it. I liked it when you first mentioned it, and I like it now."

"Just checking. Why do you think it's good?"

"Is this an interview, George?"

He nuzzled my neck.

"It's not farming," I said. "And it's not the sea. The mountains are something we can experience without triggering memories."

"Good."

"I knew a girl from North Carolina once. She said she drew her strength from the mountains. She had to go back to North Carolina every once in a while. Renew her spirit."

"I like that. Look, I've got formation flying tomorrow, then night flights. What do you want to do?"

"I might go and see Mama. She's on pins and needles with the wedding. Daddy's trying to be nonchalant."

George kissed me then, making everything warm and safe. I rested my head on his chest.

"Day after tomorrow, if the weather holds, we'll go for a walk and look at the stars."

"Love it."

Chapter 24

GEORGE AND I were married as planned on September 9, 1942, in the Summers' family church in Camilla, Georgia. We didn't have to go to the Justice of the Peace, and we were blessed that day with friends and memories. Wendy Clinkscales could not get leave from Washington, and Barbara Rucker, picnic buddy and insightful friend, was in the hospital with tonsillitis. But Mama and Melsie Mae were there for me. Haggis, Archie, and Freddie finished their Advanced training on September 6th, and Freddie was a hit with a handsomely groomed mustache. He took a lot of ribbing about fighter pilots, those 'Brylcreem Boys', and how his mustache would tickle the girls and ruin his dancing. The three of them were all over me with hugs and well wishing, but they could not resist going to one side to compare notes on their multi- and single-engine training. Their newly acquired pilots' wings were bright in the sunshine. And the American contingent was strong, of course, resplendent in USAAF uniforms and silver wings. Second Lieutenant Butch Martinelli was George's best man. Newly promoted Captain Bill Trepick, dear Bill, was there for our tiny group as usher. He didn't have much to do, but found caring ways to help out. I relished this mix of USAAF and

RAF uniforms. and I was so very proud of my parents and the way Melsie Mae was gently drawn into our small wedding party after she had hung back, the usual segregation imperative. She's in all of our wedding pictures, smiling uncertainly, wearing her Primitive Baptist, church service, Sunday best. The only concession to segregation was having her sit in the back of one of the cars to get her to the church. George was bewildered by this, believing only the rich and influential sat alone in the back. There had followed one of those peculiar exchanges between Daddy and George, borne of good will and a singular affection for each other.

Quite a day, and when memories offer themselves to me, they always start with that wedding day morning, with me in my mother's wedding dress and Mama making last minute adjustments, her mouth gripping pins. That day was a celebration for George and me and all those we loved and cared about. Mama and I could hear Daddy lecturing George on trout fishing...

"Now, George. I can fix you and Doreen up with gear, and wet and dry reels, and some extra leaders and tippets...you do fish, right? Besides that pier in Hartlepool?"

"Well, no, sir, not really. The army, then flying..."

"Well, let's keep it simple, then. A plastic dry fly box, some streamers and wet flies."

"Francis!" Mama called, her mouth somehow holding onto the pins.

"What!"

"I don't think you should push George into fishing if he doesn't want to."

"Landsakes, woman! He's gonna be up on the Oostanoula where they got trout and fifty pound sturgeon."

"Doreen's there too!"

"Hell, I gotta line for her. Now, George. If you get there after the fifteenth, the season on small streams may close on you. So try for the Etowah. It's got spotted bass, bluegill, crappie..."

I looked down at Mama pinning at my waistline and found her eyes on mine.

"You gonna let your man out of that cabin?"

"No."

And we laughed together, a marvelous free bonding in that sunlit bedroom.

"I can hear you back there." Daddy called.

"Poor George," I said. "He's only just got the hang of frogs." To my surprise Mama wrapped her arms around my legs on a quick rustle of satin.

"I love you, my daughter."

I took her in. "I love you, Mama."

She resumed pinning.

I said quietly, "I sense the rhythms of everything today. We're all part of something wonderful."

"Soon be time to pick the cotton," Mama said, "and we're already working on the peanuts..., keep still, dear, just this tuck here..., then there's the pecans and corn. Always remember, in hard times the pecans can see you through."

"I'll remember," I said. I'll never forget that brief exchange with Mama. It captured my regained respect for the land; it spoke of commitment to the farm. I would take our future challenges firm footed from a good earth.

"And it's the cadets, Mama, moving through their training, moving on. Those graduation parties at the Idle Hour Club, they seem to come faster and faster."

"You'll find life gets faster and faster," Mama said with a smile. "I've been talking with your father. We're going to bring more of the cadets down here from Cochran. We'll hold dances, chaperoned of course."

"That's wonderful, they'll love it. 'Y'know what Archie Watkins said to me, the first time I met him at a dance?"

"Keep still, dear. What?"

"He said, 'Doreen, you were born to be wicked, why aren't you?'"

"Landsakes," Mama said mildly. "No Southern boy would say such a thing."

"These boys are different. I like their manners and charm and guts."

"So, what did you say?"

"What."

"To this Archie Watkins, who asked why you weren't wicked?"

"I said, 'How do you know I'm not?' He loved that."

"Uuummm."

I hesitated. "I heard something disturbing the other day."

"Oh?" Mama's eyes were back on mine.

"We got word two cadets had been killed. In the war, I mean, not training accidents. I didn't know them, but it could easily have been the other way, with me knowing them. It's bad enough losing these boys, but what if...?" Mama's hand grasped mine and shook it. "You must brace yourself, Doreen."

"I just worry about them."

"We lost Tim Oberly."

I jerked, twisted. "Not Tim!"

"Keep still. I didn't want to tell you."

"No, I'm glad to know."

Tim, who pulled my braids in grade school.

"The dances are nice, Mama. Always in love, huddled

over our drinks and swizzlesticks, listening to Benny Goodman or Glenn Miller. And those hushed whispers about sex. So genteel."

Mama stiffened.

I kissed her brow. "No, Mama. Tonight's my night."

"Anything you'd like to talk about? There's still time…"

"No. This part of life's rhythms I want to journey alone.

"Don't forget George," she said dryly.

"Hey!"

Mama stood up, smoothing out her skirt. "You know what I like about these British boys?"

"What."

"The language. Things like 'chin chin' and 'cheerio'. I like it."

"Me too. Wendy Clinkscales tries to talk with an English accent, but then she gets excited and forgets. She's just fooling around, of course. I doubt if she does it at the FBI."

"I've noticed you've changed your own way of talking." Mama's words fell abruptly into the warmth of the bedroom.

"I…I try to speak clearly, enunciate clearly."

"Yes, of course."

"You're not angry, are you?"

"No. I'm used to it. Your Daddy's not too comfortable with it."

"I need it, Mama, to get ahead."

"I understand. I notice even George changes his speech for formal occasions, then he relaxes. But Doreen, don't forget your heritage. You're a Southern girl. Shaped here, nourished here, part of us. Please don't lose it."

"I won't Mama. I was just now thinking how I needed to keep the good things with me "

"And when you stand before God, my daughter, talk honest, not your getting ahead talk."

"Yes," I managed, twisted up inside.

Mama smiled. "Doreen, you look beautiful, just beautiful!"

"I'm lucky to have your dress, Mama."

"After the wedding we can go on keeping it here at the farm, but one day perhaps you'll have a daughter... who knows?"

"Christine!" Daddy yelled. "What've you done with my fishing books?"

"Slip the dress off carefully, dear, and I'll make the changes. Right now your Daddy needs me."

And on that lovely September morn, I remember the church foyer, the anteroom, and those quiet moments with my father as we waited for the opening bars of the Wedding March. Perhaps it was the close confines where my wedding gown rustled, and my deep red roses offered their fragrance, and our voices were muffled and private; perhaps it was looking through the history book of the church, the fading lists of names and photos of members at socials. And children playing on rope swings, and wearing homemade clothes from flour sacks, always neat and clean. There was little Tim Oberly tussling with his dog. Whatever the mood that caught us, I found my father looking at me, his eyes wet, his sunken face old and wise.

"It all went by so fast, Doreen."

I hugged him, so close, so close, crushing satin and roses. When the organ struck up I took my father's arm, and I felt the knot hard strength under the rented tuxedo. And on that lovely September morn, as we walked down the aisle, and loved ones and friends looked at me, I found it hard to discern where love ended and friendship began. Airforce uniforms, smiling faces. Freddie, my sweet Freddie, and his dashing mustache. George waiting. Butch smiling. And Mama, almost ethereal, her face delicate yet vibrant. Billy Odum, tough editor, kept looking at his feet. I glanced at the organist, Mr. Billings, who had challenged mother's talent to its present reaches of Mozart's 'Turkish Rondo'. The Reverend Clay Wilkes watched and waited. He had been our first fulltime preacher after the circuit preachers, and I wondered what he was thinking about this girl he had baptized, who had pulled away from his church on a surge of rebellion against the role of women and their place in the Bible Belt. But now he was smiling, and George was smiling. As I took my measured steps the church shimmered in sunlight and memory: The old days, when only wooden shutters covered the windows, then the hand made glass, then the addition of the single and beautiful stained glass window. Now hands held funeral parlor fans and wafted them, and ceiling paddle fans spun the sultry air. As always, bees and insects and gnats made their way through open windows. And I could see the tree, once so small and tender, and now a hulking limb. I could hear Mama's voice during the Sunday morning ritual: 'Don't set your hat too rakishly, check that hem and shoes, and don't look at that Willard boy, because he's goin' to come to no good.' Beyond the hulking limb old gravestones teetered, protective still of babies lost to a hard birth, and elders who lived strong and devoutly and endured.

I looked at George.

Who would stand beside me as I faced God in my Southern heritage? George the leader, the cool RAF pilot dreaming of an airline career, who spoke with good but studied diction? Or would it be the George who kissed me under the stars and spun lyrical tales of fishing boats and monkeys and North Sea storms? I was wrong on both counts. As I turned to face him in our betrothal, to look into those marvelous brown almost black eyes, I got the boy turned man who had once carried coal for a crippled father, and I rejoiced.

At the small reception I whirled and talked, relishing the attention, smiling brightly. Fussing with my train, my lifted veil, I moved around the church basement, standing at the buffet with the Reverend Wilkes and Daddy, recalling names and photos from the church history book, then hugging Melsie Mae who was swiping at tears with a lace handkerchief, and telling Billy Odum and Mama that I was glad they knew each other. And always, always, George was my focal point; I was ever conscious of where he was, and when I looked at him I found his eyes on me, quiet, exquisitely loving, as he held his chipped cup and triangle sandwich. But the key to that basement and its memories was the emotional underpinning to it. Beneath the banter was a growing sense of extended family and the priceless but moribund relationships as war took us forward. My father dancing with me, awhirl in memories, holding me as if to hold back time, and I remembering, remembering. Then George, to cheers and applause, taking my hand as no one else could and offering me the world. Butch danced with an old country flair, comfortable surrounded by joyous voices and spontaneous feelings. Haggis danced to a voiced concern for his pigeons and the chance now that he could get back to them. And his words fit as we turned to the rhythms. Archie sought a high, profound plane and failed — the greatest compliment — and he settled for, 'I know you'll both be happy', and I squeezed his hand. Billy was stiff and uncomfortable, this shaper of destinies, soother of wounds, wellspring of hope.

When Bill Trepick cut in the record ended, scraping in circles, and he looked at me in that difficult silence.

"Just a sec," Freddie called. "Technical problems."

Then Glenn Miller's 'Serenade in Blue' filled the room.

"You look lovely, Doreen." Bill said.

"Thank you."

"I wish you and George every happiness."

"Thank you." I waited, but the silence between us hung in counterpoint to the music. "George tells me you've got a B-17 at the Air Depot."

He brightened immediately, shaping a comfortable world. "Installing two new superchargers. And George gets nowhere near it, except as co-pilot." I laughed.

"Mom and Dad send their love." Bill said, turning me on a low siren of saxes. "I'm surprised you didn't get a shipment of cheese."

"I'll write them, Bill."

"Thanks."

We danced in silence until the song died.

It was Mama who reminded me of the time and the need to open gifts, and there was a marvelous kaleidoscope of wrappings, ribbons, and packing paper. Mama and Daddy gave us linens, second hand from the farm because of cloth shortages, but they were newly and beautifully embroidered and hand stitched by Mama. There was a brand new portable typewriter from Billy Odum, and he had added six spare ribbons. George declared it was just what he needed and he received a lot of catcalling; and that grandest of prizes, a generous supply of gasoline 'C' coupons. But what took my breath away was an heirloom necklace I didn't know existed. "It's over a hundred years old, Doreen," Daddy said. "Came from England with your forebears. We've been kinda saving it."

"We didn't know if we should give it to you before the wedding, or wait." Mama said.

"I'm glad you waited. It's beautiful, Mama. And Daddy, I'll treasure it."

There were other gifts from friends, sustaining gifts in difficult times ahead, and George and I handed out to Bill and Butch I.D. bracelets with USAAF wings embossed on them. It was Archie who pointed out Freddie to me. He was off in a corner. "What's he up to?" I asked.

"Search me. I think he's got a record he wants to dance to, and he's hiding it."

As Archie spoke 'Moonlight and Shadows' filled the basement and Freddie came towards me. His smile pulled at his mustache. He was a bit red, suddenly realizing everyone was watching him. He held a neatly wrapped present in his hand that looked suspiciously like a book.

"May I have this dance, Mrs. Westcott?"

"I'd be honored, Freddie."

We danced to cheers and applause and I watched Freddie's face color in discomfort. "I didn't think we'd have an audience."

"They're just happy, like me."

"I want you to have this." He handed me the present, but he whirled me, making sure I just held it and didn't stop dancing. As if I would.

"You usually hold me closer, Freddie. We have our comfortable way to dance."

"Well..."

"Let me feel that mustache, my dashing fighter pilot. Come on!" We fell into our comfortable embrace, the one that had offered sanctuary when George was an enigma, a million years ago.

"How is it?"

"It does tickle, but it brings out the rascal in you."

"Good."

It was Mama who reminded me of the time. We all listened to Haggis and Freddie do their rendition of Gilbert and Sullivan. 'Captain of the Eddystone Light' is how I always remember it. They held up their iced teas and didn't miss a beat, with Archie providing wonderful backup.

"Make the most of the iced tea, boys," Daddy said. "When you go home you'll miss it."

Mama ushered me into a study room and helped me change into my going away outfit. Jesus smiled from a fading print, his arms around children. "It's going so well, dear." Mama said.

"What do you think of Billy, my editor?"

"He's rather shy, isn't he. I thought editors were bears who bossed everybody."

I laughed, easing out of the wedding dress bodice. "He is, he's just out of his element right now. Mama, the dress is so beautiful. And I bet you looked lovely in it. Your wedding picture doesn't do you justice."

"I'll store it," she said, as she turned to get my new tailored pastel rose dress.

The dress was a knockout. Pleats. "I'm undermining the war effort."

"You look lovely. George will be thrilled."

"Mama?"

"What."

"Keep an eye on Melsie Mae."

"Of course, Doreen. There's no need to worry about that."

"She misses Uncle William something awful."

"Your Daddy and I know that. We've redone her home, inside and out. We're getting help for her with the heavy laundry. When she wants to, she can retire. She's safe, she'll always be safe, daughter."

I kissed her. "Why do I keep saying the obvious, talk about things you've taken care of ages ago."

"Because you care. But you've got your own life now, Doreen, and your first job is George."

I crinkled my nose at her. "Not news reporting?"

"No."

"Not a journalist's career? Becoming famous?"

"No."

I ran my brush through my hair, eyes bright with excitement. "You mean I have to feed him?"

Mama poked me.

"Hey!"

"By the way, be careful getting into your car. Melsie Mae put her present there. She was too shy to give it to you."

I put the brush down. "What did she get us?"

"She made you some of her favorite preserves to take with you. Peach and strawberries, I think."

"That's lovely."

"You have my eyes, Doreen."

"And I use them shamelessly. I learned that from you."

"Do you know when they're gray and when they're blue?"

"Yup."

"I watch you use the light to best advantage."

I laughed. "Again learned from you. Good old straight ahead Doreen. Not above feminine wiles."

"I should say not."

"But you know, Mama, for all your traditional

Southern ways, you've changed. I was blind to it from my own impatient ideas, but it's there."

"Yes. A little. Your Daddy and I are alone again, like in our courting and early marriage days, we're looking to ourselves. I think the British boys have given me a lot. And your Daddy loves them."

"While we were waiting for the Wedding March, Daddy and I got very close. His eyes teared up."

"He's a good man, Doreen."

"I know."

"Here now, let me look at you. We really need a full length mirror" she mused, looking at a stack of hymnals, "but..."

I turned slowly. "Hems, tucks, shoes..."

"We'd better get you outside now. Doreen?"

"What."

"Daddy and I are proud of you, and we love you always. Live a life good and true."

I held her close, so close.

Outside, George and I were greeted with a shower of rice and yelling airmen. We made it down the steps to the sound of bells, and got to the Chrysler. It had been polished and a hubcap had been found, although it didn't match. The grill in front was still offering its gaptoothed grin, and empty tin cans were tied to the rear bumper. Two small flags were mounted on the radiator cap: a Royal Air Force Ensign and the Stars and Stripes. Butch opened the trunk and laughed at the fishing rods, wondering out loud where we would find time, and in the raucous, good natured hollering that ensued I became acutely aware of Bill standing close by. He got me with a face full of rice.

Chapter 25

THE CHRYSLER NOSED its way along the old logging road, probing with its headlights. We had the heater on against a north Georgia September. Beyond the windshield the Blue Ridge mountains were black shadows blocking out the stars against the clear night. I sat close to George with Melsie Mae's preserves tucked in beside me, along with Freddie's book. It was a marvelous small volume called, *Famous Steps from Fred and Ginger*. The inscription, written in Freddie's distinctive British hand said, 'For Doreen, who always made me look good.' The car's instrument lights glowed and the seat leather was pleasantly warm. We were alone, it seemed, in the vast northern wilderness. I looked out at the scenery trapped in the headlights. Dead trunks of giant chestnuts, victims of ruthless logging in the Nineteenth Century, were like old bones bleached by rain and sun. As the car rocked over a hump, the wedding tin cans clinked in the trunk. I cuddled closer to George.

"Different up here," George said, one hand resting comfortably on the wheel.

"Yes, it is."

"You don't have this feeling of isolation back in middle Georgia."

A deer teetered off the road ahead of us, its eyes luminous, then it was gone.

"The mountains do it. And the trees. All kinds up here. Black walnut, red maple. I like the Sycamores."

"Hold the wheel for me while I light my pipe."

"Okay."

"Hope we're on the right road."

"We are." I turned the flashlight onto the notepaper with our instructions written down, along with a hand drawn map.

"Bring enough tobacco for the weekend?"

"Of course."

"What did you think of the wedding?"

"Doreen!"

"I know. I keep asking."

"And I keep answering. It was good. I just wish Mum and my sister could've been there. All the people close to us were there." He squeezed my hand. "It was a beautiful wedding, Doreen, just right for us, who we are."

"I missed Wendy and Barbara."

"I know. These things happen, it's wartime. We could've ended up in a J.P.'s office."

I fingered my wedding ring, turning its gold round and round. "How does your ring feel?"

George smiled into the gloom. "I give up!"

"Come on, this is my big day."

"It feels different, how's that? It taps against my pipe sometimes."

"But you like it."

"Yes. And I'll always remember when you put it on my finger."

"And it'll never come off. Just like your mother's ring, even with her arthritis."

George hesitated.

"George."

"I'll always wear it, Doreen, but on flight ops I think all crews must leave their personal belongings in a locker."

"The Ronson lighter with the drifter on it...?"

"Coins, pens, everything."

"Oh. But what about that air gunner who smoked sixty cigarettes on a mission?"

"I forgot him. But I think that's what the orders make clear. Then we put it all on again when we get back."

"Oh," I shuddered in the dark, feeling the war closing in like some prowling beast.

"That's the turn ahead, isn't it? The cabin should be just back off this road."

We got out of the car, leaving the headlights on to see our way. The cabin was a functional single story giving off a smell of cedar and a feeling of shadows, mysterious in the moonlight.

"Got the torch?"

I handed George the flashlight.

"I'll try the key. Supposed to be a note inside on the kitchen table."

I breathed deeply, stretching my legs, smelling the freshness of the air, the mix of pine and cedar. "I'll get the groceries." My voice was constricted by bomber operations and the war that lay thousands of miles away beyond the mountains. As I opened the trunk I resolved to be brighter, carry it, not wallow in it. Young men were over Germany right now, while I clinked around amongst wedding tin cans.

"Good," George called out. "There's a can opener and matches next to the note."

I got to the door with the grocery bags just as the match flared and I looked inside. "Oh, it's so nice! What does the note say?"

"Hey! Don't come in!"

"What?"

"I get to carry you across the threshold."

"Oooooh!"

"Put down the groceries."

"s'okay."

"Put down the wretched groceries! Where's your romance, woman?"

He carried me into the cabin, and I had a quick panorama of the big chairs and table, nature pictures, and a mounted deer head, its glass eyes glistening like marbles. "My Viking," I said.

"My southern belle." He kissed me and put me down, then he swept me up, crushing me to him, while outside night sounds echoed against the mountains, and car headlights offered harsh beams, and grocery bags tipped, letting cans roll and cookies slide. I buried him in kisses.

"George?"

"Uuhmm."

"I have some things planned for tonight."

"So do I."

I pinched him. "I...I've got to get changed, I've brought this outfit."

"Ah."

"So we need to slow down."

"Set the stage."

"Yes."

"Pick up the groceries."

"Yes."

"Turn the car lights off. Close the front door."

"George!"

He kissed me brusquely on the forehead. "Let me look around the kitchen and check on things."

"Okay." I watched him look again at the note on the counter. "Says here there are tea bags for me. That was thoughtful."

I took his hand. "Let's look around. There's another oil lamp over there. Let me light it."

"Okay."

"You swept me up and you don't even know where the bedroom is," I said, blowing out the match.

"It's over there. I checked."

"Done this before, have you?"

He stood there, his gaze not unlike the deer's on the wall.

"Just so long as I'm the last, George," I said, kissing his cheek. "First in this bed and last everywhere else."

He took my hand and I shivered. The quiver ran through me and he felt it. "Tonight in so many ways, is yours, Doreen."

"You were right. I am nervous."

He kissed me then, gently holding me and stroking my hair. "I don't know what you're going to wear, but I know you'll be beautiful."

Once in the bathroom with my overnight bag and the door shut behind me, I closed my eyes and exhaled, listening to my heart. When I was ready I looked around. The bathroom was cedar log with bright yellow curtains on the window and a heavy-duty shower curtain. The washbasin sparkled in the cozy flicker from the oil lamp. A pine smell came from the lamp, mingling with cedar, unobtrusive and comforting. I had the thought that this fragrance was not offered to everyone who ventured to this cabin in the Blue Ridge foothills. My face was calm in the mirror, my eyes and pupils wide, the line of my jaw touched by deep shadow at my throat. I stared at me. I stared at this outer expression of who I was. Some maturity around the eyes, but also anxiety. I had learned to trust my body with George. There had been boundaries, some of them lowered in heat, some in a giving joy, but the final rite of passage remained.

I held up my impossibly small silk nightie and the most gloriously impractical underpants a farm girl ever wore, and I made a face at me in the mirror. My giggle slipped loose, alarmingly loud.

"Just what's going on in there, Doreen?"

"Nothing."

"I want heavy sighs, not giggles."

"Phooey."

"Come 'ere. I'll give you giggles."

"I'm not ready." I looked at my silk encased breasts.

"I've found a Reader's Digest."

"Don't you dare!"

The bedroom was a dusky amber from the lamps, a comfortable place for journeys and barriers, and long roamings across familiar landscapes. I need not have worried. We gamboled in known joys then ventured forward, nerve-edged and excited, this time not having to rein in, to hold back. I explored my lover with fingertips and found the Dunkirk scars, but he gave no sign, no intake of breath, no word, no twisting away... We entwined and turned, close, so close, in a dreamy halflight, but I knew a quick fear. This should be easy because I was helping, and I wanted, I wanted; but we clung on that brink in flickering shadows and I bit down on my lip in frustration, then he pinched me — hard! I yelled, then everything imploded and he was part of me. Roiling senses and discovered textures, alive and raw, and greedy. So greedy. Later, sweating and vital, my intellect kicked in.

"That was some pinch," I said.

"Never to be forgotten. Where's the champagne?"

"How long have you planned that pinch?"

"Didn't know if I'd have to."

"All those pinches I gave you, and you had that one in store for me. You were saving it up."

He held up the champagne. "I have two glasses for the occasion," he said, reaching under the bed for them, "to celebrate Womanhood."

We lay on the bed, watching the bubbly go into the glasses. When they were full he put the bottle on the floor and got up on one elbow and looked at me. "I love you, Doreen. You're my bonnie lass and my beautiful wife and I'll love you always." Then he kissed away my tears.

Tap, tap, tap.

"What's that?" I said.

"Me. I'm tapping out Morse code on my pipe bowl with my wedding ring. Guess what it is."

"I don't know."

"Guess."

Tap, tap, tap.

"'I love you'?"

"Terrific. Got it first time."

"George."

"What."

"Please don't tap Morse code on your pipe bowl with your wedding ring."

"It bothers you."

"Yes."

"Okay."

Thinking back, that was the most bizarre thing I had

ever said in my life.

"George," I said, as he refilled my glass of bubbly.
"Uuhmm."
"Do you know about moonshine and rev'nooers?"
"Revenuers?"
"No. We say, 'rev'nooers.' The people who chase the people who make moonshine and sell it."
"They're up here?"
"They're everywhere."
"Really."
"Some of the moonshine chemicals used to ferment the mash can destroy your stomach lining, nervous system and brain."
"Potent stuff."
"Right. But the moonshiners are not criminals. Not really. Did you know that?"
"I think this second glass is enough for you."
"Did you know that?"
"No."
"Anybody turns him in becomes an enemy. Like in the Hatfields and the McCoys."
I sipped my champagne. "Moonshiners work in hard times, trying to add a little to their tiny farm income in this poor rocky land. Sometimes they teach their wives and kids how to make it."
"Uuuhmm."
"And law officers must catch the moonshiner working his still, or he's not caught. You can have moonshine machinery in full operation on your own land, but if no one's around, the rev'nooers can't charge him."
"Ah,"
"What ah?"

"You didn't get those panties in Camilla."

I looked at the diminutive pile of silk on the hardwood floor. "I made them out of a parachute."

"You lying wench."

"Just allow me some secrets."

"Straight ahead Doreen, willing to bend things when expedient."

"Absolutely."

"These rev'nooers and moonshiners. Maybe we can find a still around here."

"I don't recommend it, George. These mountain men are not to be messed with. They're likely to spit a stream of tobacco juice in your eyes, blind you, then kick you where the bullets didn't go."

"Tell me about Hartlepool."

"I've told you about Hartlepool."

"Tell me more, while I put this butterfly kiss on your cheek." I began blinking my eyelashes on him. "What's that in code?"

"What's what?"

"That. Feel." Blink, blink, blink.

"Three short, three long. Good grief, SOS!"

"It's all I know. I remember it from the girl scouts."

"Doreen."

"Uuhmm."

"Don't blink Morse on my cheek with your eyelashes."

"Okay."

"We're sweaty." I said.

"You still smell nice. Is that a new perfume?"

"Mama gave it to me. I'm hungry, are you hungry?"

"Yes."

"Let's get Melsie Mae's preserves and some bread."

"Okay."

"And we'll drink a toast to William and Melissa Horton."

"Okay."

Later we fell asleep across each other, with our peach preserves and champagne, exhausted and sated, while the Blue Ridge Mountains pressed their infinite weight to the center of the earth and blotted out the stars.

Midmorning of the next day found us on an Oostanaula stream bank with fishing rods and trappings. George had chosen a beautiful restful spot with maples and spruce leaning across a quiet pooling backwater. The sun was gaining height and it dappled the grass and shadowed leaves. The air was fresh and pummeled by bird cries. I watched George's first cast. His hand came back as he talked.

"Casting grip must be firm yet light, your Dad says. How's this?"

"Looks good."

"Then the backcast like so, don't tangle in the trees, and..."

The line whined out and plopped into the pooling waters. Ripples went out in lazy circles. George stood stiff in his waders.

"Not bad," I said.

"How about the spot I'm in?"

"What did Daddy say?"

"Well, he said a great deal, but what I remember was, pecking orders for fish are based on size. Big ones select a choice spot to watch stuff drift by."

"And where's the choice spot?"

"Well, I aimed for that undercut bank. I'm probably too far out from it."

"Leave it. See what happens."

"Okay."

I watched a rabbit lurch quietly in a grassy bank, its nose twitching. "George?"

"What."

"What are those planes like, the ones in our codes for when we write letters?"

"Well, they're all four engine bombers. I'm likely to be assigned to one of them. But I've never been near them, Doreen. All I know is scuttlebutt stuff."

"Such as?"

"Oh, the Stirling is a gentleman's aeroplane, flies well, but has a low ceiling. Keeps it down near the antiaircraft fire, unfortunately."

"Don't you like the Lancaster?"

"The Lanc? From what I hear the Lanc is a superb bombing plane. Every bomber pilot wants Lancs." George reeled in slowly and looked at his fishing fly. "Y'know, I'm not even sure if this is the right thing to use."

"And the other plane?" I prompted.

"The Halifax, a bit of a clod hopper, I hear. Heavy on the controls, a drudge. No breeding at all, you have to heave and jerk the thing along."

"I see." I sat in the warm shafts of sunlight and bending grass. Dank, mossy smells wafted from the water. I tried to calculate my husband's chances of surviving a tour of bomber operations.

"Nice of Melsie Mae to give us those preserves," he said.

"She's a gem, she really is. Daddy's fixed up her little house? (I could not, even then, say 'shotgun shack', which is what it really was.) "No more 'shiverin' an' a paperin.'"

"What?" He looked up from the water, turning in his waders, a surprised look on his face.

"That's what negro hands call it. Mushing newspapers into sodden wet clumps to fill in cracks between the siding planks, then laying newspapers flat to keep out the cold. That won't happen for Melsie Mae."

"I'm glad! Hey! Did you see that!"

"What?"

"Over there, a flash of silver."

"Sorry, I missed it."

"I'll cast again. This is really quite nice, restful."

"You get your rest, George."

"You have plans."

"I have plans. Try over there, by that tree branch."

"Okay. Hold it like a ping pong paddle, not too tight, there we go!"

"George."

"Ah, that went well, a nice snap to it. See that wrist flick?"

"George."

"Uuuhmm."

"When you come back here to live, after the war, what will you miss from Hartlepool and England?"

"Not much...too cold up there, damp!"

"Seriously."

"Seriously?" He was quiet, gazing at the water as if reading secrets there, then, "I'll miss Mum and my sister, Marian, of course. And I'll miss the sense of history, of age and traditions. I'll miss my home looking out on the North Sea, and the binoculars on the windowsill to study ships and porpoises; and Mum and Marian playing the piano while I look at the sea. I'll also miss the sense of close community, like New Year's and 'First Footing', and carol singers at the door, and inviting them in for a glass of port or sherry. Here our distances are considerable, the car is central, and it changes things a bit. It sounds odd, but I'll miss the general mix of people, old and young, going to the shops with their shopping bags. Watching middle aged women bundle up, riding bicycles, their knees and faces red from the cold. When I was a boy, my first job was rushing to the shops and carrying a woman's shopping bag for her. Then she might give me a penny or two, and I'd go haring back to help someone else. Picked up some good money like that, and I knew a lot of the locals. From there I got a job on a milk round with a chap named Tom. A horsecart pulling crates of milk. Mostly, I'll miss the North Sea and the pull of it in my life. But now I have my lucky North Sea pebble on a Savannah beach, so I've got some home here too."

"I hear Greenwich Village is a community of sorts," I said.

"Probably is. When you go, just watch out for that Bohemian stuff."

"So you delivered milk on a horse and wagon." My farm girl curiosity stirred.

"Right. I'll miss that too, the clink of milk bottles on a morning. And Old Nigs, the horse, he would walk forward to each house, he knew his route blindfolded..."

"Nigs?" I said.

"Yes."

"Short for what?" I watched George stiffen and go silent. "Short for what, George?"

"Well…?"

I stood up, incredulous, outrage pumping through me. "It was Nigger, wasn't it! You're horse was called Nigger!"

"Doreen, this is hard to explain, but…"

"Jeezus, George!"

"I'm sorry. I hadn't given it a thought for years and years, and now all of a sudden…"

I launched myself from the water's edge, landing on his back, wrapping my legs around him and pounding him on the head. We both went under and came up coughing.

"I called him Nigs, you daft woman!"

"You devious bastard!"

We went under again and the fishing rod floated towards the sparkling fast water, then it disappeared.

The cabin was quiet and soothing. We closed the curtains against the sun's rays and rekindled the oil lamps. We tore the Reader's Digest in half so we each had a section and stretched out on the bed, with me cuddling in. The sour earthy smells of the Oostanaula River had been washed from our bodies, and our clothes lolled on an improvised line.

"Soon be going home." George said.

"Three days isn't enough. Not with the car travel."

"You're still glad we came here, though."

"Yes."

"I could have done without the dunking."

"You deserved it."

"You must have the last page to my article on Victory Gardens."

I squirreled away under the covers. "Don't think so."

"Yes, you do. Let me see."

"No."

"Let me see!"

"No!"

"Wretched woman!"

We rolled and rolled around the bed while our wild-eyed deer looked on. Somewhere in that jousting our moods changed, and our flailing arms settled into a cradled loving. Our needs for each other, fresh and exciting and barely explored, consumed us. I cried out his name over and over as our needs took us, until I could stand it no more and I clawed him to me. Fright, fright, ride through, ride through like the Greyhound...scream...

Afterward, I could see through a crack in the curtain our fishing clothes lolling on the line, drying out. The sun was descending, molten gold. I ached, my body hot and slack.

"George."

"Uuhmm."

"That was a bit frightening."

"No." He kissed my eyes, my cheeks, my forehead, neck, throat.

"I lost control."

"But you were safe."

"I was safe."

"Yes."

I moved my arms around his neck, keeping him close. We lay like that for a long time. Long enough for the sun to withdraw, streaming its pink veil, for animals to curl and burrow, relinquishing the brightness of day to the dark creatures. Out at the pooling backwaters, trout bellied over rocks. Then came the moonshadows. A long time. That was when George shook, just once, as if chilled. And against the warmth and musk of me, he gave up his burden. "What is it?" I asked. I thought he wasn't going to say anything, just stay there, embedded in me.

"Did I kill him, Doreen?"

I held my breath and my reply. No fast words. Gather them carefully, you wordsmith, you all too cerebral creature: find something in your little girl's heart that was safely stored for Uncle William and give it now, give it now...

"Clive chose his defining moment. For himself, for the honor of his family, for all he lived by. Don't take that from him, George. When you ask that question, that's what you do. Don't strip him of his gesture, his courage and everything he held good and decent. You mustn't do that."

We lay still, so still, and the moment passed, and I wondered if I had helped or added to his burden. The mood lifted, like a fog scurling off some landscape of the heart. I poked him. "Penny for them."

"Sorry, I didn't mean..."

"Come on, what're you thinking?"

"Actually, I was thinking about Roy. Remember Roy? At the Americus train depot? He got told off for making a joke about Scottish kilts in front of you."

I smiled. "Jarrell's Feed and Seed."

"So long ago."

"Yes."

"He just got the DFC."

"I know you're proud of him, George." It would be years before I heard the rest of it. Roy bringing back his Stirling bomber with dead and wounded on board, his hands burned to sticks. 'Shouldn't he have got the Victoria Cross?' 'The British are stingy with their medals.'

"Remember John Piggott?" I asked.

"Yes, the lad killed in the training crash, when I came to instruct."

"He called you a tough egg, did I tell you that?"

"Some tough egg."

I wanted to answer, but I let the words fall back, unsaid.

We drove back to our small rented house in Ft. Valley and George immediately resumed flying duties. Archie, Haggis, and Freddie were gone. Butch, Bill and George grew very close, bonded in part by the old Chrysler which they shared to get to Cochran Field. Logbooks grew fatter with flying time. We got into the habit of dinner once a week, with me cooking and getting 'new bride' help from Mama. One night Butch took over both our meat ration and the kitchen and prepared a magnificent meal of sausage and meatballs. It was prepared with wine and spices and wonderful talk about growing up Italian in Chicago. During those days I wrote news copy and PRO announcements, with Billy Odum even more strict on my writing now that I had a genuine contact in Greenwich Village. My Chinese puzzle box was kept under the bed. It now contained more than pilots' wings. Freddie's signed small volume of 'Fred and Ginger Dance Steps' was in there. So was a small card onto which I had carefully printed SCARLATTI. A reminder of that day and my comeuppance, and my deepened respect for my mother and father.

As war production gathered momentum the telephones became a problem. George couldn't get through on his limited time between flying classes. We got into the habit of dropping the St. Bruno Flake tobacco tin with a message. I would watch the BT-13 curve away against the sky, and I would study the cadet's flying with a critical eye. My own flying was coming along, although I was not held to cadet standards, and it was strictly off the record. I had done a couple of spins and had performed one, rather erratic, barrel roll. But George would not instruct me in landings or takeoffs. It was something I never pushed, because I think the answer lay with losing Jimmy Peterson and John Piggott; and our trip to Hawkinsville and the mortuary records: 'Cause of death, multiple head fractures, incineration...' It was one of those quirky things, intensely private and irrational, but all too real in the fear of great loss. There was an almost childlike holding on to what we had.

Georgia crops, nourished on sun and soil, moved towards bloom and unfurled leaf, and we went on picnics when we could, I still went to cadet dances and offered support at the Idle Hour Club. But now that I was married, and to an instructor at that, I was perceived as a rather matriarchal figure. Cadets began talking to me about their personal problems. 'What do you think about...' And George and I grew exquisitely close. A montage of jazz concerts, usually bebop sessions by young sidemen on their way up: Bud Powell, Dizzy Gillespie, Kenny Clarke, and the incredible Charlie Parker. We had everything, everything, and we rejoiced in it and were grateful for it.

His Majesty's Government summoned George in early November, and we joined the millions of other young men and women in the search for words, for assurances, as we prepared for our parting. The heartache we pressed back into those hidden places, awaiting the night, where it was assuaged in loving embraces and sweet murmurings. That's how it was on our last night together: in the darkness of our bedroom, the door closed on balloons and party hats, full ashtrays and dessert plates piled in the kitchen sink, and dance band records in sliding stacks on the carpet. We were so needful for each other as our time unwound, holding each other, filing away tactile memories for when each of us would be alone. We said our talk, the things each of us had secretly prepared to say at this moment. We planned how I'd get letters in Greenwich Village (care of the newspaper, at least at first). We talked about possible gaps in the timing of letters across the Atlantic; but we talked of them being late, never lost. Throughout that last night in Ft. Valley, the Pilot and the Reporter drew into one, in flesh, spirit, and heart. How blessed and lucky we had been. We held each other until the sun came up.

Chapter 26

I SAT ON a bench in Washington Square wearing a fall coat against the New York chill. I had an egg salad sandwich fixed in my cold water-shared bathroom walk up. The marvelous pastrami on rye that I craved had run amok in my digestive tract and given me bouts of throwing up. It had also attacked my wallet. So, egg salad on white. It was a beautiful sunny day, and I took the time to reflect.

First in priority after my terrible ache for George, was New York's contradictions and paradoxes. Not knowing a neighbor across the hall, yet knowing a father confessor, a greengrocer, three blocks away. I had such a grocer. He cared when my feet hurt. He cared about George as he threw an extra carrot in my bag. In closeness was anonymity; in distance, closeness. In the Spring, I was told, and I took it on faith along with my guidebooks, 'everything bloomed', a noble surge of growth in window boxes and brightly displayed greenery on the chilly brick of buildings.

I swallowed a bite of sandwich, chewing carefully, making it last.

But I was starting to fit in and I was holding my own. I had arrived to the raucous, racy surge of City life, my enunciated diction lost on the babble. I ached for George, forever looking at my watch, adding time zones, allowing for Double Summer Time, and wondering if he were flying through a hostile night.

'I miss you, my Darling Doreen, and the South, especially those pecans...'

Halifaxes. He was flying Halifaxes, the drudge, the clodhopper with no breeding, the four engine bomber you had to heave and jerk along...

Somewhere in England. November 30, 1942

...I've been able to see Mum and Marian, which has been wonderful. I've told them all about you, how your eyes go from blue to gray and back again, and I've shared photos. But they're insatiable! I know you're busy, but if you could write them again...

...I played my Duke Ellington records! Remember when we saw him at the Biltmore? Marian has done a bang-up job of caring for them. Bombing here has eased, Mum tells me, and it was quiet during my overnight...

My walk-up room and shared bath was off 8th Street in the Village, close to a jostling meld of odd bookstores, tailor shops, groceries, drugstores and dimly lit cafes with poetry thumbtacked out front. I had been lucky on two counts. I was close to the Village 'Opinion' and Mr. Sam Rowland, editor, my long-term hope for permanent employment; and also in just getting the room at all. Rents were skyrocketing, and as it was I had to go over budget. I had dug in, investing in sensible flat shoes for walking and a full-length coat against the cold. My funds, made up of George's money, my own nest egg, and my parents' money, were going too quickly. But while I searched for stories for Sam Rowland, I used my ingenuity. My triumphs included typing papers for New York University students, rapidly using up Billy Odum's extra ribbons given with my wedding present typewriter; and ironing shirts for an itinerant poet one flight up who had a white shirt fetish and a little money to support it. He was a mess and he smelled of stale sweat, and he read his poetry for food at the Village Vanguard. But no one could find fault with his shirts, thank you very much, as Freddie would say. With time I got more savvy, a respected trait in Manhattan. I began bartering 'straight dope' about the South to students and newspaper people I was getting to know. 'Your poem suffers from cliches, Maxwell. You've got to get inside a Southern belle's guts, not just her bodice. Don't be content with northern stereotypes...

Somewhere in England. December 2, 1942

...I'm enjoying English tea! Dark and strong, with an occasional tea leaf floating in it. Marvelous! I tried to explain iced tea to Mum and Marian, but I just got this look...
...I'm sorry I can't give too much detail, Darling, on flight ops.
...a lot of training, of course, getting used to our aeroplane. But I can tell you that I've got the best crew! My navigator is Jamaican, very black, with a marvelous lilting English accent. When he gives me a change in course it has such a lovely lilt that I think we're flying to rainbow's end. When we were choosing crews, a typical British, muddle through, find somebody operation, I found Cyril, my navigator with Jock, my tail-gunner. Jock insisted they were a package deal. I liked their grit... I daydream (when off duty) about landing our four-engined bomber in that small town with that bad cop. (Thank God I had Billy to turn to. I never did thank you for that, Doreen.)

I was digging deeper, sending down my Southern roots into the cracks of New York concrete, learning and making mistakes, but going forward. I picked up on lore, adopting it, chameleon-like. Villagers retire late, rise late, and a true Villager is born facing Washington Square (and a true Cockney is born to the sound of Bow Bells). I finished my sandwich and folded the wax paper and bag. It was not yet greasy. Good for a second usage at least. Wendy, where are you? Hobnobbing with J. Edgar? How long will my wax paper last, Wendy? I'll barter an apple and delicate sandwich and a wedge of cheese. And John and the Cockneys, and an egg sandwich at the London Science Muscum. I knew what I was doing, of course. I was sparking off old memories of loved people. Homesickness and heartache for one's lover and husband can do that. Where was I...yes, lore..., a Village saying has it that there are many hours before midnight, and I had read in a discarded pamphlet George Bernard Shaw's admonition that nothing makes a Bohemian faster than a regular paycheck from doting parents. That one I filed away. Straight ahead, Doreen. Make it on your own.

Somewhere in England. December 5, 1942

... when I fly, Darling, I do not think of you. To do so, to relax, is to court catastrophe. We're on the job right from briefing, if not sooner, to engine shutdown. I ride my crew hard, but they understand why. To get us to the target and back! And nobody sneaks a smoke on board. We're constantly checking and rechecking. I polish the cockpit perspex (Plexiglas) until every speck is erased. Next time I see a speck, it could be a nightfighter or an off course bomber, but it won't be a bit of oil or dirt. Seconds count in this business...
...but on the ground, off duty, I'm greedy for you. I stored up so much, Doreen, so much. I hope I gave to you as much as you gave to me. Sometimes my wed-

ding ring taps against my pipe bowl and I smile... I'd give anything if you could bat those eyelashes on my cheek. SOS! Thank heaven for the Girl Scouts (Girl Guides, over here).

I ached to the fringe of sanity for George, living on his letters in my mail slot, and coming to grips with the Village in particular and Manhattan in general. I referred to the Village, romantically, as my beat, even if I still didn't have a fulltime job. I'd go and stand outside El Chico's and try for a news piece on the introduction of the Rumba and Flamenco (Freddie, where are you when I need you). Or pick up on Communist dialectic in the political ferment, a source of trouble in years ahead for the intelligentsia. Or stand outside Nick's jazz club, or hang around Julius' or Goody's. A shattering of Camilla dreams of Greenwich Village was the inundation of soldiers and sailors who turned Saturday nights on Sheridan Square and upper MacDougal Street into Honky Tonk, Anywhere, USA.

But the Village was a membrane, absorbing, using, excreting. Clifford Odets, Edgar Allan Poe, Jackson Pollock, the air was redolent with artists and their work. I don't think there was anywhere below Fourteenth Street that was untouched by art or literature. It was sunk into brick and mortar as well as collective memory. I sought out trees in Washington Square, and studied the egalitarian mix of Fifth Avenue well-to-do, college students, and impoverished Italians from the southwest neighborhood, all enjoying the scenery and sunshine. The first time I had done this, I found myself drawn to the Italians. T h e y interested me, and I remembered all that Butch had shared with me. I filed away some thoughts then went to my first meeting with editor Sam Rowland. Already it seems ages ago.

I handed him his letter to Billy Odum. I waited, trying to weigh him up. He was an elegant man, turning to fat as he moved through his late fifties, and he spoke with a lazy resonant voice and fine diction. He was rendered slightly less imposing by his ashtray with its cigar stubs, and a fleck of ash on his shirt.

"Ah, yes, Mr. Odum. When did you get here? How'd you come? Train?"

I told him of my pilgrimage while he cut the end off a cigar and lit it.

"Cigar bother you?"

"No. My father smokes King Edwards'."

"Great. Your husband is in the Royal Air Force, I understand."

"Yes, sir."

"You're bucking a trend, Doreen. May I call you Doreen? Most people around here think that once you're married, there's not much point left in Village life. Who wants children in with the struggling and the anguished?"

"Are you married, Mr. Rowland?"

"Yes. Okay, I live here. Touche." He smiled, the cigar glowed, growing the first of its white, quality ash. "Mr. Odum told me a bit about you. I had a hard time cutting through his accent."

"He probably had trouble with yours," I said, bridling.

He gave me a granite look, then softened. "Loyal. I like that."

I let my purse drop back to the floor.

"Doreen, your big advantage is a fresh pair of eyes. That's good. But you can be distracted by the obvious."

"That's bad," I said.

He smiled. "No pieces on drunken poets, anguished painters, or New York glitter. Try for something else."

"Any tips?"

"Nope. Good luck." He flicked the cigar at the ashtray.

"Any objections if I have that piece of shelf over there to call my own?"

"No. What do you need it for?"

"I've a new typewriter at my room. I'd like to leave my old one here. Also I keep index cards in a shoebox. I'd like them here too."

He nodded. "I want you to meet Eddie, he's out right now. Brilliant with a flash camera, but don't say I said so. Bring me a good story, Doreen, and who knows?"

Somewhere in England. December 7, 1942

A year since Pearl Harbor. What a year it's been. The U.S. Eighth Air Force are taking heavy casualties with their new daylight bombing. It's still trial and error for them, and errors from learning the best tactics are costing them. Fine men, such fine men. There is a U.S. base near us. We sometimes end up at the same pub and Jock, my tail-gunner, kids them about the B-17. "There goes fifty thousand rounds of ammunition and one small bomb." They get back at him by calling him a Limey, which sends his Scottish blood into a turmoil. They get his goat every time. It doesn't say much for Jock that he keeps falling for it. An endearing fact has been Cyril mixing in at the pubs. We know that some communities haven't been so lucky. I keep writing "Somewhere in England" on my letters. I'm afraid I've been influenced by your journalism! John Steinbeck is over here as a war correspondent and he's covering the U.S. and British war efforts. He wrote a nice piece on American versus British ways of talking. He made the point that whether the Yanks said, "They shot the hell out of us", or the British said, "Things got a little tricky", it makes no difference. Boys were doing the best they could for their countries...

I watched the Italians walking around Washington Square. I went searching for an Italian restaurant, my only guide being what would Butch think? "Don't be taken in by a bunch of wine bottles in straw baskets with candles stuck in them, Doreen. You wanna eat Italian, check the floor corners for dust. And look for family photos in alcoves where the family and not the trade can see them." I found it. Nello's. Like the corn crib it was rich in amber light and golden mood, with sunrays shafting in. It was warm in atmosphere but cool on this Fall day. It was closed, but two small tables were outside. Strings of red and green peppers lay across them. A dark, round-faced man was hanging them on walls splashed with Mediterranean seas and billowing sails. He had large, gentle eyes and a freshly ironed apron. I smiled too brightly but he was patient. We found our common ground, Butch's sausages and meatballs, this spice and that spice, in another world Down South. "And Chicago, Mr. Nello? Have you family in Chicago?"

I sat across from Sam Rowland, my stomach in knots. I'd probably lose my shelf, my foot of ground in journalism, which is really what that piece of shelving was about. How would I be able to tell George I'd failed?

"This is Nello's, on Eighth?"

"Yes, sir."

"Great lasagne."

A young scrawny man sat at a desk watching me, playing with a camera. He smiled at me. I bit my lip, eyes back on Rowland.

"*Salerno.*"

"Yes. He's worried about his mother. He can't write, all he does is worry." Rowland's fingertips moved across the triple spaced type. "This here, 'I 'ave trouble, Mrs. Westcott, they don' unnerstan' I'm American, my good wife, Sophia, she's American. Some sailors come, insult me, call me lousy wop, *Fascisti!* I am as American as they are. I serve good food, I owe nobody.'" His eyes came up to meet mine.

"Good. Good piece. Stay in the Village, Doreen. Work our community. That's what the *Opinion* is all about. You'll need to develop sources. Talk to Eddie over there. Eddie! Help her find her sea legs."

"Sure." Eddie smiled at me. He could be an English cadet except for his accent, which I learned later was pure Brooklyn.

Sam Rowland studied me, taking his time. He was an editor thinking, which could be good or bad. With Billy Odum I scored about eighty percent good, the rest bad. "Got some college?"

"No, sir. I didn't think…"

"You might want to think." He flipped through the pages in front of him. "We'll need to chop it. Don't have the space."

"I can do that."

"This reference to landscapes, I like it."

"I couldn't develop it, Mr. Rowland. I tried to keep it short, tight."

"So tell me now. About landscapes."

"Well," I was at a loss, conscious of Eddy's steady but twinkling stare, some kind of setting up for a photo not taken. I think he saw life through a lens. "I…I just have a theory…"

"Which is what?"

"Well, I think that all minorities, radicals and ostracized groups like homosexuals, negroes, Jews, women..."

"Women?" The cigar rolled around his mouth then he trapped it again.

"...they resort to the same imagery in their writings and art to express their rage. I call these common images landscapes." I was acutely embarrassed and I looked at my once more short nails. I was being pushed into talking about things I was still just figuring out for myself. All in a year of upheaval and joy with George, and grappling emotionally with my parents, and the wisdom of Billy Odum.

"Fire. A landscape?"

"Self immolation, incineration." The BT-13 rolled onto its back and headed down.

"And the South?"

"The South is a landscape, it was my start point. Madness, insanity nurtured in a beguiling sultry array of fragrances, deadly flowers that end up as emotional rot — look, Mr. Rowland, I'm sorry to have troubled you, I'll edit this piece and..."

He leaned back, his hands clasped behind his head, so very much like Billy. "You're getting all this from your reading, you read a lot?"

"Some. Mostly I've just been thinking."

He smiled and his eyes were kind. "You've just been thinking."

"Yes, sir."

"Doreen, you're not what I expected."

"Is that good or bad?"

"I expected a segregationist."

"I struggle with that. Even now. My father is a segregationist, but he's a thinking man and times are different, the war and everything. My best friend doesn't like negroes except as servants. George helped me a lot."

"Helped? Not a good word, Doreen. It implies a way of thinking is wrong, something to move away from."

"Helped is the right word."

"How?"

"He took me to hear Billie Holiday and Teddy Wilson."

"He what!"

"In Atlanta. The colored district. J.J. Lemon's jazz club."

He wiped a hand across his jaw. "Jesus Christ." His hand stopped, and he looked through his fingers at me and smiled. "You like Billie?"

"She moved me. She did 'Strange Fruit'. I've never been the same since."

"We have some fine jazz in New York, up in the East Fifties."

"And Harlem, of course. Minton's Playhouse. Thelonious Monk and Dizzie Gillespie are developing Bebop. Some of it's out of Ravel, Prokofieff and Schoenberg."

He thrust his face across the desk at me. "You went up there, alone?" I took a deep breath. Tell him, tell it all. "I sit in the public library. It's warm and I can rest my feet. I research." I smiled, seeing the irony for the first time. "I read about what's happening just a subway ride from the library."

"Been to Nick's, here in the Village?"

"I've stood outside. I can't afford to go in and I don't have an escort. Ditto El Chico's."

Sam Rowland stared at me. "Mrs. Westcott, you have royally screwed up my day."

"I'm sorry."

"Don't be." He delicately trimmed ash over the ash-tray, then the cigar was back in his mouth.

"Eddie!"

"Yass-suhh, boss."

"Take Doreen to Nick's. Doreen, a jazz piece if you please, three hundred words." He grinned at me. "Paper doesn't grow on trees, y'know."

"That's a joke," Eddie said.

"You must get lots of jazz pieces. Like anguished artists and drunken poets."

"I'll play a hunch on this one."

I watched him think.

"Look. I don't want you to do anything right now, it's way too soon. But I want you to think about something."

"Yes, sir?"

"Go take a course at NYU. Comparative literature. Maybe creative writing."

"I...I don't have the money..."

"Find the money. You're holding life and limb together. Anyway, not now. Just think about it, okay?"

I nodded.

"Meanwhile, I like this piece on Nello's." He took out a large black ledger and opened it to reveal pages of blank checks. He began to fill out a check with a pen carefully taken from his drawer. "One thing, Doreen."

"Yes, sir?"

"Don't ever use this pen. I've got the nib broken in just right."

"Okay."

He looked up at me, eyes sharp. "I like the way you stuck up for Odum. I value loyalty. Too bad the poets around here don't think it's worth writing about. If I help you get established, Doreen, I want loyalty. No contract, a handshake is it."

I reached across and shook his hand, and he handed me a check for fifteen dollars. "Mr. Rowland, this is too much."

"I decide the money. Maybe next time you'll belly-ache it's not enough. Trust me. I know writing, I know money."

"Okay."

"Eddie, help Doreen clear off that shelf and buy her a soda. Tell her things. Don't take long."

"Sure," Eddie said.

"And at Nick's, one round only. Nurse it."

Eddie's smile faded.

I got up clutching my fifteen dollars.

"Congrats, Doreen." Eddie said, his smile back again. "A New York paycheck. You're big time."

Chapter 27

ABOUT A WEEK later New York began at full tilt, City
paced, complicated, a Bebop riff. Nothing ran to schedule that day: pencil points broke, words wouldn't flow.
And I got a blister on my heel when I thought I was
through with them and had run out of Band Aids. But
that night I gave a whoop and grabbed from the mail slot
the several letters with British stamps on them. I flew up
the stairs to the dismay of my clean-shirted poet.

"Doreen. I'm communing with the Muse, stop that
racket!"

"Sorry!"

"And more care with the shirts, one had a wrinkle."

"Sorry!"

George's letters. What can be said. They were life, a
desperately beating heart. They gave everything meaning.
I always carried some in my purse, and others were kept
in my room bundled under a rubber band. George had
written six letters while we were in our rented house,
after our honeymoon. He had given them to Mama with
instructions. After he had left for England, Mama mailed
them to me one at a time. I devoured them, and I tried to
bully Mama into giving me the rest of them, but I was
firmly told, 'George wants it this way.' I still had an anx-

ious and interminable wait for those English letters with the distinctive King George VI stamps on them. And I would read my own name written in George's distinctive writing. It was childish but needed. I would soak up every aspect of each letter, pausing before opening it, saying a quick prayer. Soon the first one arrived at the *Village Opinion* office, then George had my Village address, and I fell into a reading ritual. It would begin with checking the mail slot for 'English' letters. Sometimes the slot was just a void filled with slanting sunlight, and my day would be dampened and I would lose myself in my work. But then a letter would arrive and I would greedily grab it from the mail slot. I would feel it to see how thick it was. Those would send my heart pounding. Usually our love was limited to flimsy airmail fold and lick forms. But with a letter from George in hand, any of his letters, I would charge upstairs and collapse in my special comfortable chair with its end table and photo of George and me at the lake. I would draw the framed photo closer to me, closer, closer. Then I would open the letter.

Somewhere in England. December 9, 1942

I'm a bit tired tonight, a bit tense. We have the wireless on (radio), which is cheery and relaxing. One of the chaps got a Labrador retriever named Nigger. I find it rather difficult, and I don't call him by name.
Usually I say, "Here boy!" Oddly, Cyril takes a rather superior road with it. His poise and force of character are so strong that I think the dog owner's feeling a bit defensive about the dog's name choice. Give it a couple of weeks and Cyril will have him begging for forgiveness. Seriously, Darling, after this war is over, people won't be the same; there'll be air travel, people mixing in, rubbing shoulders. It will probably get "a bit tricky"...Remember on our honeymoon when we were fishing? You made that Carole Lombard leap onto me

while I wasn't looking! (You really did thump me good, y'know!) Was I supposed to be Cary Grant? If so, it's damned strenuous playing opposite Lombard!
I love you, my Darling. Flying time is building nicely. I'll stand a good chance with Delta, I think; but I'm glad Bill wants Pan American. I don't need that caliber of competition!

My full tilt day had been spent with photographer Eddie Medlock. I had learned a lot from Eddie over a series of sodas, and we had taken an instant liking to each other. He was an artist with a lens, a man of images, not words, and he knew I understood this. So he was relaxed in talking to me, grammar and syntax not on display. He showed me the mortuary where Dorothy Kilgallen and a photographer had pinned open a corpse's eyes with toothpicks to 'make the shot.' And he had taken me to see at least the outsides of the Colony, Twenty-One, Stork Club, Toots Shors, and of course, Sardi's. 'Watch 'em, Doreen. See how's the celebs come late, so udder celebs notice? Whaddaway tuh live.' And Eddie took me to his Brooklyn and showed me, at my request, the Navy Yards. I wanted the docks, I wanted the seagulls and ships, and the smell of the sea at the Atlantic's threshold. I wanted to be close to George. By chance a Royal Navy destroyer was in for a boiler repair. The next thing we knew we had a mad party of British sailors in my small room. The accents made me homesick not for England, where I'd never been, but for Cochran Field and the South. I called out for Geordies but there were none. I showed around photos of the RAF cadets. Lots of talk about the 'Brylcreem Boys.' The jazz night at Nick's featured a once in a lifetime chance for me to hear 'Yardbird.' I blazed my story from the heart, trying to put into words my responses to Charlie Parker's lightning phrases. Sam Rowland turned it down as pretentious. No check...

I have your letter dated November 12th. I've read the ink off it! The perfume fingerprint is absolutely marvelous. Please don't stop. I have to watch the lads. They mustn't see me sniffing pages or they'll put in for a new skipper... We have a new squadron leader. He's like us in that he's not pre-war enlistment. (The tough NCO's view pre-1939 enlistments as the real RAF!) I get off lightly because of pre-war army service. The Sqn/Ldr was schooled at Eton, and yes, he does have a posh accent. But he's a fine, unpretentious sort and the chaps like him. He's not a 'make it look easy' sort; just a cool, fine man with guts. We're lucky to have him...

Somewhere in England. December 17, 1942

Just received a grand letter from your mum and dad. It's "Christine" and "Francis" now. Your dad told me to knock off calling him 'sir'. Said it was a requirement for U.S. Citizenship!

P.S. You never did give me my missing pages from that Reader's Digest.
P.P.S. Have a wonderful Xmas, darling. I love you more than words can say. Remember me to Melsie Mae and Billy. Sam Rowland sounds great!

Somewhere in England. January 15, 1943

My Darling Doreen,

I'm thinking of you right now, I'm sitting by a stream close to the field. I saw a frog and yearned for my croker sack! But England's streams are more sedate than our Georgia cypress ponds.

No croker sacks here, but no water moccasins or coral snakes either. Remember when we looked at the trees and thought about music in their branches? I do that here, too, and I wonder what melody or composer you would detect in them...

I miss you, my darling, and now in the quiet of off-duty time, I daydream about being with you, perhaps at the farm or in our Ft. Valley home. We didn't have it for long, did we? When I'm back I want us to look for a nice place to call our own, buy it, I mean...I want you in my arms, Doreen, now, right now...Remember my eunuch days? I couldn't have kept my hands off you much longer, darling, it would've...

I sat in the quiet of my room and dug my fingers into the chair arms. I drew his words from the page and enfolded myself in memories: his embrace, his indescribable touch. Then I pressed the letter to me, this lifeline to my world with its past joys and experiences to come. He would hold my hand. I moved my fingers on the chair arm enfolding a memory. He smiled behind my closed eyes. I brought the letter to my nose and sniffed at it, searching out a tang of St. Bruno Flake tobacco. It was never there. If it had carried on those letters, it had long vanished under the weight of other mail to other lovers. I remained quiet, eyes closed, savoring.

When the knock came at the door, it jarred me back. I set the letters aside and went to the door, ready to face my smelly itinerant poet. He would have to take his shirts back upstairs. But on opening the door I found Bill Trepick, dashing in his dress uniform, what they called the 'pinks and greens.'

"Bill! For heaven's sake, what are you doing here! I just got a letter from your folks, and a couple from George came today." My words tapered off as I watched Bill's face. I knew his face. I knew its laughter, intelligent eyes scanning the lake. I had seen it troubled, like the time he stayed beside the Nash, knowing George was the one. And I had seen its sadness at Oakland Cemetery as rifle volleys sounded. But this was different. A reporter's fine edge is a curse, you see. Don't let them fool you. The blade cuts both ways.

Bill pushed gently by me and closed the door. He just stood there quite still, surrounded by my New York world of chair, photo, story file shoe boxes, ironing board. He looked at my winter coat. "You going out?"

"No. I just got home and ran in with George's letters." I slipped my coat off. "What is it, Bill?"

"Doreen..."

"Because if you're in trouble," I said quickly, "you know I'll help all I can. What is it, the farm in Wisconsin?"

"I'm not in trouble. It's not that."

I smiled, but something tightened inside me, somewhere deep inside a beast prowled. "Well, that's a relief! You looked kind of tired at the door. Too much flying, I guess. Are they increasing training schedules?" I pushed the words out, using a reporter's skill to keep the concern on him, not me. Dear God, not on me.

"Doreen, look..."

There was no place to go, nowhere to dodge. The prowling beast sliced at my insides. I shook my head, backing away. I hated the anguish now in his eyes. I hated him. "Get out." I said. But he came towards me. I screamed it. "Get out! Get out! Get out!"

When his arms enfolded me they were wrong and strange, not those of reveries in a lonely bed, and I fought against them. My own anguish flailed at me, my heartbeat some cold ugly lurching; my brain closed down. I fought him, some atavistic creature in total fear of its world being consumed, its life shriveling into nothing. Then I collapsed in Bill's arms in endless sobs. The room turned, my stomach heaved, and I threw up.

Tremors die. They do. Because raw flesh can't take it. I burrowed into Bill like a seal pup, blind and deaf. I clung through the night, not moving, not speaking. I remember Bill reaching and turning out the lamp, and the ensuing darkness. I remember the darkness. In a gray dawn I found my eyes focusing on the photo of George and me at the lake. His deeply tanned face and neck, the crooked tooth smile.

"He never cared about suntans." I said. My first words, as life slowly moved forward.

"No," Bill said. "He didn't."

It was quiet in the room. So quiet.

"Bill?"

"Yes?"

"I want to know how it happened. But not now."

"Okay."

"And when the time is right, you must give it to me as a pilot would aive it to another pilot."

"I understand."

"Right now, I don't have the courage."

And that was all we said on that. I looked at his pants. "I'll need to wash those pants, and I can iron them dry. It'll only take a few minutes."

"Okay."

Bill helped me pack. There wasn't much. Shoeboxes, typewriter, some clothes. And photographs, my Chinese puzzle box, some clippings. My beautiful wedding necklace was with Mama for safekeeping. We made a stop at Sam Rowland's.

It was a lovely townhouse, its door embellished with an elegant brass knocker and kick plate. We watched the lights come on through a crack in the blackout paper. There was a rattle of locks.

"What time is it?" I asked.

"A little before six."

Bill's phonecall had given Sam Rowland some time. There was coffee, with Mrs. Rowland quietly moving in the background against fine antique furniture and photo galleries of Sam with politicians and VIPs. One had him smiling with La Guardia, another with Cordell Hull. I had met Mrs. Rowland only once before, and now was not a time to reach out and bridge unknowns.

"I'll mail your old typewriter, Doreen." Sam said.

"Thank you." I stared at my coffee cup.

"And I'll explain things to Eddie."

"Yes, please do that."

"Doreen?"

I looked at him. He looked older. Stubble on his jaw, his dressing gown baggy, his hands restless.

"You're a good reporter. You'll always have a job with me if you decide to come back."

I nodded. There was really nothing else to say. Bill and I left quietly, Sam standing in the doorway. Then we were back in the Chrysler heading south. The car ached with memories and for hours I had to fight them.

"Bill?"

"Yes?"

"I'm pregnant."

He looked across at me, his eyes quick with concern, then pain. "Oh, God, Doreen."

"No. I want this. Don't see it the wrong way. I want this baby."

"You'll have your folks."

"Yes. And Melsie Mae, and my home."

"You know I'll be there for you, Doreen—and George. Anything. Just say the word."

I reached over and pressed his hand. "I thought it was pastrami on rye, for God's sake."

"What, the throwing up?"

I nodded, staring out at the gathering day.

"I'll get you home."

And that's all we said on that too. Bill understood. There would be time later. There was always plenty of later for some of us.

"Thanks for coming, Bill."

He pulled a face. "News travels slow. Sometimes it takes four weeks. You didn't have a phone, and I couldn't say anything on the phone anyway."

"You wanted to be there for me."

"And George."

"Thank you."

"Heading into Virginia now. Sorry I couldn't get a flight. They're packed with politicians and VIP's."

It was later when I was ready, the prowling beast gone, only a numbness to be healed over by knowledge and insight. I cleared my throat around the words. "How did George die, Bill?"

Bill's hand pressed around the steering wheel. He was ready, and he told me the way I wanted to hear it. "They were bombing Hamburg. A Halifax had an engine fire, you could see it all over the sky. Its flames reflected on another Halifax—George's. The Germans manning the searchlights were good. Either by accident or design they left the Halifax with the burning engine and coned George. All lights superimposing on his plane." Bill looked across at me. "There's not much to be done in situations like that, Doreen. Movies show planes sideslipping out of the beams, or performing violent maneuvers to get away, but in truth..."

My voice was cold. My fire hot reporter's imagination seared my brain. "What happened?"

"Some say a nightfighter. There were reports of tracer before the detonation."

"His plane exploded."

"Yes."

"And the plane with the burning engine?"

"A nightfighter picked him off."

I looked out at the countryside. The landscape was different up here, running behind Georgia's more sultry climes.

"Do we need to stop, Doreen? Get something to drink, anything?"

"Take me home, please."

"Sure."

I clutched my Chinese puzzle box. I felt nothing. It was the Chrysler and its warmth and memories that brought me back. *Tap. Tap. Tap.*

"Bill?"

"Yeah."

"I want his pipe, and the Ronson lighter, and his wedding ring, if they're in his belongings."

"There's a good chance, Doreen." Bill said softly. They do have procedures for that."

"They are for his child." I said.

Epilogue

THE ROYAL AIR FORCE MUSEUM, HENDON, LONDON
SEPTEMBER 23, 1996

IT IS OUT of place, this creature of darkness, displayed under bright but not unkind light. The information plaque tells us that it is a Halifax Mark II, shot down over Norway where it made a forced landing on the ice of Lake Hoklingen. The crew survived. It soon sank through the ice and came to rest on the lake bed, ninety feet underwater. There it remained until it was recovered in 1973 by an RAF salvage team and some eager Norwegian volunteers. It was then transported to the Museum. I have looked at it several times over the years, as has my daughter, Marian. It is for her part of the puzzle, a dimension of knowing. For me too it is a way of knowing. My first visit had been uneasy, a stirring of long quieted remembrances. I had stared at this aircraft, tracking from it the last moments of my husband, George. I could look at the cockpit, the left-hand seat, and know that this is where he sat, flying his own Halifax. I could look at the remains of the perspex and imagine him cleaning it, getting rid of every speck of oil or dirt. Later visits had been easier but just as necessary.

The Halifax rests in its display area on a bed of sand, representing, I suppose, the lake bed. It is moss green in color, as if still dappled by sunlight filtering through the depths to her resting place. Part of the starboard wing is missing, and so is the outer engine. Front and upper gun turrets balance on the broken airframe. The tail fins reveal the exposed ribs of the rudders, all their fabric gone. Behind it, with a happier story to tell, there is a Vicker's Valiant atomic bomber, handsome in presentation, its pristine tail soaring to the roof lights, its paint-work immaculate. But I am old, seventy-five years to be exact, and I gravitate to the Halifax and hone sharp my memories and reflect on joys which are ongoing.

What rides the heart so lightly and stills our breath is how young we all were. Eighteens and twenties. George was considered old and wise at twenty-six. But to remember the age-that we-were is not a good exercise. Pursued, it only points out that meaningful things are timeless and an earthly age is meaningless. Marian, named for her aunt in Hartlepool and George's sister, is now fifty-two. Old enough to be George's mother. Her two sons are George's age at the time he died. I am staring at the Halifax when my daughter, Marian, comes up.
"Where's Dad, Mama?"

"In the American hall, looking at the B-17 with Bill Jr. Those two! Totally enthralled with that plane. If they could, they'd crank it up and take off down the Edgeware Road."

Marian laughed. "I'll go find them. See you in a while."

She is George, she is me. George's eyes and my jaw-line. She is quite buxom now, the result of poor food and erratic living on a rolling, refurbished fishing boat. I look into those eyes as I have done for over fifty years and I spark off them, remembering. I like her fire, her spirit, as she tilts at her activist causes, making every iota of her energy count.

Bill Trepick and I married in 1944, surprising no one, a gentle coming together amid the harshness of war: faithful visits to me and baby Marian. And we had long talks into the night about Marian, then barely a year old. When the talking was done, and more talk was shared with Mama and Daddy, it was decided that Marian would call Bill Dad, or Daddy, or Pop, or whatever she chose. Bill and I planned on having children and we wanted Marian fused into our whole, a part of who we and our future babies would be. But we laid out a careful plan for her to know George, to have his memory, his essence as part of her. Her memories would be good and strong. Not just a pipe and a Ronson lighter, and not even just a beautiful, most beautiful, wedding ring that symbolized the abiding love in which she was conceived. During her growing years, she came to know George. And there were holidays in Hartlepool with George's mother and sister, and she learned more, bringing home precious facts about where and how George grew up: the tradesmen and their horses, the Spanish Onion man, the sea coal sold door to door, the knife grinder pushing his cart, working the blades across a lumbering grindstone. Free enterprise is in vogue today, but I recall her excited stories about peas pudding and toffee cakes sold from homes. And the quiet rhythms of quiet living. The lamp lighter lighting the gas lamps on an evening, and trades horses moving unbidden from house to house. And the sea, the working sea, with its fishing boats and beaches, and the pungent kipper houses with rows and rows of herring being cured for market. Once she talked to me about Elephant Rock, a rock formation that looked like an elephant's head and trunk. It had been viewed by men leaving on the Crusades, and was no doubt being looked at today by new generations. A will o' the wisp thought had tagged me that day: 'the aim is to become elephants, not chickens...'

"Okay, hon?" Bill said.

I nodded. "Just thinking. The usual." I looked at Bill, checking him out. I watch him closely now. He is still a handsome man, but half a lung removed from cancer had left him careful in his movements. At the farm a photo has a younger Bill smiling confidently in his Pan Am uniform, the captain's braid very new. His passengers had been in good hands, this former BT-13 instructor and later P-38 Lightning fighter pilot in the Pacific.

"Sorry we're late, Mama." My daughter's eyes appraised me, probably the same way my own checked out Bill. "Y'know, this doesn't have to be your last visit here."

"It's the right thing," I said. "But I know you'll be back."

She kissed my cheek. "I think you want to hang around some more. We'll go check out the souvenirs."

And I was alone again, with my reflections, but with a sense of urgency now. I looked at the Halifax, its nose softly at rest in the sand. Silent. Small interior lighting shone through natural and battle damaged openings. There were mysteries in there, the rituals of war of a bygone time. God, I was feeling old. Not much of a dancer now. That was it, that was the thought that had been just beyond reach. Cochran Field and the dances, center of our world had we all but known it at the time. Archie and his 'once around the garden', dance intro survived two tours in Lancasters, which made him something of a walking statistic. He still pops up on television specials and serves as an adviser for BBC documentaries prepared for American cable television.

Haggis, whose idea of a good Cochran dance was sitting with a drink and working a shilling across his knuckles, took a morose class activism into Glasgow's slums and developed a unique blend of social work. Over the decades he built a reputation for helping troubled boys by having them race pigeons.

And Freddie, dear sweet, Freddie, was shot down in his Spitfire over Burma. He died of his injuries in a prison ship en route to Japan, and you will forgive me if I say no more about it.

And the girls, Wendy and Barbara. I miss them.

"Excuse me, madam, but could I ask you to move just a little to the left so that my class can see?"

I stared, startled, at a young schoolteacher. Children under ten years of age smiled at me. Some were black, and there were two Asians. They all watched me, until a black child said in his cockney accent, "We don't want to trouble you, lady."

"You're not troubling me, young man. But thank you for your consideration. It's nice to see such good manners these days." He smiled at me, revealing teeth in need of care.

"Are you American."

"Yes."

"I'd like to go to America."

"I hope you do. I think you'll like it."

The teacher was pleasant but firm, drawing their attention away. "Now this aeroplane is very old, not like the jet propelled aeroplanes. They found it at the bottom of a lake..."

Wendy,... 'This one's a foxtrot, Archie, you kicked me last time...' 'Just you hold on, girl...'

After the war she returned to Macon, battling with the inevitable changes in society. Her world was atrophying and it was difficult for her. But I valued our friendship and the tension that drove it. She married a high school teacher and found an uneasy happiness. Wendy died of leukemia in 1966. Life, it seems, cycles like the crops: inevitably, gloriously, and sometimes tragically, torn from a nurturing earth or pushed back into shadow.

Like Barbara, old reliable. Gifted, astute, who had provided me with the priceless insight about Bill's feeling for me. Thrice married, dying of acute alcoholism in 1976. A sadness stays with me always for the loss of her fine mind and delicate sense of things.

The children moved away on a clatter of shoes, some looking back at me. Black and Asian kids. Who would have thought. But George had known. He had predicted the rubbing of shoulders of people from all over the world, and that was demonstrated with this museum public. And Butch Martinelli, too. He understood. That day at the lake, the picnic, George and Butch, both of them laughing. Butch runs a trucking company and sneers at Mario Puzo's, 'The Godfather'. He still cooks sausage and meatballs with style and passion and that's what Bill and I get when we visit him in Chicago. In 1943 he was assigned to the Eighth Air Force and flew B-24 Liberators. 'They burned easier than Fortresses,' he said once, pouring more wine into the simmering meatsauce. After the war he never flew again. But if you look in his office, at the wall not readily viewed as the door is opened, you'll see photos of his parents, his wife, and their six kids.

I looked at my watch. It was new and uncomfortable, but Marian got it for me because it had big numbers on it, which helped my eyesight.

My darling Marian. My activist. She had been innately drawn to the sea. We all heaved a collective sigh when Jeremy, a brilliant marine ecologist who had a wonderful way of gentling her, married her and challenged her to work with him. She wore her grandmother's wedding dress, which continues a family tradition. Today they patrol the North Sea in a converted fishing boat called 'The Monkey Hanger'.

The bomber rests on its sandy bed, its green coloration seems to change in the artificial light, but it is only one's eyes playing tricks. Old eyes, cataract prone.

Mama and Daddy and Melsie Mae are gone. Daddy died from complications of stomach surgery. He died in a spotlessly clean hospital bed in 1948 surrounded by those who loved him. I miss his strong arm, on which I had held firm. Mama died in 1985 in a church bus accident. What does a journalist do with that? What spin, as we say today, do we put on that? I miss her spunk, which blossomed in changing times, and I miss her Mozart. Melsie Mae grew increasingly feeble as she got older. The fat arms which heaved the wash around in the wash pot, sending up billowing clouds of steam in the winter cold, and that protected her from smoke from the fire, these became thin and timid in their movement. Bill and I moved her into the farmhouse, taking care of her until she asked one day for her pastor.

She's buried beside Uncle William. Flowers bloom. I still have Melsie Mae's preserve jars. Each year I plant a seed or two in them and they sit in my window bay, where I can see the road leading to the house. I've set up my computer there, in full view. No tuckaway person I. Involvement. I thrive. I connect. And I get word out in my syndicated column.

Billy died at his desk at the *Macon Dispatch* of a heart

attack in 1964. He lived long enough to see the curtain go up on Civil Rights, and that's all he needed. He knew the play and its denouement. His son is proud of the brass spittoon that catches a morning sun like burnished gold. He claims Doc Holiday himself used it before heading west, and his young clerks never challenge it. I felt the arm go around my shoulders. I have known that arm for all our years through a golden anniversary. "I'm ready, Bill."

"Okay."

"Do you remember what you said when we talked about George? I asked you if it would trouble you, having him in our life. You said, 'Suppose it had been the other way around, and I had not come back instead of George, would you have forgotten me?'"

Bill smiled.

"I thank you for that." And for so many things. Like that day we had talked about the BT-13 and my flying lessons with George. It was Bill who located a restored BT-13 with the Confederate Air Force in Texas; and it was Bill who took me up and taught me how to land and take off. What's the word so common today, closure. Bill gave me closure, and I know George would have understood.

George...George...in that infinite moment when you knew your plane was lost, I pray that you thought of me, of my love for you, and that you left this life enfolded in it, not consumed in the foul landscape of war. It's odd. Our life goes on in memory, with no beginning and no end; with no ups or downs, no tragedies and triumphs; just lives that entwined and became suspended and idealized. Yet still, there are moments. An English accent in a crowded room, a Geordie lilt; or a wraith of pipe smoke, rarer these days, with just a touch of rum to it; and once in a while, someone pronouncing my name, DOReen.

If George had lived we would have loved each other in a more fully dimensioned way, tender and seasoned and different; rather like the way Bill and I grew together. I have been blessed beyond measure, and I weep. And on certain days, when my youngest grandchildren play with my Chinese puzzle box, and laugh in delight when they spring open the hidden compartments, I remember. I think back to the way George and I edged towards each other from our different worlds and shared our dreams and fears, and yes, our passions. And I guess, if truth be told squarely and I don't look back with an old woman's sentimentality, there was a common glory to it.

BIBLIOGRAPHY

Cash, Wilbur. *The Mind of the South*. New York: Vintage Books: 1991.

Cheshire, Leonard, Group Captain. *Bomber Pilot*. London: Goodall Publishers, 1989.

Collier, Richard. *The Sands of Dunkirk*. New York: E.P. Dutton, 1961.

Currie, Jack. *Wings Over Georgia*. London: Goodall Publishers, 1989.

Deighton, Len. *Bomber*. New York: Harper and Row, 1971.

Dring, Cannon, and Maguire. *Recollections of Our Hartlepool*. Hartlepool: West View Writers Circle, 1993.

Georgia World War Historian. *Georgia in World War II*. Solinet (Microfilm Archive), 1946.

Gibson, Guy, Wing Commander. *Enemy Coast Ahead*. New York: Bantam Books, 1979.

Harmon, Nicholas. *Dunkirk: the patriotic myth*. New York: Simon and Schuster, 1980.

Hastings, Max. *Bomber Command: the myths and reality of the strategic bombing offensive, 1939-45*. New York: Dial Press/James Wade, 1979.

Head, Dr. William. *Prepare for Combat*. Georgia: Robins Air Force Base, 1994.

Holiday, Billie. Lady Sings the Blues. New York: Penguin Books, 1992.

Hunter, Bill. *Down Memory Lane: a series of talks on the BBC*. Radio Cleveland.

Journal of Negro History. Atlanta: Morehouse College, 1916-.

McGill, Ralph. *The South and the Southerner*. Boston: Little Brown, 1963.

Tripp, Miles. *The Eighth Passenger*. London: Heinemann, 1969.

Verrier, Anthony. *The Bomber Offensive: American and British strategic bomber offensive, 1939-45*. New York: Macmillan, 1968.

ABOUT THE AUTHOR

Robert Middlemiss was born in England, educated in Canada, and has been a U.S. citizen since 1970. His background includes library administration at York University, Toronto; Adelphi University, N.Y.; and Indiana State University, where he taught in the graduate school on censorship and libraries. His other interests include adult education and adult literacy.

As writing instructor Middlemiss has, for over twenty years, taught adult education courses on writing the novel; served as fiction group leader at numerous workshops; served on the board of trustees for the Dixie Council of Authors and Journalists; and currently serves on the advisory board for the Tennessee Mountain Writers Conference. He is listed in *Who's Who in Library Service*, *Contemporary Authors*, and the *International Handbook of Authors and Writers*.

He has published several spy thrillers which were well reviewed by the *New York Times*, *Publishers Weekly*, and *Booklist*. Now out of the spy thriller genre, he writes fact-based mainstream novels.

This book was typeset in Sabon. A descendant of the types of Claude Garamond, Sabon was designed by Jan Tschichold in 1964 and jointly released by Stempel, Linotype, and Monotype foundries. The roman design is based on a Garamond specimen printed by Konrad F. Berner, who was married to the widow of another printer, Jacques Sabon. The italic design is based on types by Robert Granjon, a contemporary of Garamond's.

∞ The paper in this book is recycled and meets the guidelines for permanence and durability of the Committee on Production Guidelines for Book Longevity of the Council on Library Resources.

printed in the United States of America
by Thomson Shore, Inc.

www.irisbooks.com